Sex

is the

Antigravity

of

Metamorphosis

a novel by

Michael Lyons

Vol. 1 of the Sextet
My Years of Apprenticeship at Love

HiT MoteL Press
www.hitmotel.com

Copyright 2008 by Michael Lyons
All rights reserved.
First Edition

Library of Congress Cataloging in publication Data

Lyons, Michael
        Sex is the Antigravity of Metamorphosis
Vol. 1 of the Sextet *My Years of Apprenticeship at Love*
I. Title

ISBN: 0-965584291

Published by HiT MoteL Press

Designed by Michael Lyons

To s/S, the passionate Friend

Wild travelin' has always been, a miracle cure.
It'll heal raggedy reflexes 'n' give you time to decide.
So hit the road, if you ain't sure.
For there ain't no tellin' what's at the end of your ride.

Table of Contents

Agog at Magog by a Magnetic Lake

So it's on the highway toward the crossing at the border from Quebec into the States. She is driving in her green Mercedes and I am some guy standing by the side of the road hitchhiking. She sees me, a tall skinny guy in blue jeans with long hair and glasses. Looks like he could use a ride.

She has just dropped off her son at his father's farm. Later I would come to know how these encounters with the child's father always left her seething with rage over the divorce, how he got the farm. They used to be husband and wife, mother and father. The farm used to be their home, their dream. Now it is just a memory. She was working on a film about it, editing some raw footage she had just had enough time to shoot of the place before she was run off. It had that tune from Crosby, Stills and Nash: "Our house was a very very very fine house, with two cats in the yard . . ." playing over it. So she was very adverse toward getting into any new relationship. Perhaps that is what made the idea of picking up a stranger appealing.

Picking up the man was lucky for us both. For me, because I was noticing the dark clouds hovering over the distant mountains as they appeared to be moving in from the States and I was starting to think about an uncomfortable night hunkered down in a farmer's barn somewhere. Things can turn edgy fast in Magog, by the shores of Lac Megantic. It was lucky for her too though, because she hoped having a man along would make it easier to avoid the inevitable hassle she always got into with the customs guards when she crossed the border as *une femme seul* (an unaccompanied woman). She was anxious about it, as she soon would tell me of having to submit to the dreaded internal cavity search when she crossed the last time. She was anxious about having to encounter this gloved-bitch servant of the state again.

I was very surprised to see this fine old green Mercedes with Quebec plates pulling over on the shoulder of the road for me. My lord! It's a girl! Checking me out. I opened the door and there is this intense-looking, slightly-older young woman. Her faced looked angular like Patti Smith, but tanned and framed in soft light hair. And her petite frame had curves.

She gave me a rueful smile, both teasing and sheepish. I would come to know the smile of that twisted little mouth — it was her way of suppressing, like always, the rage she felt at the oppression of women by letting the curl of a snarl on her lips unfurl — and she said, "I'm just going across the border to visit some friends in Vermont." (And as she would later tell me: Who knows? This long-haired man by the side of the road didn't look too grotty.)

I am delighted. She looks like a stylish gypsy. She's wearing older expensive secondhand clothes: a full-length warm dress, and a colorful knit sweater. It looks like Quebec country hippie but a little more utilitarian and stylishly warm than her American counterpart.

Of course, I got in.

It felt good to sink into the cushiony bench seat of exquisite tan leather. When she roared back onto the road, I thought our phaeton is being pulled by a dog sled of Canadian geese under the hood. We eyed each other from across the well-appointed cockpit; we were an arms length apart. Her light hair curled out in a flip from under a beret or *toque* (knit hat). She took me in: He didn't look too bad — blue jeans, long hair, thick lips and big meaty hands. She later told me she thought I looked like a taller, more scholarly Mick Jagger with John Lennon glasses.

The first thing she said was, "You got any dope?"

"Nope. I travel clean."

"Good, cause we are goin' across the border."

She said, "Reach back and empty out all the ash trays in case there are any roaches."

I could see her admiring the length of my stretch out of the corner of her eye. She told me her name is Rayne Luce. Spelled it R-A-Y-N-E.

I introduced myself: Walker Underwood.

I was up. It felt good to be on the road again. I told her: "I left Montreal this morning; crossed the Jacques Cartier Bridge on public trans. Then a couple of rides through the eastern townships and then turned south here before getting into Sherbrooke. I'm going to Nova Scotia. I'm pretty sure it will be easier to hitch across the States."

I was some kind of hippie in those days. I would hitch-hike all over the US and eastern Canada, taking off from San Antonio, Texas without a map; with a little back pack mostly full of manuscripts. Something had happened to me after reading Whitman and Kerouac and Sartre in my early teens and I had become driven by a restless and existentialist wanderlust to more fully *experience the moment.* This I satisfied on the wide open road in the poor man's style; they called thumbing a ride in Quebec *a faire l'auto-stop.* Or *Post,* presumably because one stood by the side of the road like a fence post. I was so existentialist about it, that I had actually done hitchhiking on one side of the road then run across to the other side, like Paul Newman in the movie *Long Hot Summer*, just to get going somewhere — any-where? I fancied myself a Knight of the Road: trained in CPR, street wise, gifted in gab, able to wheel it like Neil Cassidy.

Rayne told me that she lived in Montreal and was on her way to meet some friends in West Glover, Vermont. She was not tall. She wore her hair in a flip like the French girls from Montreal. It made her look coquette. Yet she had a noble face, dark, Mediterranean, with a high tanned pate and flashing eyes. She might have been French except she did not have that blasé look they sometimes have. She looked kind of goofy-sincere with a tinge of authority, which meant most probably American.

To put her mind at ease about picking up a hitchhiker, I told her a story about my mother: "I was born in Montreal. Raised in Texas. I can speak three languages. My mother once aptly summed up this brew of nationalities, regionalisms and languages with the phrase: '*Bonjour*, how are y'all, eh? *Por favor*.'"

Rayne laughed at that.

The girl in the Mercedes. She was cool, she seemed so self-assured. She had smiling eyes. It makes the whole scene brighter. Outside the green car, the sun is shining down on the green fields that we can see from the mountain pass. Closer in, along the gravel roads through the hills, near the lake, the trees in those hills were beginning to glow in fall hues of gold, red, brown. A warm beautiful day in the Vermont autumn, which might soon be darkened by rain.

As we drove I told her about how over the years, I had made several attempts to reestablish myself in Canada. I worked at Expo 67, got my first bachelor's apartment in Montreal after high school. During high school I worked summers at the CPR hotel in New Brunswick. And then later in the small town I had grown to like as a knock around laborer staying in rooms rented out by widow ladies. I went to college at St. FX in Antigonish, Nova Scotia. "And I was living in Quebec City when they landed on the moon. We were pleased at the excellent comment Trudeau made the day after (I quoted): 'Man has reached out and poked a finger in the tranquil moon.'"

Then looking out the window at the land drifting away to the horizon, I said wistfully, "Yet Canada could not hold me."

Rayne had an almost jeering, teasing aspect. As we traveled on, she told me stories of how they really hassle her at Customs. She told me the border crossing horror story, about how "The last time this ugly woman crossing guard searched me internally!"

I teased her back. "You don't mean," (exaggerated fake gasp) "the anal probe."

"YES!" she snickered, squirming in her seat and grinning at the humiliating prospects. "This public servant stuck a gloved finger in my butt, while looking for dope. Oh, it was ever so degrading."

We laughed. She was a pretty straight forward chick, I thought. And, I'm going to get laid tonight, if I play my cards right. But I could tell she was a very liberated woman, and it wouldn't do to come on to her too strong.

It was her wicked mouth. That was the reason I would never be able to tell about her. She was always caught up in more than one emotion at once. At one moment she looked like a punk teasing me, the next she looked mystically serious. I told myself: just be her friend because you admire her. Maybe that is what she needed most now. Certainly I needed something. Let it gel, let it gel.

At the border, agents waived the couple through. It was the easiest boarder crossing she'd ever made. She was amazed. "They just waived us on through!" she exclaimed in relief. And because she was so grateful and since it was getting late in the afternoon, she invited me to dinner with her friends who lived down near Barton, Vermont.

We pulled into Newport and went into a bar called Gantrys. This was a freak's paradise. I was relieved to see that there were whole communities of long hairs who lived up there. I had never seen so many hippies. I felt kinship. I was flying. On the road. No attachments, just passing through. Though I had but four dollars in my pocket, I bought us two beers. Outside a couple of local boys were in some kind of contest to see how big a round of hardwood they could split. They had huge axes that looked to be about 6 feet long, and the axe head was as big as a small anvil. These stout lumbermen swung it easy.

Later when we pulled into a large modern supermarket to get some fish for the dinner I had to tell her I was almost broke. So she bought two big fish.

We headed down toward Barton where we stopped in a little yellow farm house with white shutters to visit a friend of Rayne's named Victoria. This woman had a great thick mass of resplendent curly Jewish Italian hair. She looked like a placid cool mountain Madonna. I thought I recognized the sly, yet aware, knowing moves of a dope dealer in her. Though it might be that she was just a beautiful woman, stoned. She put me totally at ease the moment I saw her. She made us some tea, and we drank it with fresh home made ginger almond cookies. Then Rayne and I headed out into the country to West Glover, to visit more friends. I admired how she wheeled the Mercedes over those narrow gravel country roads with a kind of reckless mastery. The scenery was gorgeous, the hills, a quarry and lakes. Off in the distance the soft green landscape rose up and dissolved into mountains. The Vermont farms with bight red barns are so much more opulently maintained than those in Quebec. In the fields and forests the leaves were flickering into the onset of Autumn display.

Everywhere we stopped, people were glad to see her. And accepting without much prying of this tall long-haired man she was with as her consort. We stopped to visit a guy who was an editor at Something Else Press, which I had heard of. The Situationists, and the Fluxus Movement people. We pulled the car off the road, parked it in a driveway near the editor's trailer. When we got out of the car, I was surprised to see Rayne turning modestly away, with her back to me, hike up her long skirts, to show she was completely denuded of underwear, and pee off to the side of the drive-way. The wild woman was holding the folds of her skirts draped over her arms, has her fingers down on her thing and pees like a man standing up, with her legs straight, thrusting her hips out — her smooth round bum shining like the moon. She drops the skirts back down, smooths ruffles, smiles, and heads into the house, without saying a word.

The editor, Larry Freeland was a slightly harassed, though righteous Vermont hippie. He and his wife were transplanted New Yorkers. She had been a show girl and even danced with the Rockettes. They had two little darling daughters. I had to wonder if he had taken on a movement name, until he spelled it out for me. Freiland. He was actually a Vermont apparatchik, who would much later in life join the great re-migration back to troubled Israel. He was harassed because their home had burned down last month, in a freak of nature fire — lightning had struck the propane tank outside their house. It had been a beautiful log cabin. A local biker gang had given the refugee family a tiny one room trailer to live in, while they were working their way through the insurance in order to start construction on a log cabin.

Down the road from their trailer we entered the home of another friend through a side door. It was a charming New England country kitchen with wainscot. Eveywhere there were braids of garlic and shallots and herbs hanging upside down. Therw were great baskets of squash and corn and autumn bounty. When the big man of the house saw petite Rayne carrying in the big fish he greeted her with a great All Right! He gave me a stern look. He was a stout New Yorker too. He took the already gutted fish to clean. Then later after he breaded them he placed them gingerly into two big hot sizzling frying pans to be fried in big slabs of butter. A great feast was soon in preparation. The food was delicious, organic brown rice, fish and fowl, casseroles and a couple of pies. Kids coming and going. It was grand to be part of this splendid and sumptuous spread way out on some land at the end of the road in a country kitchen miles from anywhere. Though the people were suspicious and protective of Rayne — when they asked us: How do you two know each other? I had to say somewhat sheep-ishly, "She just picked me up hitchhiking." She was confi-dently gracious at cooling them out around the somewhat unconventional circumstances of our meeting.

After dinner I jumped up and started doing my most excellent busboy /dishwasher butler routine, amid faint protests from the women of the house. But I was fast and gracious and the folks there immediately offered Rayne and her charming companion a place to crash for the night.

Later I was hanging around on the front porch, leaving the old friends to get caught up on gossip when several fine strapping young men showed up and carried in bales of what appeared at first to be hay. But they were ninety pound bales of marijuana and there were three of them — dumped onto the huge oval Tudor oak table in the center of the dining room. Though the man of the house gave me a suspicious and malicious threatening look, he as quickly let it drop, sensing I was cool. Then the next thing I saw was, coming up from under the table, and from all corners of the darkened house, came these kids, these lovely blond and long-haired kids with rosy cheeks and soft eyes, all came converging at the table and many little hands did come reaching up over the top of the table and pulling up pinches of weed began to roll it up expertly into fat bomber joints.

I was astonished and to tell the truth a little unnerved because, though this was not your biker, cowboy, dope-dealer scene — these were stalwart churchgoing patriotic New England organic farmers in the assiduous pursuit of botanical perfection — there was a slightly foreboding tinge to not knowing the local law enforcement proclivities, not to mention the child endangerment aspect and the possibility of being busted. I did appreciate being handed a gorgeous sticky dried flower as big as a fist. I wasn't so unobservant of local customs so as not to accept this generous gift to a traveler.

About that time Rayne and I took leave of the married folks and went to hear a band called New Leaf at Gantry's in Newport. This band was burning down the house in a sweating hot jam. The band created that special feeling of 'mass attack'— the dance floor was just packed, the lead guitarist yelled "I want everybody to just fuck mah face!" It was out of control — fucking bah-zerk. An experiment in mass psychol-orgy of Rock and flat-out country boogie and Roll. Me and Rayne danced their asses off.

After a little while of percolating beer through the body in aerobic dance, Rayne and I got a little drunk and started acting outrageous on the dance floor, doing the bump-butt and the grab-ass and what-not. Up until that time I had been acting cool, like one of the androgynous angels of the air, dancing with everyone there. But now she was all hot and flushed and happy and looking so fine. She was sitting at the table when I walked back from the dance floor. She looked up at me and kind of grinned and fairly shouted over the din, "Say, do you like to fuck?!"

Suddenly it was as if somebody had pressed the Pause button on the scene: everything in the place stopped and got quiet and everyone was leaning in slightly, listening in on our conversation, waiting expectantly to how I would reply. As I moved closer to whisper my answer to her question, the world around us seemed to dissipate further until it vanished into the background, so that we became really the only ones there in the dive, amid the background whirligig.

"Well yes." I said, shocked but trying to appear cool and nonchalant and offhand at this open challenge. Basically I was relieved. And although I figured I was in for some of the finest pussy in my life, I tried to maintain cool. Her challenge delivered the evening of its sexual tension. Although people might think it kind of unromantic — might prefer the usual boy chases girl machinations — I was grateful. Because now we could really have a good time that evening like a couple of old lovers on the town and not have to hustle each other. It's cold in them there hills in the fall in Vermont. And I would have the closeness of a warm human woman that night. Mammals like that.

Yes, a northern lady, approximately 100 pounds of capricious delight. We set up quilts and sleeping bags on the floor at another friend's house in an unfinished room with a vast panoramic cathedral window. The full moon shined in smiling. We became supine and started hugging and kissing. —Yes I thought as I undressed her. This was going to be a piece of ass I would never forget, my piece of white leg, yes, soft white thighs, long stems, with blooming nipples, (ever blooming) warm, cupped in their looseness within the bra that unlatches in the front, eyes blooming bright green, eyes staring back, feeding on wonder, joyous. And she was going to give it all to me as we undressed and snuggled into each other.

Swaddled in a sleeping bag I cuddled up to her warmth, as she presses herself closer to me. I whispered her name, Rayne to make it personal. I softly touched my lips to her lips with the kiss of a new love. I grew like a child in her warmth, and felt safe in her protecting embrace.

And I was polite! As I kissed her on the stomach and lower pelvis I looked up as if to say something like May I? with my eyes, indicating that I was going to kiss her *down there*. She just nodded. My tongue got her wetter. I moved back up and slipped my cock inside her. This new found land was mine to explore. Thrusting deeper, getting inside and feeling more and more up inside her body. Thrusting, thrusting and going deep, further inside to bring each closer to ecstasy. Heading towards orgasm, starting out in shuddering, bring each other close to the edge of falling off the plateau of rhythm, then stop; everything freeze. Shuddering freeze, soaked in liquid electricity, so near that time must have run out. But letting it abate a bit then thrusting more deeply until orgasm is beginning again. . . A noble gasssssss, Call us helium. The pair Bond.

Shhhh. . . She is dozing off. She is smiling. She is the queen of the underground. Take me down little sister. I think: She is the one who will shake me loose from my childish ways, but she must have her rest... I'm falling out. . . heart-beats slowing. And I look over and see the soft glory of her hair on the pillow beside me. Her hair proclaimed her mind a garden. Her eyes proclaimed her soul an animal (a she-goat). (She was very sturdy and strong could take a severe thrusty fuck with lots of pounding, no problem.) Her stature was small and wiry; she was tanned and muscular, a strong back — good to handle. If she was a bucking bronco she could throw you. The tautness of her skin proclaimed her youth. Her sinewy curves showed she was a mountain woman.

Woodland Nymph vs. Werewolf

I am bashful with new women. The next day we two newly chance-blessed lovers headed off into the woods, with a borrowed ax and lantern from our host, to be alone. We were to stay in the Geodesic DOME, where she and her son Beausolei — she's got a kid! Beau she called him — had lived that summer. Wow. I hadn't ever hooked-up with any little moms before. Little did I know what an all-consuming spell that casts. I couldn't wait to see the Dome. I had spent a lot of time with Bucky's geodesics. I loved the idea of the dome, it was a most elegant dwelling that embodied the new consciousness my generation was giving birth to. The efficiency with which it minimized material use for maximum volume; the way it was responsive like a living thing, transferring forces through its reticulated joinery all over itself to ground; the way it housed sound. The dome celebrated our desire to be efficiently in line with the spherical symmetries of nature circulating around on the globe. It expressed the network of tribal evolution emerging from the collective consciousness of my time.

The countryside we hiked through on the way up was beautiful. Up a steep fire road, past high pastures to the dome at the top of the Green Mountains. The birds are singing. There is the smell of wet duff and a freshly mowed hay field. In the meadows, the grasses licked her legs, for Rayne was wearing real tight jean short-shorts, so short that they were squeezed into her camel toe. But what really brought on the lycanthropy was the knee socks. She was wearing knee socks.

The sight of her in knee socks, the idea of girls in kneesox , caused paroxysms of lust to spasm through my under-ego, caused me to undergo a metamorphosis. I heard the bad devil on my right shoulder sneering and snickering to the good angel on my left: "Uh, he's caught a case of lycanthropy." Brought on by this cute little girl, this saucy little Circe wearing knee socks. It has something to do with young girls making castles in the sand pile. It goes way back, to kindergarten, girls wearing knee socks; nothing makes me foam at the mouth more than knee socks, unless it is a pleated skirt with knee socks, like the uniform skirts the girls wore at the catholic school yard. Lord, have mercy. Now I am back in the catholic school yard. I can remember the fear and loathing and shame when the nuns cracked a ruler over my knuckles; all those snaggle toothed little girls, smiling, wicked bitches smiling uniformed students, children with ruffled feathers, walking home (in two and fours) walking home through life, girling in a saunter, boys playing for marbles in the school yard, marbles that dazed, especially in the cat's eyes. Yes, I was subject to lycanthropy, brought on by seeing girls wearing short shorts and knee socks or kilts and knee socks or pleated skirts and knee socks.

Summer was drifting out with a feeling of great contentment, over the bountiful garden, serenely. . . drifting. I have this memory of her. We don't know each other, don't know how to be around each other, and are kind of equal in that inspired state of first love. I am 26; she is 29 or 30 but looks 18; she has a joyous elfin demeanor as she walks through the woods. The breeze tussles her soft brown tresses and the sun plays accents in her hair and splashes on her legs as she sashays through the blazon foliage. She is taking a drag on a spliff with her left hand and holding some shiny stone between the thumb and forefinger of her upheld right hand. She looks dainty and distant as she picks her way over the stones. Her face is relaxed, open to surprise and delight.

After a while we reached her garden where now there

were just giant sunflowers still standing tall, like some alien deity watching with one eye. She is telling me about how she and Beausolei fed the rabbits that came right up to their plot. "One of them became Beausolei's pet, all soft and cuddly."

I am feeling part of all this, part of her life, part of this place. Lust becoming sex becoming love becoming belonging.

"This is not Mr. McGregor's garden," she said.

"Huh?"

"Oh you don't know the story of Peter Rabbit? And how he was chased by the terrible Mr. McGregor? It's by Beatrix Potter. I can see you're not a parent."

"No. I must say, I'm a wee bit out of touch with children's literature."

Just then, to the left we see the dome. It looks like some fantastic crystalline brain, with its angles and windows. In front of it is a small Cambodian Buddha about 2-foot tall, sitting in the crook under a huge laurel, overlooking the Green Mountains with the orange foliage shooting through the green running across the horizon in distance.

The dome's exterior was plywood, painted a light green with varnished wood trim around the doors and windows. Besides the many facets giving the building a gem like appearance, it had large triangular windows that gave it a cathedral quality. We floated up onto the little deck, and entered through the unlocked door. It was spacious inside, though it looked compact from the outside. The 16-foot high ceiling had a sleeping loft. The dome's interior walls are sheet-rocked, and painted a faint green. Very lovely, with light blue accents and gold trim. It is like an ancient Italian villa. It had double sinks under a window looking out at the fields — though no running water, just a drain. Custom cabinets. There was a large antique vanity. A ladder leads up to the little loft which is just a floor for sleeping. We put down our stuff, get a few things set up, wander back outside.

It was a hot day. I was very hot. I flicked a bead of sweat off my cheek, where I was beginning my winter beard which was getting a little stubble.

She wanders around, almost dancing with lightness. She looks into the sky from time to time. Breezes gently hush. "Look at this stone I found," she says. "This is a metamorphic rock, pushed up from deep inside the earth when these mountains were formed. The Indians who used to live here use the stone as a symbol for the self. The immutable center." She hands it to me.

"Thank you." I said, accepting the gift, a round white stone with swirls of blue through it, like a miniature earth ball. "It's beautiful." I watched her wander around and pondered how women know such neat things.

She says: "Sure is hot. Isn't it?" (No reaction, she has a mischievous look on her face.) "Isn't it?"

"Yes," she answers herself. "I'm going to take my blouse off." She takes her blouse off. She has nothing on under it. She throws her blouse on the ground beside me, where I am sitting under the tree. She twirls around, kicks a leg up, dancing. "Aren't you hot?"

"Y . . . Yes," I stammer, delighted to look at her small breasts, white against her tan.

"Take your shirt off, silly."

I do. While she takes her boots and knee socks off. I pull of my sneakers and socks too. Trying to float like a cloud I waded lightly through the grass, shuffling my feet languidly over it, so I could feel its exquisite tickle on the sensitive soles. "It is nice to feel my feet in the grass."

She says, "Nice thing about this place is the total privacy. We hardly wore any clothes all summer. I used to lug a goat skin of water up from the stream every day this summer. It felt good to feel the water trickling down my bare back." She turns her back to me, and unbuttons those tight little blue jeans shorts, and bending over pulls them down. "It would trickle down my back into the crack of my ass," she said as she arches back up, stepping out of the shorts, and catching them on her foot, kicks them in an arch through the air to land near her blouse. She stands there watching, hands on her hips, standing up straight all 5 foot 4 of her, thrusting her hips out, her breasts glistening in the sun. She indicates with a toss of her head, challenging me to follow suit with her grin.

I am in some kind of trance. The heat, the marijuana. . . *Je est un autre*. He stands up and drops his pants, though he is still in his underpants. By now he's flushed with excitement and embarrassment to actually be almost naked in his tidy whiteys in the light of day. He gets red in the face, as she is grinning at the bulge in my briefs. I figured this was the right moment to use an old line from days of childhood exploration: "Will you show me yours if I show you mine?" He grinned.

"I might." She hooks her thumbs into the elastic of her panties, pulling it away from her smooth little belly and looking down into her delta. Then she pulls them down over her illustrious hips and lets them fall down around her ankles. She steps out of them. Her back arched beautifully as she bent over to pick them up. She walks over to me with her green panties in her hand and lays a hot sweet slow liquid kiss on my lips. She presses herself into me. She can feel the bulge, getting bigger against her. She steps back. "Take your own off. I know what you look like."

I slide mine off, kicked them away under the tree. My cock freed from its cloth encumbrance engorges and sways free, jutting out, erect. This is how a man likes to feel. She has been holding her panties in her hand.

"Here you can have these," she says. She drapes her panties over my cock, so that it passes through one of the leg holes, and they are suspended there, like you might drape them over a door knob. She grins in coy sophistication at my ridiculousness and says, "There. Comfy?"

She reaches down and takes hold of my cock gently like she was shaking hands with a dog. Slowly she rubs the panties back and forth on it, never actually touching it with the skin of her hand. I am starting to get a little weak in the knees and about to fall over. The feel of silk is exquisite.

Then she abruptly moves away, throws herself into a turning leap, twirls around and says, "Now let's dance."

I remove the silk panties from my ruffled, cherry rouged member and shrug my shoulders getting into this tease. She leaps, we both laugh and scramble around half-dancing, half-running and jumping in a general grab-assing the woods. Neither of us makes the slightest attempt to be graceful. I think: Here I am dancing barefoot and naked with this mad woman until the sweat runs down her back into her crack.

I grab her from behind, around the hips, lift her up a little, and scrunch myself down a little and push my hard cock between her thighs, so that it protrudes in front of her, and she reaches down and strokes it with her fingers and puts her hand around it and pulls it through a little more. She juts her butt up into my belly, and jumps up and down, jacking off this cock that she has between her legs, like she was some gross maniacal man, while I am nuzzling on the back of her neck.

Rayne was proud of her power over this cock. She played with it like it was her cock. Making psssss noises, and sweeping it back and forth, like she was hosing down the area. She looked around at me, her face almost touching me, her cheek beside mine and said, "You know, I'm a real nice girl. I have a lot to give." But by this time I could barely hear her, as I held her so tight as to squeeze some of the spunk out of her, and make her feel my power. She let go of the cock.

I twirled her around, trailing kisses over her breast and belly. I knelt, lingering at her naval, probing it with my tongue.

I kissed her hips running my tongue down to her inner thigh, lifting one of her legs and putting it over my shoulder, leaving her standing on one leg, holding onto my head while I hungrily parted the lips of her cunt with my tongue. After a little of this she was easy to pull — swooning, crumpling down onto the soft grass.

I slipped it in and she rapped her legs around me like a snake. We were now the beast with two backs. We rose and fell with him. I nailed her to the earth trying to force my body inside her through the sacred tunnel. She started moaning and breathing hard. Uhhh, uhmmmmmm ahhh. She tossed her head from side to side; her eyes scrunched shut abandoned to her orgasm. She was a hot little screamer. I made one last thrust and my body and her body seized up spasmodically. We stayed coupled together for a long time like a pair of snakes, she all the while giving my prick little hugs by contracting her pelvic muscles. We moaned and cooed, heart beats rose and fell like tides, and thoughts came warm and lazy. Then we rolled apart cool and clean. "That sure was fun," I said.

We got dressed, in the waning light. I set about to split some wood for a fire. After she saw me whacking away at it she came out to show me how it was done. I can't believe I went through all of boy scouts and a *girl* had to show me the proper way to lift the round of firewood and bash it against the block to drive the axe through. How embarrassing.

We made a good fire in the potbellied stove and cooked a meal. The cast iron stove had an accordion door that folded open and closed. It was the only heat for the dome. You could open these doors and have roaring fire, or you could close them and have a more efficient radiant heat source. The dome had been abandoned for a while, and some coons had trashed it a bit. As with all domes, it leaked a little. They are hard to caulk. I climbed up in the loft and was looking down at her. She was sitting in a rocking chair. I took this eyeball snap shot of her. Her being seemed to emanate through space, as she relaxed down there in the chair. She wore these funky granny glasses. From under her *toque*, soft brown hair curled. She had on a pair men's slacks replete with pleats. And these heavy monkey-grip boots of a moon glow color, trimmed with vermillion.

She had a broad, toothy cover-girl grin.

"I wish we could always be like this," I said. "Too bad I don't have a camera to take a picture of you."

"Well, take a picture with your mind."

And I gazed on her. And she gazed back. Something happened. I scanned her in.

In the setting sun in the dome she is looking impish in her rocking chair (where she has rocked her little son). I have a chance to take a mental snapshot, to study Rayne Luce at length, before we part, so that I should never forget her.

She held my gaze and shamelessly we looked into each other's soul, eye to eye, while I scanned her into memory. I kept getting drawn back to her mouth: her lips were thick, and even with no lipstick (she didn't use makeup, it would have been a cop-out) they were dark in color — full of blood, half opened, and one end of her mouth was perpetually curled up in a jeering, teasing smile of animal cunning. The girl can't help it. In this portrait, her long neck is arched in an upturned angle; she had hot, tanned skin, for her heredity goes back to the tribes bordering the Sinai; she had small pear-shaped breasts, which science has established meant that she enjoyed sex and said yes whenever possible; her nose was slightly wide, she had the kind of wiry sturdy little body that could take a lot of severe sexual pounding, and men quickly saw that in her. She was built for it. She challenged men with her eyes in a kind of haughty almost pitying gaze. She has that rage for life, wants to always be trying new things; her senses were sharp and her reactions were swift. She was keenly looking at me too, enjoying her power over men.

The two lover's eyes met as they were taking in each the other, she knowing she was being lusted after and loved, him feeling guilty for lusting after her, but knowing she knew and was turned on by it, and she knowing that he knew she was turned on by his knowing that she was turned on and they were locked in a kind of penetrating laser gaze, that burned away all the flesh so that they became like two parallel mirrors each reflecting the other, in infinite regression of worlds, all the way back to the androgyny — the sex force that was the entity before it split into male and female.

That night when we were hunkered down in front of a roaring blazing fire, I covered the rocking chair with a big quilt and had her sit down in it. She just relaxed, with her legs spread apart, her heels resting on the rockers arm, like the stirrups in some lecherous gynecologist's office. I am down on my knees in front of her in a naked sweat. She spread her pink pussy lips with her fingers showing me her hole. I hoped she didn't think me too oral. But I just loved her little flower cunt. I loved its little labial petals. Eating them was like brushing the petals of a rose, it was of such a fine texture. There's not another taste like it on earth. I slowly savored it, soft lips, really coming to know it, to know everything there is to know about it. She was completely relaxed, yet getting hornier and hornier. I could see the sexual blush of blood rushing into her thighs and swelling around her breasts, as she slowly spread her legs wide and ooched her cunt closer, harder onto to my hot breath as she ran her hands through my hair. It was incandescent sex, all that blond hair glowing in the red firelight, and white skin, in the roaring breath of the flames.

I entered her as she lay languidly back, neither of us having to move. I was kneeling in one place between her legs; she was riveted motionless to the bottom of the rocking chair.

All I had to do was reach up and pull the rocker forward, and her cunt, wet with eggy sauce slid over my now satiny smooth boner, as it impaled her to the limit, completely. And she would moan softly, and whisper *fuck me* in a hot little wimper into my ear. It was almost a tearful, sympathetic union, and then just as casually, move the rocker easily back, and un-cunt, a little or a lot, I had complete control. We did it like that for hours, since I had already shot my wad earlier in the day, and was now just in it for the friction, the caretza, like two rats that had found the pleasure button in some behavior modification experiment, but really having no idea how the mystery of human sexuality worked. She got real loose and all worked up, and hugged me to her, my cock inside her secret, and it was very tender and loving and beautiful. But also looking back on it, in the way that the only parts of ourselves that were touching each other were the genitals, one could say we were kind of afraid, of the full on body hug. It was not perverse, just not particularly loving — not able to be loving, but perhaps just intoxicated with the prowess of youth and what it can accomplish?

Tears Falling at the Busy Bee Cafe

The next day was Sunday which meant Rayne had to get back to her life in Montreal, had to get back to being mom to her kid, had to get back to her teaching job, had to be ready for her students. It was a dark September 7, 1975, and it was raining. After fixing a trail food breakfast of boiled gruel in a bowl, amid a feeling of foreboding at the mucky-mucky forces of destiny swirling and circulating around in the social realm, we two newly anointed lovers took off on a harrowing slip-sliding, controlled-drift drive all over those back woods mountain roads to the highway. She could really wheel it. She was going to drop me off on the interstate and I was going to continue my journey to Nova Scotia.

"It sure is a drag to say good-bye," I said as we were backing out of the driveway of the commune in West Glover — especially since it is starting to rain, I thought. "Why don't we have one last cup of coffee for the road."

We ducked into the Busy Bee Cafe in Barton. Sat at the little table with the blue gingham table cloth in the front window trying to figure the next phase of the adventure. I ordered coffee and a piece of apple pie, but couldn't eat it, as there was a huge lump of sadness forming around my heart. It was turning into a heavy scene, with our holding hands across the table and looking into each other eyes, while these hard-core old Vermont duffers, sitting-around-the-cracker barrel types, were secretly chuckling at our mooning sighs. I looked out of the window trying to think of something to say. Here we were two lovers sitting in the Busy Bee Cafe and we were being bombarded by destiny, and it was raining. And it was raining in my heart, like it is raining in the town.

Big fat splats on the window — it was getting wet out there and the fronts were going into combat.

Something was raving in my brain, it was like some kind of refrain, it was raining in my heart like it was raining on the roofs and windows of this little village, and here we are, well met, pitter-pattering too.

My mind riffed out on the hippie dippy weatherman, spit and smattering, who looks out the window, flit and flattering and says: Wanna know what the weather is like? Look out your god damn window. It's raining. Going to be raining all day, clouds will come in, rain will be falling. Nothing but drizzle and sprinkle and precipitation. After that it will be a downpour. *Après moi le deluge.*

I was being pushed around by Karma, I was being used by angels of destiny, it is falling on us here and every one here at every moment, a rain of subatomic particles passing through — neutrinos and beautinos and you'n'menos and they fall into a pool, a pond, a mirror reflecting the sky, where they form concentric rings going out entrapping you and eye, and I am standing at the edge of her circle and she is standing at the edge of mine and will they reach out and overlap? For today it is raining in all of the world, raining drops of love, the elixir of life, the potion to assuage the pain, the connection beyond yourself, pushing out of the frames of reality floating in the ocean of I. I'm just a lost cat howling at the moon, kitty take me in. Amid the clatter of dishes, propriety and decorum and decency was about to shatter as we came to the crux of the matter. There in the soft rain pitter-pattering on the tin roofs and windowpanes, we were falling into a kind of spell. Our mind told us to cool it, our heart told us to commit. I really had to have some more of her. We could make it, maybe.

Looking out the window, I heaved a big sigh and said: "It's raining in my heart." Said it again in French, "*Il pleut*

dans mon coeur." I thought, as she later told me she
thought: Is my heart so dulled, my ego so vain, that it can't
recognize when it is being called to love again. There is no
reason to it, it doesn't make sense, and yet, how sweet it
would be if we could get together for a little while again.

I wanted to say something like: Was it raining in love all
over the world? I wondered if the lovers sitting out a tropical
thunderstorm in Africa, or the amour-smitten Indians under
trees in Brazil, or the other-obsessed fanatic love objects in
the monsoons of India, or the head-over-heels hooked riding
out the squalls of Norway, or the lust-besotted infatuates
sipping drinks in posh hotels during the soft rains in Florida, or
the dharma-doomed driving around in vans in the constant
drizzles of the Olympic rain forests, were crying into their
apple pie like I was. Lust becoming sex becoming love
becoming...belonging.

What I did say was: "Did you know there are over
40,000 thunderstorms per day all over the earth?" It was
some kind of idiotic attempt to cheer us up. I have always
found a pure unequivocal fact from science to be an interesting thing to throw into conversation. It's my way of resetting
the frame to a larger perspective leading people back into the
nature of the world around them. Not knowing what to say I
idiotically continued. "I think of the thunderstorm as batteries
pumping electricity back up to the upper layer of the atmosphere equalizing the potential difference caused by falling
rain."

I could tell that she was not impressed. My attempt was
a kind of bravado to forestall the serious sadness about to
befall my sorry ass.

She wanted to say something similar too. Later she told
me that it seemed to her at that moment, the green mountains
were melting in the rain, the ravines were flooding with the
strain of living alone. Someone has come into my life, what

does it mean? She was feeling something similar as she later told me how she felt at that moment: I am getting tired of feeling like my life is on hold. This won't do for very much longer. I don't want to just be someone's mommy. My skin doesn't fit right any more. I'm annoyed with my divorce, my life's unsettled right now and I don't have the ability to change any of it. Here's something like love that has come along, the first I've felt in a long while. I hate hate hate that I can't control anything about my life at the moment.

Well, one thing led to another and instead of smiling knowingly into each others eyes with a nod at 'the affair that might have been' and me going out and standing by the side of the road, and her letting me go — making me go, knowing that we will never have this chance again, and will be forever condemned to our safe and sterile lives, forever somebody's favorite eccentric and nobody's Person, like two sane Normal people, we decided instead to live together!

Talk about instant Karma. And she has a kid besides! Somehow the requisite "must like kids test" had been secretly administered and apparently I passed.

She no doubt was thinking something like: I wonder how my kid is going to take to this. Well I'll bring this strange man in. I should know pretty quick if everything is going to be OK or if this was a huge mistake. I am afraid that either way, I'm probably going to end up with a broken heart. What in the fuck am I getting myself in for?

But it was raining in love, and I wanted some more of her. Some more of the Jewish princess with the subliminal opera massage. I figured what the hell; I'll try it for a week or two. Maybe these little mamas are all right. I'm not going to leave her thinking of herself as just another notch on some players's guitar. Maybe it's true: welfare mothers make better lovers.

On Staynor Street

Rayne brought me back to her apartment in Montreal. It was in a building across the street from Staynor Park. You entered through a standard metal and glass front door, went down a narrow hall lined with brass mail boxes. This led to the stairs and the whole central corridor which opened up into a three story atrium around which there were walkways at each landing going to the apartment doors. The stairs zig-zagged up, leaving you off at each landing to walk around galleries that brought you to your door. When you entered her second floor apartment, you were in a little living room.

The living room is in the center of a long narrow flat that went from the front of the building to the back. It is larger than the other rooms. It is furnished with an antique looking chair with a stiff back and arms, and a large TV/ book case stand. It has a closet, and an entrance to the bathroom right off of it. (Joined at the hall entrance.) The walls are a kind of blue-gray, there is another large book case, some more chairs. Across the living room from the entrance a narrow window opens to a light well. There is an area demarcated by straw mats and a large tree bough and a bird cage hanging from a smaller branch of the bough and some manikin parts so that it looks like a sculpture or a diorama.

She sees me looking at it. She shrugs, says with a slightly sheepish grin, "This is what I call one of my *nests*."

And with that, I entered the swirling whirlwind of Rayne's life. I put my pack down. She took me on the tour. Out of the living room down the hall past the entrance to the tiny little bathroom — just big enough for a bowl and a tub and a sink — we went down a long hall that ran parallel to the kitchen, into the den or TV room which you passed through to enter her son's room in the back, which had another mud room behind it and the back door that gave out onto the alley. Her bedroom was at the opposite end of the house in the front beyond the living room. It had a window facing out into Staynor park across the street. She could watch her own child playing.

Entering a woman's bedroom for the first time is always intimate. They are so together, in their boudoir — lacy sheer curtains, fabric draped over a lamp shade. It was feminine, warm. (Now, I was with a girl who wore hippie underwear (which was nothing at all) underneath her dresses.) Over her bed (a foam mattress on the floor) was an embroidered sign done in fine needlepoint thread by the loving hand of some devout woman, probably a nun; maybe her, I didn't ask. It read, *Mon Dieu, Je Voudrais Bien Vous Recevoir.* (My God, I'd like to receive you again.) I didn't know if it was religious — the thought did cross my mind that it was a romantic paean to all the lovers that had passed through here. I would come to find out there were quite a few.

She must have been reading my mind for she got a little defensive and said in a sharp challenging tone, "Well that's it. This is my world." She slammed some thing down. I fairly cringed. I felt small and vulnerable.

She must have felt vulnerable too. I could just feel her repeating to herself: What have I done? Brought this stranger into my house. What have I done? What will my kid think?

I could tell she was having second thoughts. I felt diminutive and dependent. It was crazy for two people to be moving in like this. But love had got a hold of us. Romantics believe in this kind of stuff or so we told ourselves. Follow it, and see where it goes. I did have that can-do enthusiasm of a young guy on the road. Happy to be there, into whatever the locals are into. In fact it was a privilege to be part of their trip. I thought to calm her, say something and put her at ease. I looked her in the eyes, sighed heavily and said, "Well aren't we a pair." I took her arm. "You've got a lot of courage. But maybe its fate. Destiny. Lets roll with it, see where it takes us."

She seemed to brighten at that.

Rayne is nobody's fool. I said, "I know you want your son to feel comfortable with me and not feel threatened.☐So we need to make sure everyone is happy, especially you and him. If your son is not happy about this man "sharing" you, then I'll have to go. You'll know. Maybe it will be good for him. I'm not a bad guy. I'm an older brother and know how to be responsible for kids."

She smiled and felt more relieved at that. She said, "Wait right here. I'll go get Beausolei; he's upstairs in Linda's apartment."

"Who's Linda?" I asked.

"Ah, Linda's my pal, my lifeline. Linda is Wolfie's mom. She is a single mom like me. She's like the sister I never had. You'll meet her. She's my amiga, my alter-ego, my confidante, my partner in crime."

While she was upstairs I prepared myself to meet her son. No doubt I'll have to deal with young Oedipus.

But great, here we are in this little scene, this apartment, with its rooms strung together like cars on a train. We'll be like people going somewhere. I had caught the Karma Train. May it pull its containers of beauty through my dreams.

Rayne brought her son down.

And he hung back by the wall looking at me. A nice looking kid, with curly hair. I let him take me in. He looked sensitive intelligent. Don't rush him.

She introduced us. "This is my friend Walker, he's going to be staying with us for a while."

I gave him a real smile and stepped forward and extended my hand like you might to a puppy to sniff. His father had taught him how to respond to the manly art of the hand shake. He stepped forward and we shook hands like men. I said: "Nice to meet you, young man."

Then they were off into the kitchen, and I was there stashing my pack behind a chair. She came in and cleared a drawer for me in the chest of drawers in her room.

Up until that time I had only been with single college women. I did feel some fear and trepidation about taking up with this full blown woman-mom creature with a kid in the mix. That was a lot. I've been in love before, got my heart broken. I had explored — while being a full time, live-in lover the possibilities of domestication by "wife" and had learned a thing or two. I knew how to be a boyfriend. But being a father figure? I'm not quite ready for that responsibility. I mean I knew what to do, I'm a big brother, have been the baby sitter, have changed diapers, but I don't know about this. Can I do this? I told myself: It will be all right. You can do this. Let it gel, let it gel. You can feel all you need to know.

We three headed out to a local supermarket, at the nearby Atwater Station. I told her I was a baker and would make her some bread if she had some yeast and a little flower. At the supermarket I won over the lad by giving him fast rides down the aisles in the shopping cart, mushing it like a dog sled, jumping on and riding myself, smiling, mugging into the face of the laughing boy as it got going. This charmed both the boy and his mom. It was fun to be loud and childlike, I had not done that for a long time. Now I had permission and a partner in crime. No accidental crashes occurred.

We walked past a bank showing the Temp: 20. It didn't make sense. "It can't be 20," I said, "that's way below freezing,"

She said. " Yeah, I know. I'm a Fahrenheit girl in a Metric world."

I did a rough approximation $20 \times 9/5 + 32 = 36 + 32 = 68$. That's more like it. "Oh, it's mild 68. It's a beautiful day."

She was impressed. Looked up at me with an approving smile.

After Beau's bath and his bedtime story, when the day was finally done (I had spruced up the kitchen, done dishes, mopped a floor) and the child was in bed it was time for the adults to repair their lives with love. Rayne and I undressed each other, pulling off clothes one by one, as we were kissing passionately. Rayne ran her hand over the curve of my ass, and squeezed my rigid rooter with her other hand. She had her hands full. Rayne had her own man now in her own house.

Monday morning the alarm goes off at 6 a.m. Rayne startles; reaches over and gives it a sharp whack to stop it. I try to hold her in a spoon.

"Oh my God!" she says. "It's Monday. All over again. I thought I had dreamed I had started a new life with my new boy friend." She looks me over. " Ah, there he is!"

I try to keep her in my clutches a little longer but she wriggles out of my grasp, springs up and away.

"I am going to be late," she says. "Gotta get Beausolei up and off to preschool."

We fell asleep last night after hot and horny sex. We are new girlfriend and boyfriend and I can feel her body wrapped around me. Her presence is seared into me. Okay, stop thinking about it and go join them, see if you can help them get ready. I stumble out of bed and nearly kill myself tripping over one of Beau's toys on the floor. Ouch, the little oedipus has laid out a mine-field. No doubt my days will be strewn with gaffs.

I meet Linda briefly in passing when she comes down with Wolfie. She came into Rayne's kitchen through the back door unannounced (as was their usual sisterhood informality). And there she was, this absolutely gorgeous Linda, almost 6 feet tall, big-boned and statuesque. Her hair a natural healthy blonde color that's shiny, falling around her face in beachy waves; her big blue eyes bright with interest and real enthusiasm, no makeup, no eye-liner. And here and there freckles in her peaches-and-cream complexion with just the healthiest blush in her cheeks. She is wearing a short mini skirt (blue jean), showing plenty of leg of good muscle and a pink tank top, showing off her skin tone of pale white blending into light tan. She's got white strap sandals on her ample feet with painted toes. I was stunned. Danger! Alert! The first time a man sees Linda he realizes he is in the presence of pure Celtic beauty, descendent from a long line of women going back to the end of the Ice Age when nature expressed Herself through beautiful females with blonde hair and blue eyes to make them stand out from their rivals at a time of fierce competition for scarce males. I tried to be cool, nonchalant, unimpressed, disinterested. After all I was Rayne's man now.

Linda gives me a kind of suspicious look. Rayne gives me a kiss good-bye and an extra key to the apartment; and the women and boys charge out the door to day care, school and beyond — Beausolei being driven in that big green car by his little ma.

I have another cup of coffee. It was a sweet little kitchen — blue walls, black formica counter — compact with a toaster and and some oranges in a wooden bowl on the counter. I dwelled in the smell of Montreal: burnt coffee, coal fires and wet leaves. It is a little like fine single-malt Scotch whiskey, an acquired taste. A great city going on outside beyond the kitchen window into the light well.

Left alone in the apartment, I tried to figure out more about her. In the little den, she's got boxes and boxes of comic books and graphic novels. It must be the biggest collection this side of New York city.

I called Rayne on the number she gave me for her office at work. She has office hours. I was really feeling her, and wishing to be with her. I had no excuse, just wished her a good day, and listened to her sexy voice. Told her I would start some bread.

I was a good baker in those days, could whip up a loaf from scratch using recipes in my head. After some crashing in the cupboards, I dug out a bread loaf pan from way in the back. And after a couple of rises, kneading and punching down — during which I went out the front door and walked across Staynor Park to Dorchester and back. And then later during the second rising up to Ste-Catherine Street and Westmount Avenue.

I had that kitchen filled with the smell of baking bread by the time they got home. We had it in time for dinner. It was too hardy for Beau. I told her my idea of bread was that it should be as heavy as a dictionary, as rindy as a tire and have the texture of driveway gravel. She seemed to like it OK, but perhaps she was just trying to be supportive too.

That night after brushing my teeth before bed, I hung my white toothbrush in the slot on the drinking cup holder in the bathroom. It was presumptuous of me; I thought what the hell. (I hoped it wouldn't induce shock into Rayne's sense of freedom.) Now there were three: a red one — Rayne's, a blue one — Beausolei's, and mine.

The Imaginary Dual-Status Alien

The next day — same thing. 6 a.m.: Up and getting Beausolei ready for school. By 8 a.m., they are out the door. I am contemplating the hot sex and feeling her on my body all day. But I had to get busy and start looking for a job.

Money. Yes, what did we do for money.

During the days that followed I looked high and low for a job. Although I wasn't ready to cut my long hair, I made a better effort to shave. I couldn't wait to hit the streets of Montreal. I had a lot of history with the place. A walk down Ste-Catherine Street was filled with memories and at certain places awash with feeling.

Mommy? Yes, she was a good little mommy.

Everyday she fixed Beausolei these heroic lunches and packed him off to the day care center at the Y.W.C.A. It was just across Staynor Park on Dorchester St. towards downtown. Beausolei was dropped off, set up with his lunch; his mom always made sure it contained a Johnny Canuck sandwich, a chocolate covered mound of marshmallow between a couple of chocolate cookies. Then, she'd turn around and head 20 miles out the Trans-Canada to work in Kirkland almost at the west end of the island. While there she was a wild thing caged for a while — tamed and petted, constantly at war against what she called the vestigialization of the art department. She taught two courses in filmmaking at a C.E.G.E.P. which stands for *College d'Enseignement General et Professional.* These are the hippest schools, like junior colleges, but where the students did the hiring! And they were fully accredited and duly ordained. The schools trained young people so they could get jobs. In addition to classes in dental hygienist and drafting, there were classes in

yoga and tai chi as well as mathematics or becoming a police-
man. The C.E.G.E.P. colleges provided employment to fine
artists and gave them a lot of autonomy. Rayne taught classes
in making documentary films and animation shorts.

While I had the flat to myself I did try to do a little writing.
I was a proud guy in those days. I wanted to live off grid,
under the radar, incognito with the simple hippie *cogito:* You
can feel all you need to know. I had been slowly slipping into
the struggling artist's life since college. The poetry scene
around Austin, was furtive which led to a defiant focus on
humor and absurdity. I was a member of the Church of the
Coincidental Metaphor, and had worked on the Brother
Heuman Hour, a 15 minute radio broadcast out of a Mexican
border blaster full of blasphemous word play.

For work in Austin, I started off teaching electronics in
trade schools, but let myself get fired for growing a beard. I
used the longest possible hiatus space of unemployment as a
government sponsored arts grant. I had gone to college (to
avoid the draft, then got a high lottery number.) But it was a
sudden leap in consciousness affirming my preexisting literary
obsession with time that got me into studying physics. It
happened during a mescaline trip in Quebec City, flying out of
body on the Plains of Abraham that had shown me how the
filters of rational mind could be transcended. The sudden
onslaught of philosophical maturity changed me. I wanted to
get an education but at the same time take part in the action
and passion of the times. And those were some times. But in
university I got interested in engineering and physics and math.
I somehow ended up with a degree in Natural Philosophy
which is what they called Physics in those days. I was on a
quest having to do with projective geometry: did it apply to time
as well as space? Were there fundamental theories for time
like collineation for the straightness of space? Was there an
analog to the projective method for time? Were their harmonic

conjugates of time whose quadrilateral was a tesseract where the cross product of flux was the cross ratio?

I wanted to be some kind of an alternative physicist, develop mathematical models for the occult, and alternative energy systems, and cosmic engineering, to deal with phenomena that hadn't been explained yet. I had smoked weed for the first time years earlier in Colorado underneath the clear mountain stars at Drop City in Trinidad in 1968. In order to be near these dome builders, I got myself into a nearby JC whose main area was gunsmithing. We occasionally brought deer slain by the student hunters out to the Dropper communards to supplement their larder which was just bushels of commodities from the government. The utopians were grateful for it. They turned us on, and it was amazing to be at their campfire 'neath the great swath of the Milky Way so astoundingly abundant in the night mountain sky. That was the year of both the King and Kennedy assassinations. I thought society was devolving, and that I would have to learn how to take responsibility for tech.

Rayne encouraged me to write, but the surroundings were still too chaotic for me to get down and make any kind of coherent paragraphs about them. Besides I wanted to find a job and pay my own way. There is nothing worse than being supported by a woman. Even though I did have a Canadian social insurance number I couldn't remember it. And I didn't want to hazard the convoluted vicissitudes of the governmental bureaucracy to unearth it. So I made up a social insurance number. I created this imaginary dual status alien. It was the first thing I wrote about on her typewriter, a beat up Underwood which I set up on one chair while I sat hunched over it in another chair.

> The imaginary dual status alien awakes under colorful (Telephone!) Hudson Bay hand-woven Indian blanket, a furry coat, for a pillow on a foam rubber mattress on the floor. (Telephone!) The current nest is on the floor in her room — Eddy sniffing out the

new day—his heart and lungs switch from automatic to manual. Arise — take up thy bed. Minutes slip by — There! — He's on his feet going for the first cup of java (Telephone! Student!) Some rank amateur is trying to — wants to pick s/S's brain, — on the way to the first cup.

Turbulence thought Eddy. All Life is Turbulence and Dissipation. Eddy was familiar with Turbulence.

Turbulence was the first thing he recognized in the morning, when he was still yawning, while the sun was just dawning, when he stirred the cream into his first early morning cup of coffee. He loved to watch the white marble swirls as they curl and twist in the fluid dynamics of mixing, the shape of restlessness itself, a kind of augury, coffeeromancy(?), that snaked off into the vacant air, and whose differential topology was due to the transparent tensor forces of a hyperspace of more-than-just-astrological influence.

A surge of images enters Eddy's mind and the new day proceeds upon the aroma rich steam rising and breaking into whirls, and the first of the days Eddies. He sung the praises of sweet speed.

Even though I was one of these writers pretty much committed to the confessional school, I wanted to make sure to protect the identity of this lady who was my love, my muse. Who put me through a lot. Also the symbol s/S was the glorious ratio of signifier to signified, developed in linguistics and such a fertile thing for a writer to try and give an aesthetic apperception about.

The imaginary dual status alien is me in another time line. A parallel dimension that is displaced ahead of me with a different history trailing behind. I had gone back to Montreal with a woman and ended up seeing my imaginary self in a dimension of what might have been. This other me that had not emigrated to the states, and tried to re-imigrate or is it de-emigrate and who was now trying to be a favorite son, was a lost citizen who had found his way back from the maze of the future.

When I am in an old neighborhood of Montreal I think I
see my father, from behind as if he were holding my hand
when I was small. He is taking me with him to church, I am
following him. Or I see my mother with her big fur coat, her
warm clean animal smell. Sometimes I see from below a
woman hanging clothes on a line, that runs across the alley to
the other side. I want to run up the stairs and see if it is her.
Or looking at the leaves scattered in the slant sun on the
sidewalks, I remember their pattern, of little veins and
branchings and their colors so golden and like parchment with
strange meaningful writing on them — the book of life to read.
That was the book I was looking for. The one I wanted to
write. About this other me heading down the highway with this
girl I loved, leading into shaded hollows of parallel time into
which I must follow for it is a privilege to shadow this more
real all-encompassing spectral spread of selves. Which is not
real at all.

I called Rayne at her office; I thought about her all the
time. In the first flush of love, you will want to know everything about your beloved. It was a merging of two lives.

She had gone to McGill, got a Masters degree, her area
was Blake and his mentor Swendenbourg. Heavy.

Though she didn't push a feminists agenda, I could tell she
was pretty much seething under the surface. But most women
are, aren't they?

I see her at the kitchen table in the morning light. Her hair
is thick and bushy, a mousy brown, tossed around a severe
face with an eager earnest real look — not afraid, not fake. A
full face, dark tanned skin rounded at the small pointed chin,
no lipstick on the full lips. And the upper lip easily rolled up
into a superior smile. I recognized that because mine does that
too. Some people might call it slightly snide, or rueful. I
recognize it subliminally as resigned, determined to see the
humor in it all. She did not shave her legs, or really go out of

37

her way to be pretty. That was not part a woman's job description. But she had that self-possessed air that most good-looking women have. A man assumes it comes with the turf — being desirable, looking at themselves in surround mirrors, being connected more directly to the chaos of life — though in her case it was authoritative. Later I began to understand it was partly due to the profound effect of video feedback on consciousness.

I found myself a ghost in a ghost family, paralleling my own family, with a child the same age now as I was then, and me the same age now as my father was then. Somehow I was caught in a knot of time that had looped back and closed around the string vibrating between the past and the future. It was thrilling to be in this and to know it.

I had never been married to or romantically attached to someone's mom. Though I had been in various crash pads with children and communes and scenes. From that I had come to understand that the disenfranchised and downwardly mobile hippie male needs to take clues from Latin and black families. In those nuclear families, the style (forced by economics) is that women have kids and men move in and out of their lives. Maybe that's good, for a boy to have other father figures. I did. But anyway that's the way it is.

In order to court Rayne I'd have to get along with her son Beausolei. He was four years old. I would come to find out that becoming a surrogate dad was one of the best things that ever happened to me. Rayne must have recognized that since I was an older brother I could be that for her son.

Beau didn't like me at first. He resented competition for his mama. But that second day, I took Beausolei for a walk across the street into Staynor Park. I pushed him on the swing. On the see-saw I ooched way up close to the fulcrum and tried to get it so he could balance me like he did his small friends. I also walked up it and rode it down as it flipped to the other side, which I don't think you were allowed to do. He looked surprised. After some other rides we got on the glide horse, a long row of seats built for about 5 kids. You made it go by pulling on handlebars and pushing on foot pegs. He sat in my seat and we got it going. I was right behind him and had my arms around the boy.

Then a little later, in the sand box, we got eye to eye and I said, "I really, like your mamma, Beausolei." I paused. "And I'm gonna be around for a while. I hope we can be good friends too."

Beau pulled out his gun and pointed it at me, and said "Bang, you're dead."

Beau was in a cowboy phase. He had a little set of chaps, and a holster with a revolver. Rayne had agonized over this male behavior, but thought that since she was a single mom, she should allow it. When Beau understood that I was from Texas, he was intrigued. I picked up on this. At dinner, I would lean back in my chair, so that it was balancing on two legs, then cross one leg over, making a big lap with the ankle of a foot resting on a knee. Balanced there, I'd lift my plate off the table and eat the dinner off the plate in my lap. I deployed my southern drawl, and said to Rayne, and Beau, "I worked on a ranch and learned how to eat like this from the cowboys." I winked at Rayne. "They are so used to riding horses all day, that when they eat, they like to feel their balance, so they lean their chair on two legs and it feels like being on a horse."

Beau didn't know what to make of this.

Rayne rolled her eyes.

I added: "But you have to be able to ride a horse first to ride a chair like this."

Beau couldn't get enough of the Texas stories. It was interesting to tell stories to a believer. I made sure that the Mom was always present, cause I could tell she was into the truth.

Pulgadas

After perusing the employment ads in the Montreal Star, I tried to get a job translating technical papers from Spanish into English. I knew my French wasn't any competition for the local native French speakers of Montreal. I went downtown to this slick upscale office at Place Ville-Marie.

These job applications always have a place to write in REASON FOR LEAVING in the Resume part. I refrained from writing: Because the Job sucked? Or, Because the people there were so miserable to be around it just drained my energy so much I got to a place where I just dragged myself to work and back. Or, Because I refused the requisite lobotomy operation necessary to perform the mind-numbing, endlessly meaningless menial tasks required.

But I had to get a job so I could stay and explore this new love I was involved in. I didn't have a sports coat or a tie. Of course at the interview they asked me, "Have you got a tie?" I was sure there was one in the freebox at the bottom of the stairs at Staynor Street so I said Yes.

They gave me a huge tract with all kinds of charts and graphs for a test.

After looking at it for a while, I said, "I'd like to take it home." When I got it home, I could only vaguely make out the meaning of things. There was one word that kept recurring a lot. *Pulgadas*. *Pulgadas* in front of long equations. *Pulgadas* with square root signs. *Pulgadas* along the y— axis of graphs. *Pulgadas* dressed in quotes and reclining on underlines. *Pulgadas* up the wahzoo. I began to seriously doubt my Spanish. I thought it meant "voltage", as in *pulling* the current along. Or some kind of fundamental force, symbolized by the cat, el gato. Pull gatos. I didn't know. Women are a cross between cats and angels. Men are a miscegenation of devils and dogs.

I phoned Rayne up at school. We were newly lovers then and were always trying to find excuses to call each other up in the middle of the day. When we were apart we couldn't stop thinking about each other. I'd feel her body on me from the night before, how she made love to me, held me with purpose and a fierce tenderness. Every few minutes during the day I'd think of her, wondering what she was up to. I'd call her at work to let her know I was still under her spell.

"Do you know what pulgadas are?" I asked. "I'm trying out for a job as a Spanish translator, and I've got this huge treatise full of pulgadas. And I can't figure out what pulgadas are. They let me take the test home. I'll have to buy a dictionary at a book store."

"Maybe you should try induction," she teased.

In her teasing, I felt her liking me more then. I could tell she was glad I was looking for a job.

I said, "When you get home today, I'd like to use you, my dear. You know what I mean. Use you in the sexual sense."

Not to be outdone, she said, "When I get home I might have to rip your clothes off before Beau gets home, so I don't have to wait until you use me."

After she hung up the telephone, I could almost see Rayne do this little dance step she did when the thought no one was watching. It was stepping lively and long like one of the Fabulous Furry Freak brothers trucking; I could see her smiling serenely to herself. Rayne had this bold masculine walk. Like Trucking — taking long strides. I noticed it. It was catlike almost like a martial artist. She was much more comfortable wearing pants.

When Rayne got home from work that day, we two lovers grabbed each other and hugged and swirled each other around, like man and wife refugees separated by two years of war. The man and woman started kissing and holding each other. I grabbed her ass with both hands — hard, and held her body tightly against mine. My cock rose and started to press itself against her. The lips of her open mouth were pressed on mine kissing me lusciously. I rubbed my pelvis against her. She undid the belt holding up by jeans, slid down the zipper; I help her undoing the top button. With deft hands she reached into my open pants, pulled the underpants open, and pulled my cock out peeking over the top of my shorts. Then let the elastic snap into it, slapping it to a shocked attention. All the while kissing me in a most delightful, lascivious way.

It was in the living room. She pushed me into the high backed antique chair with the armrests. We didn't even get out of the living room. Beau wasn't home yet. But was due any minute.

She stood over me as I was seated in a chair. "Get your pants off," she told me, "while I watch." I ooched out of jeans and undershorts, she knelt down in front of me and pulled them down to my ankles. "Take your shirt off too," she ordered. She made no effort to get undressed herself.

Now she was looking at my standing thing with wide-eyed, obvious hunger. I saw her swallow. She went down on me. Licked the head which glowed to bulging aching with a surge of red. "I am so horny," she said. "It's like being in a blue flick." My cock was just bulging. As she bobbed up and down, she chuckling and relishing it.

I reached to start undressing her, but she moved away. "I want to fuck you," I explained.

She looked at me and shook her head, enjoying her

superiority at the incongruity of my situation: me half-naked, her dressed. She had an almost gloating, satisfied overseer look of someone in control. She ran her tongue around her lips and said, "I've been thinking about this all day. Let me bring you off my way. She knelt down between my legs, leaned forward and placed her elbows on the arms of the chair. With her right hand she stroked the cock gently with the tips of her fingers for a moment, then grasped it tightly in her closed fist. She clutched the cock with her hands. She guided it into her open mouth. She rubbed her face and lips across the dome. And shook her head from side to side so that her cascading hair fell lightly across it to tease it with wispy strands. It stood up, tall, wonderful. She let her open mouth fall slowly down on the slick shaft.

She pressed her mouth up and down, twisting her lips out of shape around the rod. I just lay back then and let her do me the way she wants. She let her mouth fall down on it so that it sunk deep into her throat. The girl gurgled and gagged a bit. I moaned. She hummed an mmm, and was enjoying having the power, having her way with her man. I was enjoying letting her. Trusting her. There was much love and gentleness and care in her eyes as she looked up at me.

She no longer needed to hold my little soldier up with her hands, the excruciatingly rigid boner was standing, throbbing monstrous on its own. She repositioned herself. So that she was on all fours, hands and knees on the floor.

I was slouched down in the chair. Her butt was jutting up for she was arching her back so she could look me in the eye as she was holding the head of the cock in her lips, kissing it in a long sucking kiss, and Frenching it with her tongue. It was overwhelming; it started to cum, some sperm exploded and leaked out of her pursed lips. Still she held the kiss. It was coming into the kiss. Suddenly sperm erupts from deep inside, rises over her upper lip which was already covered with beads of sweat. A volcanic eruption from deep inside hurls white lava bursting like a gusher spewing out over her lips as she squealed MMM! at the thrashing, erupting, splurting mess now flowing down her chin.

An involuntary spasmodic hip thrust of my hips broke the cock free of her kiss. A large dollop of cum shot across her cheek and she held her face up for more, laughing. The next blast, was a huge promontory that flew past her right eye and went over her shoulder and down her back, leaving a wet streak down the back of her blouse. She positioned her head so that just her face would be hit. The next ejaculation went on her forehead and dripped down her nose. All the while I was moaning and it became a roar, a bellowing Oh, Oh, Oh, as she closed her lips over the end of the cock, in the kiss again, but not before more ejaculatory ejectamenta escaped, bursting upon her cheek, getting a bit on an eyelid, and drenching her upper lip.

My eyes were open in shock. Her eyes were open in love. She had her man —there, naked, with his dick in her mouth, his cum on her lips and dripping down her face, and she was looking at him with passionate love. True passionate love.

I wanted to behold this intimate horniness, study this lust. I gently lifted her chin with the fingers of my left hand. While she held my cock in the lips of her kiss, I felt the cum dripping down her face over my thumb. We gazed into each others eyes.

I felt my gaze softened from shock into love. The two lovers looked at each other. What an accomplished lover she was. I felt her tremendous power as she held the tip of my cock in the kiss of her lips. And I held her face in my hand.

Have you ever looked into your lover's eyes?

Seen the power of love in the grasp of lust?

We hung there in space for a moment, locked in each other's gaze. We held it for a while, and my cock began to slacken, and she was like a lioness with her arched back, and the sticky cum in her hair, and she let it drop from her mouth, and smiled a grin of pride, and said, "Mamma's gonna treat you all right."

It was so sexy; she was so disheveled. If she had worn lipstick, or eye shadow or anything to amplify her sexy face, men would have followed her down the street, would have thrown themselves in front of her car. It was a big problem that she had to be cool about.

"A mouth is just a cunt with brains," she said. And as she relaxed back on her haunches to stand up, she said, "I've gotta go get a towel." While I was fainting back, fey in the chair like a male Saint Theresa, Rayne rolled back onto her feet, and went to the bathroom to wipe her face. "And I have to rinse this blouse," she said.

She had a mouth like a torn pocket.

And my only salvation was in that mouth.

After . . . that evening, still stoned and blown, I started spontaneously singing / composing my first song.

I imagined myself at some point later in his life, famous, being interviewed by an ethnomusicologist: "It was a traditional western tune, you hear in the air in Texas. A lot of songs are built that way, you hear a version and then do one of your own. That's what they mean by traditional. Sort of like a transgenerational jam session of many people contributing something to this organic growing thing, over time. Like mythology or the stories of Paul Bunyan. I was thinking of the woman I loved: how she was effecting me at a very important rebirth of my life, and not wanting to use her name, (and to make a drug allegory instead) I called her Maryjane.

Song for Maryjane

Well I can't say I'm sorry /I loved to taste her too much to say that.
 But I can recognize her red eyes and rhapsodize, angry and sad.

Chorus: So won't you tell her: She's the source of my inspiration
And when she sweet talks. . . I can handle, the pain.

Maybe I smoked her, then again maybe I lied
But I was standin' by the sidelines, she put heroes in my eyes.

Chorus: So won't you tell her: She's the source of my inspiration
A-nd when she sweet a talks, you know it seems like
I can handle the pain.
(Long Inhalation on a joint)
Well now maybe I'm just a non-violent, god-fearin' sex toy
She does mama and I play her little boy.

Chorus: So won't you tell her: She's the source of my inspiration
And when she sweet talks, I can handle the chains.

I promised a post card. I just turn away and smile
You know I'm 500 miles high out climbin' heaven
and never knowin' where how or why.

Chorus: So won't you tell her: She's the source of my inspiration
And when she sweet talks,
You know it seems like, I can handle the change.

I went to the Westmount library for a Spanish dictionary.
Pulgadas in Spanish means *inches* in English.
Huh. Who knew?
Maybe my Spanish wasn't as good as I thought. I am
pretty good in a kind of "Street Spanish," and I should have
been able to pick up the material from the science in it. Alas
it was not to be that I would find a stimulating literary job
using my head and education.

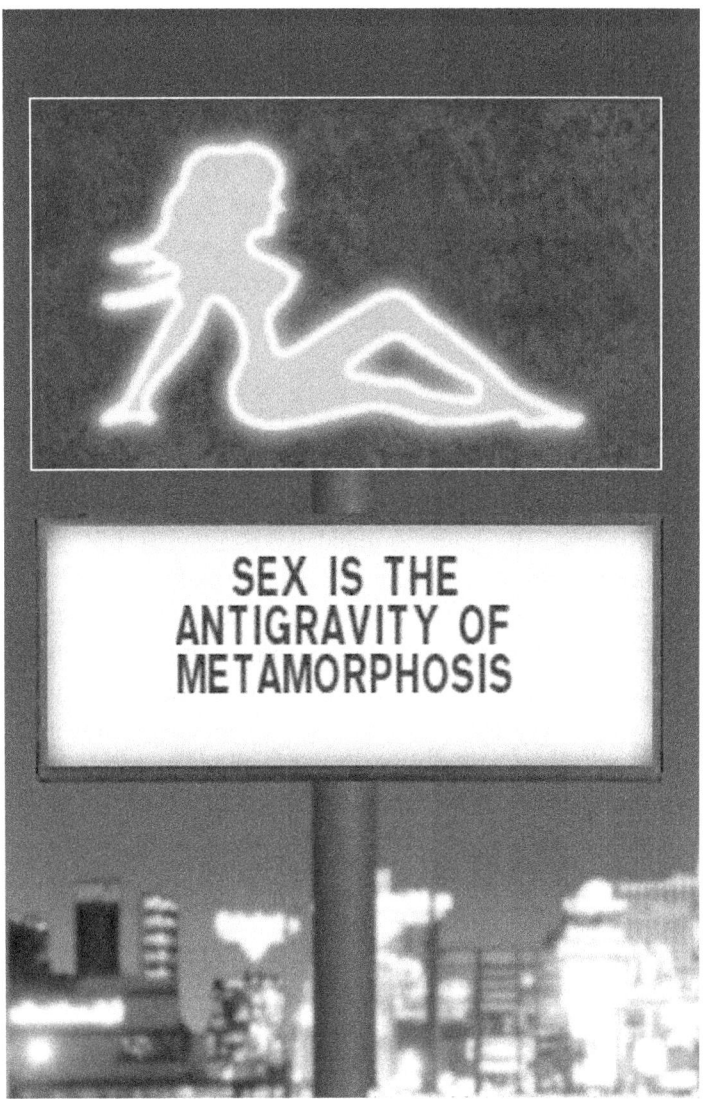

47

The Rainbow Bar & Grill

If I had to pinpoint one moment, the moment when I fell in love with Rayne, it would have to be at the end of the evening of the Friday of that first week, when she and Beausolei and I were heading home from the Rainbow Bar & Grill. She had a light day that day, and took me in to the college so I could see where she worked. I met some of her colleagues, in particular a dapper young literature and media teacher in his 30s named Palumbo.

To see her at this creative place, was different from how she saw herself there. For her it was the world of the 'white male', the world of jobs and capitalism; a foreign world, a separate reality that she had landed on. She got herself there, from having built an underground radio station, as well as having worked with a famous documentary film maker. Currently she was working on a film about mothers living in all-female communes and raising their own children without men. It was this world of the sisterhood that she believed in and whose story she wanted to tell, uninhibited by white male dominated big media. She was fond of saying, A woman needs a man like a fish needs a bicycle.

At the college she left me sitting on a chair beside her desk in a cubicle while she picked up her cheque. Then we went back to the apartment. I was supposed to wait there in case Linda brought Beausolei back from somewhere while she went to cash her cheque. When she returned she took me into the bedroom, and threw handfuls of money on the bed and said, "The eagle flies on Friday. Here is a bunch of money, take what you need. We're goin' out tonight." It was her habit to get to the Rainbow Bar & Grill on Stanley Street in time for the Happy Hour.

It turned out the Rainbow Bar & Grill was just around the corner from the Ritz Carlton, near McGill, and a couple of streets away from the McTavish Tavern where I used to drink with my cousin, when he was at McGill. Boy those Canadian college students can really put it away. They always ordered three glasses of beer, never just one. At the Rainbow, there was a cool jazz / blues band playing a few tunes in preparation for later activities. The clientele were tres chic sophisticated French / European /Anglais Montrealers.

Beausolei and I disturbed their peace when we built paper airplanes to fly them up over the booths and into the laps of the swell people around the fancy bistro, much to the consternation of some of the young and childless couples, but also to the delight of others. I had to appreciate how well Rayne carried herself, her style. She was certainly a lot more accomplished then these what looked to me to be kind of spoiled, well-to-do young professionals without any kids. Looking over at her, with her man's tweed sport coat and her army surplus ammunition bag for a purse, I thought about how together she is, to be carrying all this off. Wow I have been taken up by the angels.

The Montreal French are dark, fine featured, with dark skin and big expressive dark eyes. They talk in high speed bursts with lots of hand gestures, and they have all studied philosophy and theology. I felt like a great big rough raw redneck trying to make the scene. But Rayne was right at home, it was her living room. The dynamic of the French and Anglais in Montreal reminded me of the dynamic of Mexican and Anglos in San Antonio. In both places the majority has to be deferential to the more monied minority. Yet the down-trodden French and Mexicans seemed like the people with the most passion and *joi de vivre*. The French Canadians seemed to be really coming into their own. There had been the Separatists when I was working in Quebec in '69, and now they had their own Parti Quebecois. You could tell among the young that they knew they were headed into a marvelous time to be French.

But the young professionals seemed a bit light in the loafers too. Now that I was captured in the spell of family, it seemed a long time ago that I was just a single guy. I had never had the money to do much hanging out in clubs, and thus lacked savoir-faire to charm my way into the clubbing scene. In Austin we wore cutoffs and T-shirt, went to the Armadillo World Headquarters Beer Garden or Les Amis. Places without a cover. I enjoyed drinking and dancing, and it was cool to just go out and dance in the great human mass. At the Rainbow I was content to have an excuse to be hanging back in the booth: keeping an eye on Beausolei who, blissfully unaware of the din, would stretch out on the red leather cushions and sleep. Rayne could socialize. When Rayne is happy it shows all over her face. She had a very expressive face, and for too long it had been sad and dark.

When we left the Rainbow I was carrying Beau still asleep. And as we were strolling down Stanley Street back to the car, feeling the night, our way was lit by the windows at all the fine shops with exquisite things for sale, and we could see our little group in reflection. She looked over at me carrying her son and gave me the most joyous smile, over-flowing with appreciation and recognition. And I looked back at her — jeer , smile — and started falling in love.

Walking down a dark street late at night we gave each other a sense of security. The feeling I was having was like water plunging over a falls, (maybe that's why they call it falling in love,) because you suddenly become aware that it is an awesome responsibility. You become their parent figure.

In that moment of euphoria I could actually feel my heart rise up in my chest and come pouring out of my throat. It trembles with excitement out there in the air there between us. It had abandoned me and gone into another; but it might just have been the sense of risk at the exposure to abandonment and rejection too. So at the same time as the sense of falling — perhaps into the clutches of this woman — there was a sense of rising, being buoyed up, floating on a force field of love. That's what was moving up from my heart and out toward this other that hath captured me. And between the falling and the rising, there was a giddiness, a swoon. I did feel weakness in the knees, (some protector I was). It was a heightened state of awareness and play and energy. In Love everything seemed possible, it was being in a flow of magic.

We were a couple now.

I put my arm around her, pulled her close to me, closer, face to face, closer to kiss, lips to lips, and she kissed back, and our souls exchanged seeds of joy, like pixie dust and I said, "In Montreal, they kiss on Main Street."

It was such a sense of security, we belonged together out here on the streets at night. No one was going to mess with us because one would die to defend the other, we were a high energy dyad that was unpredictable as a whirling centrifuge — a top, and it was spinning, trying not to wobble but to stand up noble and be worthy of the state, the dance.

And love would protect with its magic if given the opportunity. It was a synchronistic vortex like Jung said, a cyclone, where the warring fronts of man and woman circled around each other and get fused into a potentially explosive thing. That's the way love likes it. Who are we to think we are calling the shots, understanding the rules.

Blue High

One Sunday we went into the great park of Mount Royal. We parked the green car at the University of Montreal, and entered the vast cemetery on the north side by squeezing through a gap between the fence and a wall. I felt happy to be out on a lark on this magical mountain with my love and her wee bairn. As we crossed the lawn into the forest, the great big silver squirrels of Mount Royal were running across the open spaces, busily hustling.

The row upon row of tombstones bristled on the hillside like sharks teeth. Some of the sweller larger family plots were built up like mini-mausoleums of marble. Some even had a tape recording of the deceased's voice; you could press a button and get a message from beyond the grave.

Soon we came upon a replica of Golgotha, a simple wood cross with an image of Christ hanging on it. I looked at the somber icon of Suffering Man, with a Woman's Figure kneeling before it. Beausolei didn't pay any attention to it. Rayne remarked: "Beausolei has never heard of Jesus."

I was a bit taken aback at the innocence of the lad. What is the mind of a 4-year old like? "Damn," — I deployed my southern drawl: "Are y'all Jewish?"

Rayne laughed. "Well, yes."

I got us into rolling down the little hill at the foot of the cross. WEEEEEE! tumbling over and over, arms tucked in like a mummy. Down close to the ground, where you could smell the grass and the flowers. Beausolei loved it. Rayne did too. A few unfortunate dandelions got bent. Beausolei almost got stung by a bee and made a huge hue and cry. This scene reminded me of rolling down a high hill here once when I was about Beau's age too. Rolling down this steep hill —

high on the Mount Royal overlooking the fluvial plain with its hard-working river of the world, I was getting intimations of my own past: I have entered through this little family — (mamma and me and baby makes three) (Jesus, Mary and Joseph) — my own family of long ago.

Rayne looked hilarious in her high-top mountain boots and skirts flailing all about as she rolled and tumbled down the hill. She came up with grass stains on her ass and a huffy laugh. Here hair was all feathers, her pendants askew. Returning my admiring gaze, the girl lifts her chin to share her sinful smile and enlighten our way with her agile wiles.

We were all flushed and high from the vertigo then as we continued walking on through the park. And I found myself walking into a recollection of having been there before. And with it a whole mindset of childhood beliefs began circulating in the periphery among long forgotten memories attached to the place. It was something I was trying to remember, maybe had dreamt about or had a fixation about, long ago. It was about tunnels that run underground in this big hill, and that trees were like elevators. They had this in Peter Pan, didn't they? Maybe I was just getting confused with that. No, this was part my own worldview back then. I used to spend a great deal of time in an ongoing story; all kids are like that, aren't they? Strong participatory magic. It was a feeling I didn't have a name for; I started thinking of it as the Blue High. It is an uncanny feeling. Perhaps the onset of creative intimations? Or it might be that kind of synchronistic vortex you slip into when drifting into a creative binge? Or involuntary memory at a node in the world mind, at the intersection of coincidences? Or the onset of powerful feeling. The moment is expanding, swelling like the surface of a hot air baloon, lifting my person, rushy feelings imbuing; a kind of possession — by furies and other chthonic deities of ancient Greek god psyche. I am floating up.

Drifting. In-between. Entering parallel worlds.

We crossed a wide Boulevard into the great Parc du Mont-Royal — me officiously and with ceremony — stopping the traffic for my little Madonna and child. We continued on up to Beaver Lake (*Lac des Castors*), where there was a model sailboat regatta going on. We stopped and sat while Beausolei studied this with keen interest.

We had joined the Sunday strollers. It felt good to be walking with my old lady and her kid. I was part of a family now, part of the great institution of the Sunday promenade taking place all over the world. In Chapultapec, in Central Park, in the Tuilleries, in Hyde Park and on Mount Royal. Everybody walking around on a perfect peaceful sunny Sunday. People smiling at each other, little waves of recognition, people playing catch, and frisbee, some sporting their wealth, others talking with god. All partaking in the sense of peace that pervades the place.

This sense of bourgeois normalcy was so foreign to me that something made me recoil with mistrust.

My "life style" if you could call it that, for it was pretty much not doing anything or taking care of anything until the last minute when the inevitable was thrust upon you — often with inexorable existential vehemence — was no way to live, let me tell you. I don't know what made me be like that. A tall skinny grasshopper fiddling his life away while the ants scurried and laid aside and prepared. The fool, the hanged man, the broken tower, the knave of stiffs — these were the cards I played. I supposed it was from sheer narcissistic sense of entitlement, from having been my mother's first born and for a while having her all to myself. In any case I just hated being the slave in the master slave relationship. I didn't want to be the master either. I just wanted to do my own thing, as they say. It was about improvisation. There is a personality type . . . Feeling-intuiting? rather than, thinking-sensing? Perceiving-judging that was it. I was more comfortable perceiving — dealing with what came up.

To bring me back out of my head I tried to enter the moment, the plane of reality before me. But something was happening to the fabric of my spacetime. Big G had gone variable, was no longer constant but getting smaller relative to the space inflating all around us, so the force of attraction between things is letting up: birds are starting to soar higher, leaves are falling to the ground much more slowly, small pebbles are starting to float when little boys loft them into ponds. My weight was becoming lunar; what use would I be with my 25 pounds? All things were becoming suspended or moving more slowly along their paths of attraction. They had been given a moment to be self-aware.

Looking up the hill we saw people hanging out on the grass, so our little family made the promenade around the lake and joined the hill people. There Rayne started dancing with Beausolei. She got into a wild fling like some Mountain Woman, twirling him around by his feet, then carrying him by his hands on her back with his arms around her neck like he was a back pack or papoose. Then she started running around frantically looking for him while he chuckled on her back.

"Hey! Where's Beausolei?"

"Here I am! Mamma. Behind you."

"Where?"

"Around here." (whirl, crouch, pounce.)

"I can't see you Beausolei!? I've lost my baby! Where are you?!"

She would swing wildly around, looking frantically every which way, jerking him around, so he had to cling on for dear life, laughing wildly.

"Where are you. Why are you playing tricks on me?"

"I'm right here, mama, behind you."

She reaches between her legs and pulls him down off of her back, bringing him carefully, deftly, through — holding onto him with both hands. She rolls him over and holds him by his ankles making him do the wheelbarrow. Squeals of laughter. WEEEEE! She grabs his ass by the seat of his pants and with a hand on his chest does a loop-de-loop. And then he is safely in her arms once more.

 She was just a girl, a little mama, with her kid playing on the mountain. Their shrieks of laughter float out on the ocean of air we swim in, piercing through the sky blue eye.

We can look beyond the blue sky out over the park in this modern city, through the canyons of buildings to zig zag out to the waterfront and beyond to the countryside and the river, out over the ocean of air that covers the world, see its turbulence in fronts swirling around each other in a dance, out beyond the edge of the stratosphere like the pilgrim in Ezekial seeing behind the arras of the horizon. We can see Venus in the Zodiac shining down her love on us. And like the lovers in a Chagall painting we are lifted. I can hold her above me with one hand like a tandem surfer team, riding breaking gravity waves. Sailing like the fiddler on the roof over the chimney tiles and dormers of the town.

She was his mother. Gave him life, gave him a healthy body, fed him, gave him immunities, will make him thousands of meals, gave him good hair and teeth and brains to burn and she will protect him like a buffer, a bubble that is there around his every given moment in some way or another. And where did she get this bubble, this manifold inflatable and deflatable space? Did it always exist? It is part of each generation's legacy. Natures gift. It surrounds every living thing with a bubble of blue ultraviolet energy, and intra violet and violent and infrared too. It's in every drop of water, in the vapour of water and feels the spherical harmonics of the atmosphere, the ionosphere, the biosphere, the ecosphere, the geosphere, the stratosphere, the zoosphere, the noosphere. Enclosing us in the their porous flexible invisible skins expanding and contracting and creating a world within and without us. While we watch like children amusing ourselves blowing bubbles in the bath.

She with gypsy eyes and hippie laughter is showing me how to play with her child. This sky air, the blue of the blue marble, plays in waves with us. . . little mamma . . . we will push through, I am trying to step into the role of father.

I was coming to understand how a man has to accept that this bond between a mother and child would forever exclude him. You can have your brotherly and otherly love; but it's not motherly love. I felt a sense of outsiderness yet belonging. She was a lone strong woman who didn't need a man. *Je suis un outremonter*. She was all that little boy needed. She was just a girl, raising hell on the mountain side, she was oblivious to the beaming of my admiration, totally at ease with my presence. I was a mere student, an observer, at the central magic of motherly love.

She's a strong little mama, and Rayne swings Beausolei around as he screams for mercy. Their screams and exaltations of joyous laughter were reverberating the whole mountain side. She jiggled him so hard that his pants fell off almost down to his knees. He sits down on the grass, face twisted in outraged consternation and this indecent public exposure. "Now see, you made me loose my pants!" he shouted with rage and pouted as he struggled to get them back on.

We continued up the mountain forest, up many flights of wooden stairs above Redman path to the Chalet and its open courtyard of massive stone pavers, out to the great lookout of the fortress ramparts overlooking the city. There we spent a long time looking at the beautiful Montreal cityscape. Place

Ville Marie, McGill University, the river with its islands, Habitat. Rayne was the first to find our neighborhood and pointed out the park on Staynor Street by first finding the Atwater Marketplace. Staynor is a peculiar street— one block long — off Green, across the park from Dorchester. There were houses only on one side of the street for Staynor Park was all along the other side.

I saw us in our green touring machine lifted, flying by flubber, chitty-chitty bang-bang through the clouds over the crowds confined in their car coffins coughing in the toll traffic. I am reliving the same scene from lost time in this great old park [maybe Mohawks and Hurons and French and English are moving through too in parallel times] feeling as I did as a child that I am being lifted. And here with this girl gifted we two are being lifted.

As I would come to find out the apartment on Staynor Street was the center of the spiral of their world on the island of Montreal, for Rayne was a very together single mom. (You have to be.) The location offered easy access for the drive to her work up the river. Also it was close to day care, and shopping and only a few block from the Children's Hospital, and the Montreal Forum and the Atwater metro station. Looking out at the city of my birth, I had drifted into a reverie. It was not your common everyday trance.

I seemed to have stepped outside of myself. A kind of separation, where you were in two places at once. I felt something was lifting me. An expansion. It was the blue high, and I could soar out over the city, and I could look at places in memory, in the past of Walker Underwood. It was like I was hovering over the schema of my own life, could see it all at once as a long and winding path that had brought me to this moment. I was a kite tethered by a thin thread held by a small boy on a hill overlooking a vast city. I saw the St. Lawrence River glimmering, winding its way in a wide silvery swath cutting through the bottom of a vast river valley, a royal road shining in the setting sun. I was the small boy, brought here by my parents to run around on the ancient meadows of Mount Royal. We used to explore all around Mount Royal. There were streams and gullies and little underground grottoes and, I thought at the time, tunnels and caves that only fairies and little people and children could get into. They were only visible to children; grown-ups weren't on the same wavelength and couldn't pick up on it. Back in that time, what other things had I believed in, going on in the mind of a 4-year old.

As Catholic children do, I believed very strongly in Guardian Angels. I was a serious boy and for a long time I wanted to be a priest. I learned all the Latin of the mass before the second grade — it was some kind of strange mumbo jumbo incantatory language said while throwing smoke at an idol. It was through the smoke that the mind rose and expanded out, mixing with the glorious sun rays filtered through the stained glass windows of the church, and could be au fait with god. I wanted to be a priest because my mother thought they were the greatest. It was some kind of insurance. I had seen my Guardian Angel on more than one occasion. What was that about? Because I think I saw Santa Clause too and we know that has been discredited. The mythology of the Catholic Church is Jungian that way, don't you think? My guardian angel had curly hair, just like mine. Beau too had curly hair; through him I am there. It felt wonderful to be protected by a Guardian Angel, I suppose he is still there, though I have not done things to make him proud. I think they are forgiving.

It was a lucid dream: something was pushing this Walker along, causing him to lift through the air, and *zoom down a tunnel and into the secrets of the earth. Into the subway tunnels, where he could fly along faster than the train. Soon I reached Mount Royal. There I climbed the Redman path. I didn't even have to walk up all those stairs I just floated up. There we climbed a leaf strewn path, my Guardian Angel and me, about halfway up the mountain and came to a little lake and then behind some rocks there was a hidden tunnel. My guardian angel said, Don't be afraid. Go right in.*

The tunnel seemed to be an opening like a subway. Once inside, I see it IS a subway station. I go on an old street car through to the other side of Mount Royal and came out at a park with a huge fountain. I think it was called Parc de la Fontain, in the old part of town. I was walking near where my parents used to have an apartment long ago. I was surprised, and I thought I'll just go home and have some of my good old mom's home cooked Canadian food.

I looked into the faces of Beausolei and his good old mom.

As I entered the kitchen with its big floor made of black and white linoleum squares, I saw my mother as a young woman, much younger than Beau's mom here now. And she was dancing with my father, who was also young, they were dancing the jitterbug in the kitchen. They just kept dancing and didn't notice me. I walked to the kitchen table and sat down and tried to think.

But then from there, I was looking out the window at the blue sky, it was just a little bit of blue you could just see it in between the other buildings, the buildings were so close. That's right! The apartment we lived in then was below street level! You could look up at people's legs walking by. But then like in a dream the windows became like frames of panels of a comic book. And I floated out the window, I bobbed along like a balloon, rising and falling over Mount Royal the beautiful.

After a while, Beausolei got bored with quietly gazing at the city and started to fidget and fuss. Rayne had to tend to her dependent. He had to take a lesson in Zen patience. She gave him a time out while she went off to get him a half moon Twinkie at the Chalet canteen. Time to head back.

The sugary food perked up Beau's spirits but Rayne was starting to turn her thoughts to the big bring-down of having to encounter her ex-husband for the child-exchange. As the day had long since folded over on itself and the sun was setting out of sight, Rayne's thoughts started to turn toward getting ready for the onslaught of Monday morning. Beausolei's father was coming back into town. Rayne and he had been divorced for only a couple of months, although separated for 2 years. They were always being punishing and defensive toward each other over the exchange of the kid.

On the walk back to the car we rested among some trees that had boughs low to the ground and Beau climbed up on them while Rayne and I stood by. And I started to tell a story, something made up that was a mishmash of what was going on for me at the moment — I tried to share my feelings in real time — by launching into what I hoped would be an entertaining story I called The Baron of the Trees. I was familiar with its outline, the rest you made up as you go along. Beau was up in the trees, looking down at his good old mom and me. And I started telling him a story about a little boy who climbed up in a tree one day and never came down.

It had him building a nest in his favorite giant maple tree he called Sugar Mama, and about how he grew moss on his feet and could walk around in the trees like it was a sidewalk. It had him being able to communicate with the tree and Sugar Mama told him about how there was a special tree struck by lightning that developed a tunnel into a maze of other underground tunnels in the mountain. There was some description of the underground world. It mentioned how the creatures of the forest, fairies, and magicians, leprechauns and orcs and trolls and elves and even what they call yidams, or sky-walkers, and even the dragons and unicorns and other magical beings all used these tunnels to get to other places fast. These tunnels looped though children's dreams and parts of town where time, which flows like a river, curls back on itself, in the counter circulating eddies of turbulent flow. Anyway this back flow of time had the effect of making people younger for a while. There were many races of people living inside the mountain, elves and trolls and spirits. Whole communities living underground. But it is very rare that the mythical beings who live underground in the mountain have a human boy come to visit them. So they got together and elected him Baron of the Trees.

We got Beau down and continued back to the car. On our way something grotesque happened. When we were walking through the cemetery Beausolei picked up what at first looked like a tree limb, but with closer inspection might be a huge thigh bone. We couldn't be sure; they don't just let these things float out of a crypt, do they? Christ! And it was too long to be human, wasn't it. Perhaps left over from a former race of giants? Beausolei carried the bone like some African king might carry the scepter of power over the tribe, like a little majordomo leading an invisible parade down a sunlit path under the trees in an ancient pygmy forest. The two adults laughed grimly at this bizarre juxtaposition of innocence and experience — it was like something out of *Lord of the Flies*. Or *2001: A Space Odyssey*. Finally parental responsibility asserted itself and Rayne made him drop it. We walked along in silence.

"Are you mad at me?" Beausolei asked her.

But the bone began to unfold its power into an incident.

Thinking of her responsibility and the upcoming encounter with her powerful ex-husband and all the trouble and rancor associated with those encounters made Rayne very uptight and hard edged. She snapped at the kid. I had seen her go off into dark moods, sometimes for hours on end; she got off into spaces where she just wasn't there. And no wonder — bringing up a child you have to be on call all the time, you have to be in your feelings even if you can't.

Rayne's ex-husband runs a game on her head. I had not yet met him, but felt his power in the family. He manipulates her through her child, like the way the Church manipulates its people through the dead here.

Back to the car, some kind of evil telekinetic energy was crackling through the dark woods and WHAM she sticks the door key into the lock, twists it so hard that it gets stuck. We spent over an hour trying various tricks with coat hangers and shoelaces to get the car unlocked. But the great green touring machine will not admit us. Soon we are the last lonely car in the infernal parking lot. The Mercedes Benz is thief proof. The feeling of inadequacy is growing almost unbearable and it threatens to wash away all the good we have done. And to make things worse, we didn't even have enough money to take a bus home. We should have packed a picnic and not spent the little bread we had on cakes at Crape Breton. Instead of walking home Rayne decides we should break out a window. Had I been a more experienced parent I might have recognized a meltdown. But I thought kids were indefatigable, but no. Little moms aren't either. And we made a wrong decision to break out a window in the Mercedes. I wished I had insisted that I walk home. But you can't walk home with a kid. And you can't leave mom and kid in a dark park. And due to my impecunious tendencies there was no money left for taxi or bus. So I broke out the back left wind wing with a rock, and reached my long arm in and got the door open. Soon our wheels were rolling again, we headed out as night closed in — enveloping the city in its light-porous skin. I am still buoyed up from the Blue High, though having to keep still, for now Rayne was exceeding pissed and had slipped into a silent burn. I tried to reclaim the dregs of the day with "Lets say good-bye to the old park. We'll be back again, many times." Beau looked at me with recognition; he was grateful that I was there to absorb some of the blue disappointment. And heading down from the summit, around through the town I steered our meteor blasted ship away from the eminent danger and got our angry and sorrowful selves home. And no amount of my clowning could change the gloomy silence that filled the air then.

At Play in the Fields of Shadows

The first job I got was basically picking pennies out of pigeon shit with a putty knife. I had to let myself be played by a petit-bourgeoisie over in the east side of Montreal. But it got me out into the neighborhood where I was born.

This fat little petty tyrant said, " I want to show you the job. It is to be done by Piece Work."

We walked around the inside of his warehouse building. It had a wall of industrial windows in steal frames. The job was supposed to be only washing the windows. The windows were really filthy. And they had this aluminum burglar alarm tape around their perimeter. It needed to be scraped off. Some of the windows were really covered in a rain of pigeon shit. When it was over I thought: Lucky you didn't catch polio.

The petty bourgeoise counted the windows. There were 15 by his count. Really there were 17. So anyway at $3.00 a window, that makes 45 dollars.

So we drove over there a couple of days later. I was lean and starving by that time The Master had a Servant by the hook then.

"Now we agreed on 45 dollars," he said. "I want you to scrape all the wood around the windows, and clean up all the floors as well."

"Wait a minute." I said. "This in piece work. We agreed on doing 15 windows for 3 dollars a window that's 45 dollars. The rest is gonna cost you extra."

We went back and forth, but I needed the job and had to agree on his terms. The Master brought me a bucket, a couple of ladders, some detergent, rags and a sponge. He found a brush in the toilet. I took the scraper and got up on the ladder and started scraping away the old burglar alarm tape. It was a bitch to get off. And the pigeon shit. It was enough to make you gag. Thin little putty knife spatula fulls of pigeon shit. It was so encrusted you had to chip away at it. It flew back into your face and hair and got on your shirt. The main shit-workers rule is: Try not to get any onya. If you do, just keep telling yourself that it will all wash off at the end of the day.

With each window getting clean, and more and more light coming into that dingy old factory, I began to see things. The place had possibilities. It would make a good artists studio, but was too expensive. On the floor was scrawled in cement, Jean Lecompt, cameraman. But the real story in that place was through the glass. Rows and rows of silent windows looking out onto Montreal's past. They were impossible to clean, like they were covered with some kind of sticky, insoluble glue. I scrubbed it with a brush, I worked for an hour on one window pane, and it would not come clean. That motha fucka would never pay me. He brought me some super strong solvent, but it was not strong enough for this emulsion. With each application, though, there appeared images of the past, embedded in the glass. (Maybe it was the fumes.) Scraping away old burglar alarm conduit tape makes me wonder what could they have had in this old factory to protect.

I took off for lunch. It was down in the east end of Montreal. This was the garment district, blocks of sweat shops, going back to a style of the 30's, steam pouring out of windows. On any corner you could here people talking at least four languages. There the air was filled with mostly Yiddish, then French, very little English — then a lot of Greek, and Arabs talking close to each other, bathing each other with their breath, and Italians. You can never know what language to speak. The linguistical heterofederation of Montreal is a melting pot, but so much ice made it too cold to ever be anything more than a tepid *consumé*.

Outside I started to realize: This was the kind of neighborhood I grew up in. What a linguistical milieu. Growing up in Texas, I had never seen so many Jews. Here they walk around in black double breasted coats, wearing these great elegant fedoras, or stingy brim hats, with long beards. Cool looking older Spinoza mystics, seeing the world through the 8-fold way of the Setheroth, living the Zohar. But I wonder what they are like as people. At a small hole in the wall I told the vendor *Donne-moi un steamy tout dressé avec patates frites* (Give me a hot dog with everything and French fries). Then I got a Molson ale from a Greek with a gold tooth at the corner handy store. I took my lunch up on the roof of my building. Across the way a woman was hanging out clothes on a line that stretched across the alley to a utility pole — or the opposite building. These buildings all had back stairs zigzagging up to the back door landing of each flat; these structures were clad in sheet metal or tin, with odd windows snipped in.

It was the sound of the squeaking, creaking, turning wheel running out the sheets on a clothes-line that took me back into memory: This was my home turf. As that creaking wheel turned, it situated me into my own very early childhood growing up in these alleys of Montreal.

I remember my mother bringing in clothes off the line and they were frozen stiff. She stood up my father's long johns against the wall — and there they were the clothes without the man.

I could see myself in the stern, dirty little boys, wearing skinny, ill-fitting clothes, wearing short pants and shirt, running, running — we were so fast in the summer streets of

Montreal. We played cops and robbers with black kids from Africa and street hockey with French kids. In this multiracial, multilingual milieux you learned to keep a balance, how to get an even number of guys on your side in case of a fight. My god I used to jump from the roof of one building across to the roof of an adjacent building, exhilarated and not paralyzed by the exposure of a three story fall.

Images began to well and billow up inside my mind, like the sheets and ghostly uninhabited clothes dangling in the wind on that line.

Walking back from work to the bus I noticed the worn smooth roundness of the ancient granite curbstone, rounded from the long hard winters. Will I be worn smooth by the shear of snow melted salt sheen and windblast too?

I saw some memories flashing quick in sequence. Me in snow suit, my mother in a great big fur coat with a hood. My father young and ruddy, with short hair. He would have been about my age, the age I am now and he would have had responsibility for me, young Walker scion of Underwood, just as now I have responsibility for young Beausolei scion of Luce, about the same age now as I was then. Wait a minute he has his father's name. << What is his Father's name. >> Not spoken around here.

Later that evening I was the working man with my little family. On our walks in the park we sometimes got riled up into a game of shadowplay. I would try to stomp Beausolei's shadow and run away when he tried to stomp mine. It was fun on the pathways of Staynor Park in the slant autumn light. Sometimes when Rayne was with us, we'd have it that if your shadow got stomped you had to freeze. You could be liberated if Rayne ran through your shadow. It was silly and hilarious, and Beau loved being able to catch an adult and stop him in his tracks and make him freeze.

A Winter Coat

The women of Canada are all about being prepared for a
long, hard winter. Rayne looked please and got all animated:
"Walker, I think I have a coat for you! It didn't quite fit my
brother. Maybe it will fit you."

While Beau and I waited, she went into the bed room,
and disappeared into a closet, reappearing with a P-coat to
end all P-coats. She held it up for us to behold.

Eagerly, she urged, "Walker put it on!"

I put on the coat. It was a coat of many miracles.

She said, "I think it was a British bus drivers coat."

The coat had stiff epaulets on the shoulders, a high West
Point military collar, with red piping trim and brass buttons.
To me it looked a little like a Marine's dress uniform; not
nearly so far out as the band uniform of Sergeant Pepper's
Lonely Hearts, but outstanding.

It was elegant in a flashy way. It had *deux cheves* in red
on each sleeve at the wrist. It would be a warm black wool
coat for the winter, like a navy P-coat but much more stylish.
It had not been warn in a long time. But on me it looked great
with my long hair and it set me off into being more aware of
my posture — activating an erect demeanor; it was totally a
stylish hippie triumph, the very image of this working man's
mod. The apparition of the man these clothes made, seemed
to startle Rayne. She kept looking at me as though she were
seeing something phantasmal, a long lost inamorata perhaps?
A soldier of fortune from a life before? She was starry-eyed
— her mouth open in surprise. She had to blink her eyes to
bring the focus back into the present. She was sitting very
erect and prim with her hands folded in her lap, turning a little
sideways on the edge of the living room chair looking me up

and down, nodding her head in inner amusement. She was once again the muse and I had the sudden sense: I am in the company of a very hip lady.

The living room was dark and I wanted to see my new self in a mirror. I went into the bedroom to look at it in the full mirror and when I saw it I shouted — WOW!

I came right back and they were both smiling.

I hammed it up, tugging at the coat, posturing and twirling around, over doing it, acting like a girl, looking at them, batting my eyes demurely, asking "Do you think it's too tight?"

It was a trim fit. It was beautiful.

Rayne jumped up and with her hands clasped in prayerful delight she said, "MMM, it looks good, Walker. Girls love a man in uniform."

I laughed, "I've got a new coat!"

Beausolei was chuckling and looking pleased that his mother was pleased. It was like I was in a family with a couple of family members.

The three of us often went out to cafes and bistros. We walked or took le Metro. I liked hanging out with Beausolei, and we engaged each other while Rayne talked to her adult friends.

I'm not going to admit that I was a slacker or a dodger; but I was streetwise from much hitchhiking. I could pull cover, and go into that "I'm with the band, man," attitude. I was a proud dude in those days. In Austin I lived doing odd jobs and could be tapped to find elicit substances. Back there I had all the marijuana, Mexican food, and siesta time there ever was. I was an artist, the true aristocrat of time. A psychedelic artist using acid and peyote to explore MIND, and leaving the treasure map of theme explorations in art. I would take acid or peyote and paint the hallucinations that projected themselves in front of my eyes.

But most of all I loved writing. Ever since third grade.

I had long hair, down my back and loved it. Loved to feel it blowing in the breeze. I had the true transcendental tourist mentality and my cover was to be self-effacing, to the point of invisibility. It was useful for getting me into places when I didn't have any bread, which was most of the time. I'd just lean up against a wall, or put hands in my pockets, slump my shoulders and walk into any night club I wanted, or rock concert or dance. If anybody stopped me, I'd just give them this impossibly wasted and pontifically benevolent look, say: "I'm with the band, man."

Who am I to interfere. Let the universe take care of it. You can feel all you need to know.

And it felt good to be wearing this excellent coat, man, walking hand in hand with my lady, feeling like a prince or a soldier, yes a soldier in the service of Art!

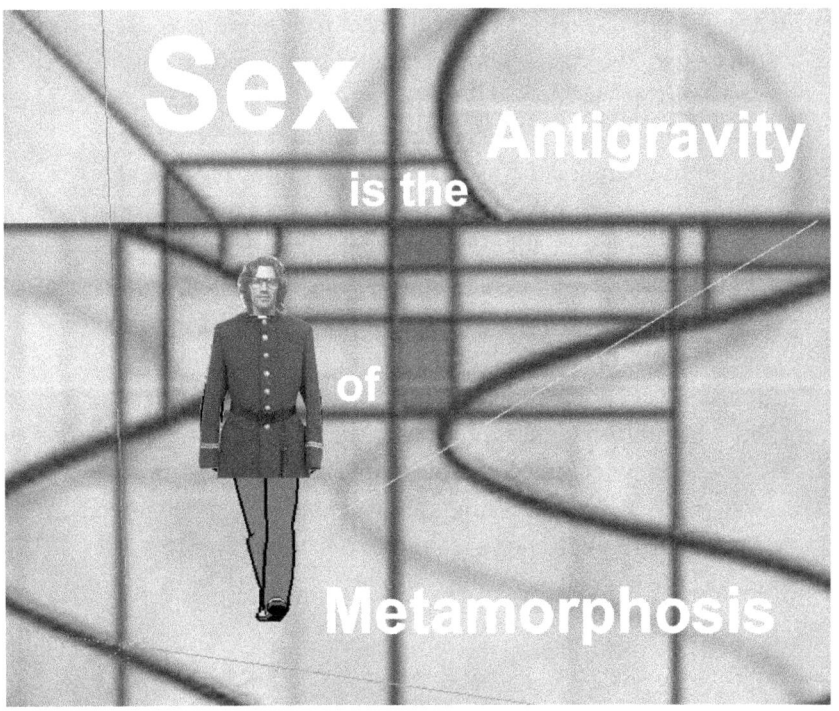

Mr. In-Between

And Staynor Street is a bunker, so much is going on. I was surprised she would even attempt to fit a man into her life. I asked her about it and she told me, "It is no longer enough to be someone's mommy."

The three of us would be walking on the streets of Montreal. Beau liked shouting into cavernous car parks to hear the echoes. One day we visited the firemen in their station and he got to *essayer le chapeau de feu* (try on a fire hat). We went into the swank bars and bistros she favored, to hang with some of her friends. In the clubs in Montreal, she had a lot of friends, a lot of people coming up to her. A lot of guys, many of whom I imagined, were former lovers. She knew a lot of people in bands, in clubs, at school. They didn't always act happy to meet me when she introduced me. She was sometimes vague about our relationship. She called me her friend. She liked to flirt with women too.

When we went out dancing she mixed with other people and cruised around, I was left on my own. I'm shy and introverted and not very social. I liked it when her kid came with us, cause we could just entertain each other.

Her friends and colleagues were a great bunch, and she could relax with them as peers rather than having to maintain that mentor role required for her young students. Her colleagues were doing things with video and sound, with feedback and tape recorders, and I wanted to learn.

The Staynor Street building, with its internal gallery /stair well was a wonderful configuration to encourage community. The people often visited each other. Canadians smoke a little pot, a little hash oil, occasionally do psychedelics, but really, like the Scots, they are into drinking. Canadians are a great bunch for gab and sweet silly innocent verbal play. They are driven inside by the severe winters and like to hole up with great quantities of booze bought from their Government Store. They say that Scots can talk the ears off a donkey well Canadians can talk the tail off too. The central light well with galleries leading to apartments, though absolutely plain, was designed with this sense of village in mind. As the winter progressed, doors stayed open and denizens wandered aimlessly from abode to abode effecting a constant floating party. The Canadians were like beavers in their boroughs who yacked their winter blues away.

Rayne Luce was an "instigator", a chaos attractor, — no that's not right, she was an *eminence gris* — what I am trying to say is she worked in the background. Constantly working in media, being herself in front of a camera, making others get in front of a camera, had liberated her, had made her ready to take chances to improvise fun actions. Maybe it was just her personality type — extrovert, thinking, judging sensing; she'd make a good president. She was having to be both mother and father to her kid. I tried to keep it light, tried to have fun with the kid, make it fun for him. He had a father, I could be his buddy.

One morning Beausolei woke to his mama's moaning coming down the hall. She was setting up a banshee wail. I was inside her and really working. Beausolei had gotten up and walked down the hall to our door.

Standing in the shadows he heard: "Um, uhm, Jesus, gawd! Oh baby, uhhh! Fuck me, fuck me!" from his mother as she moaned with me on top of her. The blanket was pushed off the matress on the floor. Beausolei could see there was movement under the sheet. He could see my butt under the sheet, and us rocking back and forth.

Rayne was carrying on, zoned out in orgasm, long shoulder-shuddering sobs. She was a hot little screw. But you could see, to the innocent, with his mom carrying on moaning and breathing heavy that it could look like this big interloper guy was somehow hurting his momma. I don't know how long he was there. It was easy to misconstrue that I was pounding on his mother. I was. Rayne was laughing. Beausolei stepped forward into the light and surprised us. He had such a righteous expression on his face. His fists were clenched, he was gonna defend his mama.

Suddenly we stopped, looked at him with big eyes.

And he was looking at us with concern. Well, there it was, the beast with two backs. With two heads, and four eyes, looking over at you.

After a pause, I said, "It's OK, yer mama and me were just playin'. I guess I was tickling her too hard."

Rayne looked over at him kind of dazed, her eyes glazed, and said "Yea, it's OK, honey."

We invited him to come on the bed. I said, "Come on, get on my back and I'll give you a horsy ride. We'll have a mommy sandwich with me in the middle."

So he got on my back, and I gave him a horsy ride, meanwhile still driving the pink buckboard into the tunnel of love. And he wasn't none the wiser. We were three partners, riding and laughing, yahoo, across the Texas badlands taking a bouncy-bouncy belly ride. I had that back in the saddle again grin.

Since Beau was in a cowboy phase I made some Texas chili. I told Beau, "This is what cowboys ate on the trail and at the bunk house." Though I did not make the really hot chili. I'd tell him stories about the old west. I told him, "I am unusual in that I was raised by Comanches. Yes. These wild Indians of the plains attacked our settlement in Texas, and kidnapped three of the children and I was one of them."

I told these stories always while winking at the mom. She kind of disapproved of lying or anything that was made up or too fanciful. I told the boy that they were only stories. And I always told them in the most atrocious southern accent, so Beau knew they were made up. He would even effect a southern drawl himself, as part of the game. I told him: They weren't mean to us at all, in fact after a while I got adopted by one of the Indian families and grew up with them on the prairie. I have only recently discovered that I was white, and that's why I still have my hair long. I had to learn their language. There language is real concrete specific, makes descriptions of things you can see like "see that hill with this kind of grass growing on it, bending in the wind." Or "the spotted palomino horse with the silver main." It was all very concrete. I told him, "The word for thunder is *bam-wa'wa*. Cool huh?"

He repeated it. Bam-wa-wa.

"And," I continued, "they have many words for the moon — depending on what time of year it is and what is growing. Like the moon of the falling leaves, this time of year, is *binaakwii-giizis*, it sounds like a baby saying 'binky Jesus'. And the moon of summer strawberries is *ode'mimini giizis*."

"Mini-Jesus," they both repeated and laughed.

I told him: "It was really nice living on the plains with the Comanche. Those people love horses, they are crazy about horses. We rode all over the place. That part of Texas is really open so a horse can go through it, but it is dangerous because of giant cactus with spines so big that if a horse stepped on it the horse could get crippled."

I knew Beau was afraid of dogs, so I told him: "Now dogs, Texas is a good place for dogs. We had a lot of dogs. There was a special kind of communication — the dogs would give you a kind of look, you know, like they liked you and wanted you to run with them. They were really protective of us. Dogs are almost like angels that way. Have you ever heard of angels?"

And I'd rattle off weird stuff like this, always in Rayne's presence, cause I didn't want her to feel like I was filling the lad's mind with nonsense. When I was telling him this, he would look over at his ma, to see how she was taking it. She was smiling, so I guess he figured it was all right.

No lie it was fun, to tell stories to a believer. He even began to mimic the Texas accent, the little actor. It became our in joke, and we did it all the more to torture the mom.

Another night we were watching Beau in his bath and I said, "I can give you guys an honorary Comanche name, if you like. They name the boys after animals and the girls they name after elements. Like boys are Bear and Crazy Horse. My name was Skychief because I have eyes as blue as the sky. Now your name could be Otter, because of how well you go in the water of the bath and at the pool in the Y. And you mama here, well she would be named Rain. Because she creates all this life around her."

And amid this great swirl of her parenting and being a daughter and being a college teacher, which meant being a mentor to beginning artists of creative projects, was Rayne, cool, classical, free-box beautiful. Energetic, intelligent and in charge. Everyone was in love with her, her coworkers, her students, her girlfriends, her old boyfriends, her kid and me.

Rayne in love was something to see. She'd get a little manic, and be racing around on the freeways, in that big Mercedes, looking over at me and talking. She looked happy, smiling. She had a smile that made her face light up, and was kind of a jeer of cheer. I thought that her mind might not be always on the task at hand. We were just so excited to be together. This was a pretty big change in her attitude too and her coworkers noticed it immediately.

Once her joyousness spilled over into giddy fun when she

had us, Beau and I cutting up figures out of transparencies and sticking them onto the TV over the show. That one night Rayne brought out: 1. clear colored transparencies; 2. scissors to cut out shapes; 3. wash cloth to glue the transparency figures to the TV set; and to clean it off. And Rayne and Beau and I proceeded to have a grand time sticking these things on the TV. So that the shows had to appear like our puppet projections. This was the start of my media education. I told her about how the burbling video white noise in between the channels was the background radiation of space left over from the Big Bang. How it proves the expansion of the universe. Also since I used to be a TV tech, I told her about how skip made those ghostly images of the people in TV, slightly phase-shifted — a harmonic away — as though in a parallel dimension. She listened patiently, kind of lost but enjoying the spaced-out hippie, gee-whiz factor of it.

I started going with her to her class more, became sort of a factotum, dogs body, roadie, teacher's assistant. I kidded with her: "Do you know what the second oldest profession is?"

"No." She looked mischievous.

"The TA."

She laughed at that.

But I did want to learn about video, about being a camera man. And feedback, and chaos too. One of the books we had showed how to create a vortex of chaos by pointing a video camera at the monitor making a self-reflexive feedback loop, in which the output became the subject of the input.

Rayne had allowed us to start "The Wall" all up and down the apartment hall. She just let Beau draw all over the place with his crayons. Not just chalk drawings but we used push pins to hang pages of art from comic books and other found sources, magazines, posters, poems.

I finished a poem I started at the dome in Vermont, inspired by the statue of the Buddha in the crux of a tree looking out over the landscape of time.

Mr. Buddha

What was that evolutionary time, Mr. Buddha?
a meteor or an asteroid could have put an end
to all that was emerging — almost did,
several times in époques past.

In my little time
I have been allowed a space to breathe
to feel the air as trees do — bending in the breeze
fluttering through their leaves.
Time dissolves all like water.
And carries all along — nourishing
— though in the end drowning it too.
If I can put down roots
and let the world shape me to its will,
then I ask what is there for me, in my time?
In order to be present, I question now.
I have this habit like Proust or Buddha
of inhabiting lost time.
But I question not Love.
Love lights up the memory jewels
in the Fort Knocks of my experience.
If I have found
how to play in the splitting of the Way
then I am not lost,
but enlivened
in my undertow.

Rayne could be just really happy. Apparently this was fairly different for her. A lot of her friends and coworkers, Palumbo, his significant other Marie, Kirkwood, Poetete, Linda were all coming up to me and saying they were glad I was in her life.

She was two different people depending on where she was. In Montreal she was a mom and a lover, someone's girlfriend, someone's ex-wife; in Vermont she was more of a male hunter figure, a mountain lady, given to dancing the highland fling. When we went to Vermont, or the woods in Quebec, she was dressed in her survival mode: pants, a man's plaid flannel shirt. She had a ranger's Smokey the Bear's hat. Sometimes when she got dressed up in the survival outfit she was almost like a small compact elegant man. I must have looked surprised. Even she seemed a tiny bit — not embarrassed, but perhaps chagrined as if someone had become privy to something private in her nature. Once while dressed up like a man, she told me a story about getting dressed up like a man and infiltrating what was called "The Dirty Show" at the Orleans County Fair. This was a sex show, for men only.

She got done up in male drag, wearing her "busher's hat" pulled down over her face and a vest and entered the big tent. There were lots of strippers, and other areas; further in the back was an area in which men paid for open sex. She said she saw one scene where a woman was on her knees sucking off several men at once. "And she just let them come on her face," she said. Rayne seemed slightly sad for the woman. "These men were OK with being multiple partners of a carnival skank." She said this with a note of disdain in her voice that indicated she thought men were pigs. With her male choice of words, I was confused; it made me feel, as a man, like some kind of oppressor.

She was open enough to invite me in to these different groups. The group of colleagues and friends at school, and the group of friends of country people in Vermont. I was privileged to see her in and out of either context.

When we met, Rayne was 29 and a mom; I was 26. And though I was older than her students, I was very much lacking in confidence about becoming an artist. Texas will do that to you. There they think they have the power given to them by god almighty to smite down with righteousness any deviant thinking. Or maybe it was just hippie ambivalence, a hesitation due to awakened second order apperception of perception and how it is programmed. Or a 60's perspicacity. But for me it was more of a Cartesian doubt. It was my personality. She was an extrovert, I an introvert; me thinking, her feeling; me perceiving, her judging, me intuiting, her sensing. They say couples should have at least one of the personality traits the same. Though too, they also say that opposites attract. I wasn't naïve. I thought I would be Mr. In-Between, the man after her divorce until Mr. Right came along. Although I began to wonder if it might be Mz. Right.

I began to understand she had a fairly extensive life with her girlfriends, and there was a lot more to it that she was telling me. I was too shy to pry. I sensed she used to be more a part of a feminist club scene but was cooling it for her new man. And it was odd that Palumbo called her Tyke, which she didn't like. It might have been about her diminutive stature, and I let it go at that, but it was also about Dyke. I began to wonder if that had been the grounds for her divorce. Here in Catholic Quebec a mom could still get in a lot of trouble for lesbianism, if someone had enough money to inflict the proper lawyer on you in a divorce court.

There was something about her, she was just wild. The doormen and ticket sales people at clubs often just waived us through. I was used to this; I used to do an "I'm with the band, man," routine in Austin, but here it was more like she was some kind of celebrity and we were her entourage.

Her colleagues at school, Palumbo seemed to me older and wiser — he was into his 30s. Louis Potete was a long-haired man of property, his family from the ante bellum south, a town of the same name in Texas.

And Rayne was sophisticated, elegant. It was amazing how she could throw on anything out of a free box and it looked like an expensive creation from a boutique.

Yet on the other hand she could be wild. At a film night at Palumbo's, she let us see a couple of her films. One was the one she made about the farm she used to live on. It was sad and gracious. Looking out through the windows of her past.

The other one just showed her licking a lollipop. It was hot. It was a close up of her face. She had put on very red lipstick. She was doing obscene things with those hussy lips and that wicked little mouth to arouse, all over and around a round red lollipop on a white stick. She was wearing dark shades so you wouldn't know it was her, unless you knew. And she had big spangled earrings. There was no sound. The bright red lollipop went in and out of her red lips. It was a round lollipop on a white stick. We followed it with our eyes. The red lollipop went in and out of the embouchement of her kiss. The bright red lollipop on a white stem withstood the forceful assault of her tongue licking all around it. The head of the lollipop disappeared into her lips. Then it was dragged out again, slowly being sucked on all the way. She gives a kiss to the head of the lollipop. A bit of sticky red lollipop juice pools up on her tongue. She swallows. Then her mouth opens and the lollipop comes to rest in the shallow valley of that tongue. The round lollipop head was touched by the tip of the tongue. The roundness of it slid in and out of her lips, pushing past her soft red glossy lips. All the while she was looking at us from behind the shades with a saucy attitude. Every man in the place was in silent awe. The red lollipop forced its way deeper and deeper into the kiss of those lips, until just its little white stick was sticking out of her mouth closed around it. Again she swallowed some of the sticky red sweet juice. Again in and out then the kiss, and this time she lets is just rest on her lower lip, the lower lip pulled down in a pout. She slides it back and forth across that lower lip. Then around the mouth on the upper lip, around and around the mouth, then the most delightful open smile, she knows, she knows that she is teasing us and we are enjoying it. She finishes with a kiss good-bye on the head of the lollipop, and removes it out of the picture and we see her smiling face as the cameras pulls back. Wow. We were speechless. I thought, My god she's got brains. . . AND she's tough and sexy. Ooof.

She was physically so sexual and attractive, I fell in love with her in that male, logocentric profane sense where she was probably more used to girl love. Some time later, I sensed something about her world view, brought up modern Jewish and intellectualism, a sophistication very different from my own upbringing. She was just way more mature. Girls usually are but being a mom she came to own her own self. I thought perhaps it is from the feedback of seeing yourself on video but she was already this way long ago. She was destined to be the center of attention and she couldn't help it. She did not wear lipstick; she did not shave her legs. It was not a woman's responsibility to be pretty. I was intrigued by the way when light shone on her face from different angles, it would seem healthy tanned Mediterranean, and then sometimes sad and ravaged. It was inspiring to the suffering artists, and it was honest.

I was getting somewhat obsessed, sometimes feeling like I had fallen into a trap. I had gone out with various college girls, had even lived with three really fine women for extended periods and felt truly in love, or so I thought. But then now drifting in between women through life, wondering if I had ever really been in love or if it had just been something like a kind of comfortable convenience. I was trying to find my way in art, at least that had been a constant in my life. I was becoming more and more committed to that muse, devoted to that path. Perhaps giving up on love. But then came Rayne to reinforce me.

She was the essence of hip, in charge and on her way. Together. And she had all these friends, this wide circle of friends in Montreal and in Vermont, some of whom were fairly well off, compared to me, I was — well, a *bomme*, a knight of the road, almost a street person with my old shoes and old back pack. Finding any kind of work just to get by. Not on any career path, not even employed at the moment. I would have to live on my wits and charm. Hopefully it wouldn't fail me.

I was intimidated by her friends and colleagues — these sophisticated Europeanesque expatriate American Montrealers. Compared to their sense of responsibility and careerist gravatus, I felt like I was a lightweight, a fairy: my feet barely touched the ground. I felt like I wasn't secure enough to be part of their snappy conversation. I half expected her at any moment to apologize for me: You'll have to excuse my boyfriend, he's a rescue.

She reaches over and snaps the seat belt on me, catches herself and smiles.

Chagrined, "Oh, my god," she says. "I'm so used to doing that for my kid. I've become totally momicized."

I knew I would be her transitional man. She was really hurting from this divorce. No doubt some sort of man-hating was seething below the surface. The surface that girls always present, and that they hate to present.

She was not the perfect girlfriend. For one thing, she would go off on these mood swings. She could even get vicious, breaking cardinal rules, like talking about former lovers. Once talking about how she let some garage mechanic have her because he bragged on the length of his cock, and she just had to see it.

She was not the perfect house wife: there were dust bunnies in the corners and under the chair. We crashed on a bed which was a foam mattress on the floor. But who am I to criticize. I was a recently arrived boho ice-back from Tortilla Flat, little changed. My needs were basic: food, art, women, sex, visions. Not necessarily in that order. I certainly wouldn't have been with her is she was some plastic doll. She could belch with the best of them. Like a lot of Canadians she tended not to bath as much when the ultra cold weather set in.

She was good at managing people. She was expert. She could distract Beausolei easily, I was a little more difficult. She gave me a lot of space, and I gave her a lot of space. Peace ensued along with pleasure. Sometimes she exuded a glow of joy, other times seething demonic despair. We are all more or less like that, and when you live with somebody, you have to become witness to it. That is how you get to know the Other, and the Other inside of you too.

Divorce and motherhood. A lot to have. She was really hurt by the divorce, and had to hold herself back from running venomous diatribes against men.

And yet Rayne was a bundle of energy getting into everything, make a world for her child, teaching classes in community video and comic drawing. She did her own art.

My idea of what a family might be like certainly was different than my father's. As his was from his father's. I had never given much thought to settling down and being *en famile*. I was too immature, too poor, too irresponsible. My goals were to write a new art that was some kind of cross between physics and metaphysics and psychics. To create perceptions of ideas.

If there was any influence on how to be a parent it might have been Elridge Cleaver, the black man's family, which was very hands off. Absent. You got in the way of her collecting welfare.

Rayne is moving through a field, the state of Luce, Princess Rayne of the land over which she reigned. I was talking to her about Descartes and Desargues, and how the imagination requires a healthy doubt.

I said the cogito: I think therefore I am.

She replied: If I am not thinking, then I might die?

Better cool out white boy, I said to meself. You are running your brain too much to be with these earth mothers. But still hot thought ought not to be for naught. I have always confused eros and logos. It's the French in me. To find ideas sexy and sex profound.

Building a Log Cabin.

Rayne and I went back down to Vermont whenever we could. She was a different, more joyous person when she got into the woods in Quebec or Vermont. It was some kind of earth mother goddess affinity for wilderness, though she wouldn't have used those feminist proselytizing terms. Rayne and I were on hand when the log cabin kit that Larry had ordered was delivered. There was a pressing need to get the cabin build before the winter snows set in. The truck delivered it in banded bundles.

It was fun to work with the guys on the cabin. The system was like a Lincoln Logs kit that we all had when we were kids, except these were real logs. We got to work. Broke the first bundle and started moving the logs into place. They had been milled on three sides, so that the outside still looked like the log. They were about 6 inches thick and cut to the right length and labeled 1-13 going around each course and A-Q for each level. Thus 5C was on top of 5B.

John was the most experienced; Larry was a poet from New York, and had even less experience than me. All the logs have been cut to interlock at the corners and special situations like where there might be a join or where they were cut to accommodate windows and doors. As you can imagine, these 8, 10 or 12 foot logs weigh a lot; even the smaller sizes. So it took 3 or 4 guys to lift some of the logs into place; anyone who could, or who came by to visit got put to work. It was mostly men working on the building, and the women were cooking up some excellent food. It was like an old time Amish hippie barn raising.

The foundation had been dug, there was a concrete slab

in place and the crew build on top of that. We laid the first course all around the perimeter, then started placing the next course on top of it, spiking through the course into the course below it. It was a pretty good size cabin. It started to take shape. Soon they had enough of a wall to set in the front and back door frames, which were held up by long braces and wedges. More logs were set in place and we started to see the frames of the windows.

It was particularly important to have lots of lifters when the height got up above the 5 foot mark. We had people up a couple of ladders and people pushing up from below. Rayne and Victoria helped then too.

The guys got into macho, and tried to see who could drive the 9-inch nails through the log with the fewest number of blows of the sledge hammer. The hammer person had to have a good eye because we had another guy holding the nail so it could be hit. And the strike was a two handed full force sledge hammer swing from around the shoulder and over the head. Even though the hammer was not one of those really long sledge hammers, maybe only 3 feet, you had to be careful not to hit the hands of the holder!

The crew was trying to beat the onset of dark, when we got the logs going over the top of the windows and doors. By then we were able to drive a spike through in about 6 hits, swinging fierce, deadly-accurate blows. There was a big basic frame for a fireplace.

When we had the walls up and there was one log above all the window and door frames, we went home exhausted. Larry was really pleased, as was his wife and kids. The corners where you had interlocking logs were intricate and strong. With that and the nails this was a really strong structure. It looked amazing this straight up wall of logs, the light colored wood lit up in the setting Autumn sunlight.

Rayne and I stayed sometimes at Kerry Sher's place, sometimes at John's. Larry and his wife and kids were staying at Sher's too. In trying to get some insight into the "being a dad" experience, I found it interesting and refreshing when Larry got mad at his little daughters and called them "little fuckers." I had never heard an adult address a child that way. But maybe it was just that straight forward New York thing. I was interested to get another perspective on being a father figure. I really didn't know how to act around Beausolei.

The little daughters just looked at each other, as if to say: Here's daddy going off again. They were completely un-phased by it; for Larry was a loving father, and though he could be sweetly, tauntingly nasty to his kids, it was just his New York Jewish humor. They knew he loved them; there was a deep bond. I thought he talked to them that way out of love, get them ready for New York city. I hadn't had much recent experience being in the contemporary American family and was ready to learn from anywhere I could.

These Vermont hippies were splendid people. They were self-reliant and high on the fresh air and lived a peaceful pace. Being in these natural enclaves of Vermont was quite a different world from Montreal. No wonder Rayne loved it so much.

I was now in the role of the new "husband" for I was living with her and was perhaps the first lover she had presented or at least one who had lasted longer than her previous lover(s). I was Mr. In-Between, between being the kid and a father to the kid; I was a man who was using the man part to meet others in the community and be in this relationship.

Larry had a tone and way of talking that was old. His hair was thinning and he wore spectacles. His style was informed by his moral orthodox Jewish upbringing in New York. He and I talked about Poetry and Philosophy for he had been an editor for Something Else Press and had published books of his own poems and others. He was quick with derision, though I could tell that he liked that I was serious. He might launch into a mini-tirade about some stupidity or other and could be funny to listen too. He'd go around kvetching: "Ultimately, everybody is a sick bastard. We're all just total animals living in a spell of desire, that we use to distract ourselves from the fact that our voracity for love and attention is always pushing us around."

Larry had spent a lot of time in his orthodox Jewish youth reading mysterious religious texts. He had no problem talking about the evil in the world being manifest through devils. Though I am sure for a modern person, this is just a convention, there might have been some truth to it, though perhaps he was rephrasing things he had heard from the elder generation. He felt like it was his job to shock people awake from their merely autonomic existence. You had to take what he said with a grain of salt for it was salty from a crusty older persona upon which he styled himself. "Where did I go wrong," he would lament at his long suffering wife. "How did our love flounder and perish? Are we hooked like fish in a tortuous net of our own making? Or have we been programmed somehow to play our parts, for the survival of the race?" I didn't know if Larry talked to his wife and kids like that all the time or just did it for my benefit.

The next day Lois and a friend were out working as were the girls, helping place the chinking between the logs. This was foam weather stripping, then sealed on the outside with some white waterproof sealant, caulking, applied with a knife between the logs.

To make sure the walls were plumb straight, we attached long stiff rods across the room from one wall to the one on the opposite side of it. These rods had turn buckles in them that you turned to tightened and pull the walls plumb. Later they built big fires to heat up the wood so that the big logs could go through normal settling and checking; and if cracks occurred they could be dealt with if need be

On another day they delivered the roof beams. These were shaped like an A and already made. They had a truck with a crane to lift them into place. And another crew put them in. These roof support beams would be cross rafters and used for internal walls. Another crew did the plywood decking on the roof. Then roofers roofed it. Electricians ran wire. On another trip I helped a stone mason put a covering of Vermont field stone over the wooden chimney frame. It had a ceramic flue in it running all the way down to the fire pit. It was a lot of fun, and you learned a lot. It was good to be accepted as one of the guys.

Norm and Eddy

Rayne and I were good traveling companions. We used to run the roads back and forth between Montreal and Vermont. I told her about the Norm and Eddy stories and on the way back into town slipped into one.

These two guys liked to travel the road, and the guy who did the driving was Norm, cause he was a staunch commander of the ship. He made all the important decisions, while the other guy, Eddy, hung his arm out the window, and rapped, admired the scenery, twiddled the knobs on the radio to find new stations and rolled joints. And hollered things like: Hey Beatnik! at freaks he saw on the street.

See, the roles were defined by the positions that they had in the car. Whoever was driving was Norm, and the other idler was Eddy. But one could put the other one into situations for either could engage in behaviors that were not always a paragon of good judgement. Like once during a moment of drama in a bar when the Eddy one is being threatened by a citizen who has lost patience with his hyper-enthusiastic rap: the one in trouble looks up at the other and says, "How do we get out of this one, NORM!?"

Eddy had a way of continually bringing on new situations which Norm had to handle. Eddy was a wonderful traveling companion, though. Sometimes, on the road he would make up stories in which he starred. His name was Eddy Heraclitus; or he played the part of bounder Loller Taller; or adventurer Dusty Rhodes; or con-man Roland Hayes.

"All life in Turbulence," Eddy would say. And thinking about how we all get swamped out of it at the end, add, "And Dissipation."

I wasn't ready to let Rayne read any of my writing, it was too personal, and not ready for others.

Eddy was troubled with multiple realities. There were always three or four things going on in his head at one time. He never knew when an Eddy was going to emerge by splitting off, branching, or budding from a main flow. Of course he naturally expected them. Eddy lived in a world of Multiple Realities, which was all knew to him. Eddy Wavicle Heraclitus they called him. He got knocked around in his world, in an aimless fashion by following girls. Eddy was a ladies's man. He was a drifter. His was the way of the watercourse, an erratic and meandering way. But more and more the patterns in of his life were starting to reoccur more rapidly now as he got older, or at least now he could recognize them. And too he was getting hell, from his psychiatrist, Dr. Markov, who told Eddy that he could not predict his precise presence of mind in the flow through his being at any given moment. But worst of all was that there was no way of predicting how, in the event of confrontation, how he and other eddies would interact.

Norm. Good Norm. Good ole true blue Norm. Norm lived in a nice apartment, in the suburbs. He needed to surround himself with a certain amount of cush, in order to insulate himself against the onslaught of the city. He was a practical man, good at his job, and he liked it. Mild mannered, he never, no never gave anybody the slightest bit of trouble.

He had gone far in the world, had learned a thing or two and was actually quite clever with in the accounting firm. Norm was a big man, a take charge guy in his own quiet way. Women admired his inner strength. His coworkers would say he was a spokesman for the silent majority. He puts on his tennis shoes after his jogging togs and runs at least a mile every day because it is good for his heart. He chews each mouthful of food well, and he brushes his teeth each morning, before his cup of coffee, and at night before retiring.

Eddy on the other hand goes around and bums cigarettes; not just because he never has money, but because he was drawn to human contact. It makes him feel better to round. The eddies whisper in his ear, strange fun things to do. All around him he could see the pretty, little eddies dancing in the moonlight, which shone through the trees. Eddy learned how to treat these eddies as random occurrences, and stay closer to the Norm in his character. Any given eddy is determined by other eddies, and those in turn are determined by still other eddies and so forth back to a certain Ur-eddy.

But we cannot describe this Ur-eddy who was the original to split from the Primal One. The Ur-eddy contained so many dissatisfactions and was a veritable caldron of bubbling belching dilemmas that compete and countermand with each other so that Norm was forced to treat the resulting eddies as chance events.

It is only bored people who can never see the eddies. Some of them are not taller than the breath of a finger, and they sometimes had flowers in their long flowing hair. Little homunculi doing a slow-mo mirror-mime — two together playing Touch Hands inside the dew drops, the large dew drops with which the leaves were sprinkled and the high grasses were spangled. Sometimes the dew drops would roll away, and then they all fell down between the stems which waved like long arms in elbow length gloves, and caused a great deal of laughing and noise among the other eddies.

They did not last long. Dr. Markov had given him a Law of Logic, which said that an Eddy moves a distance about equal to it's own character, before it generates small eddies, called first eddies, that move more often than not, in the opposite direction.

Norm was a Scorpio. He had the energy of a Scorpio. He was always able to do things more quickly and efficiently than anyone else. He was a drummer, and an engineer. When he argued he spun suspension bridges to palaces of rigor and truth, which hung proven in the air.

Barbie and Ken

At the CEGEP where Rayne worked, people were remarking on her smiling. Remarking that she looked pleased. They all knew Rayne had a boyfriend in her life. She told Palumbo who told just about everyone else. This made her a lot more pleasant to be around. Apparently she could be quite a bitch. But someone in her coterie at school was ambivalent about Rayne's obvious happiness with her new boyfriend. She mentioned to me that someone had left her a message in her cubicle but I really didn't pick up on it. So she brought me out to her school to see it. Barbie and Ken were placed in a *mise on scene* that was pretty grisly. It was a shocking mini-diorama about two foot by two foot — spilling out of a kind of stage made from an open box; it was a painstakingly constructed scene all set about and festooned with a texture of candy wrapper and plastic junk food packaging trash. Barbie is being mounted by Ken, but Ken has some kind of hideous cork screw appendage. Barbie's head is turned and her luxurious hair is cascading down. She has that glassy-eyed, dazed look, like she is experiencing some kind of mindless pleasure. Ken is fiendishly made up. He's in a crossover glam mishmash of women's clothing. His lips are outlined in red and black. He has big eyes with black eye shadow (marks-a-lot) lines running down his face like he is crying black tears. He looks like a bizarre kachina doll from some unearthly glam rock religious pantheon. The voodoo fetish object altar-stage is scandalous. Wicked. Appalling.

Ken has got long straight dark hair from some other doll. His face is painted half white and half dark. His body is painted a ghastly white, except for scars and burn marks and red welts. You realize from the welts that someone has tortured these dolls with a soldering iron?! And different colored eyes! That was chilling, the perpetrator of this obscenity had taken the time and meticulously cut out and removed a tiny little blue eye from a blond doll and transplanted it to the brown haired Ken doll. The obdurant depravity of that bespoke someone with way to much time and deviant dedication on their hands.

The clothes are atrocious. Ken is wearing a set of Barbie's hose on his legs and another set on his arms, with the feet cut out for the hands to come through. His finger nails are painted black. He has a corset around his middle, and is wearing shorts that have been severely cut into a sharp v. These were the days of David Bowie and Ziggy Stardust, the long-haired boys of rock had atrophied into a androgenous glamour.

And wedged, glued, to Ken's crotch is a long corkscrew — like for opening wine bottles. Barbie is impaled on the corkscrew, apparently she has been turned around it so that the tip goes in.

These two plastic dolls are bedecked in miniature chains. They are evidently in pain or extremis of sexual congress. They have been drawn upon, painted, colored , somehow melted — repeatedly flicked with a bic? Micro waved?! Tortured with matches and cigarettes?

There is an inscription. "I see you are really happy with your new love." This also has been painstakingly created by cutting letters out of magazines. It is like a ransom note.

The whole scene is a nest of candy wrappers and tins and labels from the trash, carefully arranged into a swirling chaos of flashy bright colored plastic paper. The thing is over a two feet tall, as big as an ice chest. Upon closer inspection of just the clothes on Ken you realize it must have taken someone hours and hours to create this scene of obscene torment. I began to wonder about who it could be that has this obsessive focus on my girlfriend. My "wife." I felt protective of Rayne and was rightly outraged. Frightened. Then secretly I thought it funny. As did Rayne.

Barbie is surrounded in a fulminating plethora of food rappers. Her body has scars and marks. She has one little pump on. Her lipstick is lavender, as is her eye shadow and it is running down her face. Her face is a disgrace. One eyebrow is torn, and hanging, yet she has a great head of luxuriant curly auburn hair. The hair is quite natural looking. They are facing each other, she is kicking her long legs in the air.

I exclaimed, "Wow, that's amazing!!

Rayne looked kind of chagrined, almost blushing.

"Who did that?" I asked

"I don't know."

"You don't know?"

"It could be student; it could be the staff. Or somebody who works here at night."

"This must be the work of at least a couple of people," I surmised.

"They have done others before, but on a much smaller scale. At first I thought it was kind of creepy, but it seems harmless enough."

"Wow, what a puzzle." I began wondering if it was some jilted lover. I could see someone in love with her, being left, but them still being cool about it. "Maybe it is someone who knows you are cool about it," I said.

"Well several people have noticed it."

"Have you reported it to security, because this is a bit out there."

"No I haven't. I don't think it is that big a deal."

And we left it a mystery.

Driving Madam Dostoyevsky

I got a job, driving an old Jewish woman who was one of the most powerful wedding caterers in Montreal. I drove her and her assistant around Montreal in a fine old black 1953 Cadillac limo, with a wonderful old car smell for almost four days. The limo had a glass partition with a little sliding door between the front seat and the back seat. The back seat was set way back: a tall passenger could stretch out. Madam Dostoyevsky was a tiny dark woman hunched over and shrouded in mystery, huddling near the right rear door as if she meant to throw herself out in case of trouble. She always kept her head wrapped in a scarf, and had fierce, black, contemptuous eyes. She was the Queen of all Sheba, a dark eminence calling the shots. The queen never once spoke directly to *moi*, only through others who would speak to me.

It was extremely odd to get this job because for 1, I was a goyem, and 2, I didn't have a valid Quebec driver's license, never mind a chauffeur's license, and 3, I hadn't a clue where anything was! It was only through the good offices of M. Dostoyevsky, the queen's son — I guess that makes him a prince, and he was a prince, a prince in a bind who hired me, even though she did not want me; they must be desperate; their other drivers and assistants quit. Even without being given the details it was pretty easy to surmise that somehow she had driven her other chauffeurs to madness. I did overhear M. Dostoyevsky say *«Elle es passee par des chauffeurs comme des fous. »* (She went through drivers like crazy). *«Les six chauffeurs en autant de mois. »*(Six chauffeurs in as many months.) *« Et des aides aussi. »* (And assistants, too.)

By now I was ready to grovel and grateful for any job. Madam Dostoyevsky was dark and grumpy, but she did lighten up a bit after we got going. She saw my natural caretaker solicitous demeanor toward old women and perhaps mistook it for the kind of existential role-playing the sycophant needs to be good at in order to work in the service sector. Anyway she was used to being treated like royalty. It was fun to see powerful rabbis jump to and do the step'n'fetch-it when the Queen and her driver stormed into a synagogue. In these great halls and somber gothic dwellings of god she moved with devout purpose.

I would take two busses over to her old mansion in Outremont, on the other side of Mount Royal. Their mansion was by the park. I entered the grounds through the fence at the tradesmen's gate, knocked and waited at the back door, got the car keys and backed the Cadillac out of the garage. Though I did not wear a uniform, I held the door open for her. We would ride around the swell areas of Montreal. We would go and park right in front of the Spanish – Portuguese Synagogue. It was across the street from a park on Kevin St. further west isle, almost to Decarie. In spite of its name it was definitely English. M. Dostoyevsky told me it was in the Sephardic tradition, which is from ancient Spain and North Africa. Though it was English, the Jewish men there wore some very elaborate costume, and hair styles. To me it almost looked like little bull fighting outfits with short vests, with loafers and everything. These were worn under coats, which were more like little capes, with short elbow-length sleeves made of shiny, glossy material inlaid with flecks of gold to resemble stars in a firmament. They even wore what appeared to be wigs, or had their hair in braids and little bullfighter scull-caps that were sideways. I was accustomed to seeing the black suit, with white shirt and fedora ubiquitous in Montreal, but these ancient costumes signified even more ultraorthodoxy. Even so, Madam Dostoyevsky struck fear in the hearts of their rabbis there and they were quick to kowtow. We stormed the great dark arched double doors of the Main Sanctuary and she moved through quick — talking Yiddish to old people and Rabbis. The Queen was here to help these people fulfill their destiny in the eyes of their god and since that was her assigned mission on this earth, you better not get in her way.

We also went to a great colossal synagogue in Westmount, on Kensington just around the corner from where me and Rayne lived. Traffic wasn't so bad, and M. Dostoyevsky was vary felicitous in seeing that I got Madam where she wanted to go.

She never spoke to me, though I did get a beneficent smile out of her once at the bakery. Every day we would pull up in front of an ancient Jewish bakery in Outremont, where they had great loafs of chalah bread, bread that was made from twisting fat strands into a shape that looked, to me, like an armadillo. The place had a great big brick oven in a brick wall with a giant steel door and smelled heavenly. There were huge loafs of this braided bread, cooked to a dark reddish amber perfection and sprinkled with poppy seeds. They did not even have time to cool in the bakery display window, being snatched up as soon as they were put out. There were lines of people at the counter. The bakers always moved her to the front of the line, or even took her and her chauffeur back into the work area. He was to carry great bundles of bread out to the back seat of the limo.

I watched a baker doing the braiding: he had six strands and was working them back and forth, crossing alternate strands. It looked like a *ménage à six* of dough boy limbs, a wonderful topological confection. It was good. I had to try making it. When I went home and talked to Rayne about it, she dug up a recipe and I mixed some up. It called for a lot of eggs. That is what made it so shiny.

She told me, "The braiding of the strads obviates the need for the loaf pan. You can just use a sheet."

"Wow I get it!" The weave provides structure. I was puffed with pride to serve this bread to my love and her child.

The assistant   always looked at me as if I were speaking in foreign tongues and was from some other world. She grunted acknowledgments to anything I might say. I didn't have much to say. Just drive.

The Rabbis hovered about, their bearded faces looking slightly fearful, almost ringing their hands, in consternation, stooping, trying to get their head lower than hers, which was impossible. Or were showing her something they were proud of. A beautiful wedding was set up in front of a wall of Stars of David linked in interlocking tiles.

I was not dressed polished enough, and the old Queen seemed to be the only person who didn't mind. Going in and out of those institutions was a trip, people in costume, exercising mannerisms, speaking in conventional script.   And for four days it was OK. After parking the limo on the fourth day M. Dostoyevsky informed me that my services would no longer be needed, that a former employee — a relative — had returned. I was sad to be let go.

Starting Out on rue Ste-Catherine Street

I'd take long walks down Ste-Catherine Street starting out at Greene. Long walks traversing time.

The autumn sky — clear and blue above the buildings casting long shadows in the slant light. I walked first passed The Forum and the Montreal General Hospital where I was born. Past the movie houses my mother liked — the Strand. Past Eatons — now accessible by Le Metro — McGill station was a vast labyrinthine underground mall with Macy's too. Montreal is a shoppers paradise.

The great Notre Dame Cathedral, once the hub around which the city gathered itself like sheep around the Shepherd has an all inclusive forgiveness. Now the city is centered on commerce and the railroad whose headquarters — Windsor station for the CPR and Gare Central for CNN, are nearby.

I remembering hitchhiking from New Brunswick to Montreal in 1966 with Ian Lavoie. He was a wild hellion. We would run pell mell down the escalator through the Gare CNN, scare the tourists. That summer I saw LBJ at Campobello, flashed him the hook'em horns sign. It was awesome to run into Ian again one night when I was in the Rainbow Bar & Grill with Rayne. He told me he had bought some land up in a little village way up on the St. Lawrence and had a business making toys. The whole village made toys. He thought Rayne was hell on wheels.

Here at the meeting of the waters, an island in the St. Lawrence, *la plus belle ville*, Montreal. It was hyper-real to recall, to resonate in and out of time with my life.

Outside staircases everywhere on the houses standing in attached abutment side by side against the cold — winding staircases, made of graceful curved wrought iron, with *fleur de lyse* and star ornaments in the balustrades. It was so stylish in the warm summer months to be above it all in the Montreal community of passers-bye. And of course! So well-designed and necessary: you had to have this egress above the snowline where the snowplow blew the snow in winter making huge piles up to the first story.

What was I looking for in Montreal, in this new little, sudden, instant, family? I was trying to affect some kind of return, I was trying to know myself by finding myself in the little family I was born in. In my wanderings I would suddenly be on a street of 20 or more years ago.

I had hints. Rosemont, De Baubien, a birth certificate. (In those days in Montreal your baptism certificate *was* your birth certificate. The name of the church on mine was St. Dominic's.)

I had memories of walking with my father through snowy, slushy streets to church. We were stamping our feet in the vestibule. I learned the word *vestibule*. I had memories of horse drawn bakery cart. From that cart you could get the awesome *tartlette au beurre* (butter tart). I used to look out the second story window at a horse drawn junk cart. I remember the iceman stopping his horse drawn cart in the street on a sunny day, I can see him bringing huge blocks of ice up the stairs with terrible tongs, and loading it into the box on the top of the refrigerator. The iceman wore a white T-shirt under a big black rubber apron. My mother shouted some hip greeting to him using the *moé* and *toé* in *joual*. I remember going into a used clothes shop, the door made a bell tinkle when she closed it, and my mother telling me it was a *haberdashery*.

From photos I know I went on a Sunday outing in a park; I assume, (wish) it was near where we lived at the time. I must look for that park. From other photos I knew we made many a picnic onto Mount Royal.

Walking up the Main, Ste-Laurent Street, I noticed the marks of streetcar track — covered up. I remember taking the streetcar with my mother somewhere. I had her to myself for a while before my sisters were born. I remember my mother and father taking me skating. They were both accomplished and graceful skaters, and I only had rubber boots on. They hoisted me up between them and we flew across the ice.

And of my mother in a big fur coat. I remember the feeling: it was so nice to run and plough into that coat with her smell and her warmth. I remember my father having to stay up on really cold nights, going down into a basement to shovel coal, making sure the fire in the boiler was stoked and us huddling around a radiator. I cringe to remember running into their bedroom and my father getting very upset when I stepped into the chamber pot (on more than one occasion!)

I was trying to return, up the steel staircase, the narrow back porch, amongst the many clothes lines, that the women ran out of the windows on a sunny day. I was trying to go back up, to watching my mother and father jitterbugging in the kitchen, it was wild, my mother doing these vulgar jive moves and my graceful young father lifting her high up in the air and her kicking her legs at the ceiling! Then him plunging her down between his legs, never letting her go, then him lifting her high up in the air again. Then them jumping apart and looking each other in the face, moving their shoulders forcefully and pointing their hands at the ground and her encouraging him, clapping her hands like she was dusting them, teasing, excited, shouting Jit, Daddy! Jit! What a rumble. What a time it must have been to be part of the Great Generation.

I was trying to return to before that, to being pushed in the giant heavy perambulator up Rosemont? To the little girl who was my mother so skinny, so enamored with style and movie magazines. There used to be a vacant lot with an abandoned car. I liked to go over and kick it, saying "Pfft! Dirty old car!" I remember the strangeness of walking out onto the streets of Montreal by myself one morning before anyone was up. Looking down the long rows of houses with their spiral staircases and seeing the weather coming up from the river. The gutters lining the street were filled with tremendous drifts of autumn leaves. The Montreal maple trees in fall, with colors and hues of gold and red in that slant sun season. Each leaf was a day, in which the sun made its golden imprint; each leaf was a foliation sheathed in a book of time.

I remember going out and catching a snowflake on my tongue. And seeing the symmetry of single snowflakes frozen on a window pane, where you could study their exquisite symmetry up close. I would like to go back into that field that formed the snowflake, that formed the egg inside my mother that was to be me, go back up to the field trying to find where I came from, to see if my face was already there, if the pattern of my destiny was already written down.

See how it was that I got past limbo, to see if I would hopefully avoid hell, though I might have to do some time in purgatory, before I make it to heaven? Silly old medieval catholic cosmology, in the time of DNA, quantum energies, and morphogenetic fields. Morphogenetic fields, in which the lion vouchsafes the antelope its speed. That field in which the long drought from the mountains after having been pushed up from the land by the subduction of plates so blocked the rain that the forests thinned out bringing the apes out of the trees to walk upright. That field. Between men and women, sometimes a battle field, sometimes a playing field, some-times a field to seed. Bringing forth this season's people.

The Great Aquarian Novel

I was working on The Great Aquarian Novel. It was supposed to be some kind of vast wide *roman-fleuve* like Proust. The river novel, that would run with the flux of time and capture the moment and would flow on forever. *A la Recherche de Temps Perdu*. Remembrance of Things Past? Shouldn't it be: To Research Lost Time?

I was writing about my character Eddy, a good trope for an Aquarian Novel. Yes, the roman-fleuve set here in the *nouveau monde* by the *fleuve* Saint-Laurent. A Mississippi of a novel, *el Rio Grade des novellas*, the Amazon of all novels . . . well, can't do that; already been done by the master Joyce. (Joyce in heaven steals pencils and continues his novel from the P.O.V. of the sea — beyond dreams, beyond stream of consciousness.) (Proust in heaven, goes to bed early, props himself up on his pillows and drifts down memory's river, looking for spots to put in to time's dimension.) No, could never touch that but you have to try. (Mark Twain in heaven pilots his Victorian river boat among the clouds through the American summer, working at his writing table in the wicker wheelhouse on a history of *patois*.) No, no way you could touch that. But you have to try.

I had started my first novel years earlier when I lived in Quebec City and was working at Le Chateau Frontenac. I used to take the ferry across the wide St. Lawrence to Levis on a summer's day for fun. I used to go to the Historical Society of Quebec Library. This English library was a most beautiful ideal of library, with a grand salon reading room — open, two stories up to the domed ceiling, with a walkway that went all around the perimeter at the top of the first floor. The tall windows opened admitting a breeze off the St. Lawrence to loft the yellow curtains. The building was classical, elegant. The ancient French edifice was inside the old walled citadel of Quebec behind gates that separated it from the modern city.

I was trying to understand about time. I had read J.W. Dunne earlier in the semester at St. FX library. It was in Quebec City where my girlfriend and I dropped mescaline, and the filters that the mind puts on the doors of perception opened their gates and the world flooded in. It was terrifying, enlightening. Later after we broke up I was in a lost state about it and finding the pages of my writing wanting, I drowned them in a bathtub one day. Took the whole manuscript and dumped it into the tub and turned on the water. Sometimes I wish I hadn't done that. But as the old poet says, "You got everything you need, you're an artist don't look back."

Actually I had started out in my so-called writing career in Montreal earlier than that. In the summer of Expo 67 I set out to be a street poet. I styled myself to be some kind of cross between Bob Dylan and Lord Buckley and Brother Dave Gardner.

Now living in Montreal again, with Rayne, I took many long walks down rue Ste-Catherine. I liked to see the old spot where I first tried my luck at being a word busker, near the now boarded up Strand Theatre. It was back in 1967 Expo Montreal and I didn't know anybody and nobody knew me; and so — completely anonymous I could stand and deliver. I was kind of blue and lonely. Everybody was planning on going to college but not me. I was on the road — wanted to see some beatniks and become a writer. I have often found solace in the movies and one day I went to see a second run feature of the Sidney Portier movie *A Patch of Blue* playing at the old Strand movie house on Ste-Catherine Street, in the same block as the entrance to Eatons. Movies there were only a buck in the run down movie house, though I knew my mother used to think very highly of the Strand back in her day. Captivated and enthralled by movies, she bought those magazines, and like her young girl friends did her hair like the stars to look mysterious and glamorous. Anyway seeing that movie made me feel a lot better. No matter how severe I though my life-sadness was, I wasn't blind. It was a breakthrough movie, for a guy like me coming from the south to see a white girl with a black man.

Just remembering that movie was all it took to lift my spirits and whenever I walked past that theatre it did. It became a kind of power spot. That summer of Expo, I decided to pursue my dream of poetry no matter how trying and confrontational to my mortal fear of public speaking it would be. So when I embarked on my career as a street poet it was near the Strand, actually in front of Christ Church Cathedral a few doors down. So there on the sidewalk in front of the cathedral with its tall wrought iron fence at my back, I began laying siege at ramparts of western lit. It was the time of heroes and synthesis from Buckminister Fuller to Bob Dylan to JFK who admonished us all "to take part in the action and passion of the times."

I would be a street musician, only my instrument would be words. I had something like a rhyming Bob Dylan thing going. At first I was standing there with a little music stand with my run on story set up. A little bohemian beret beneath it for contributions. I for sure, didn't want it to look like it was about asking for spare change. I was a busker — *busquer* (seek, prowl), a *bricouler*, a practitioner of the science of the concrete — improvising with what was at hand coming from a long line of crofter Scots; there were buskers all over the place. Montreal of Expo 67 was wild — clowns in the parks, acrobats in the squares and fortune tellers in the forest, musicians and mimes in the metro, surrealists drawing on the sidewalks. I wanted to be a Street Poet.

The run-on rambling blues story I had was one about hippie philosophy using some of the slang terms like "cool" and "hip" and "vibes." It was a rap to address the new found strengths of my generation. It started I think,

As I was floating through the daze. . .

(I had not yet even gotten stoned for the first time though I knew all the words to *Like a Rolling Stone* — how inauthentic.) I had been cut loose; or I had cut myself loose, from my culture, I had dropped out . . .

Hip is advanced appreciation not just for what is, but what is becoming; it is taking part in the action and the passion of the times. But not being dogmatic about it.

Cool is engagement while keeping composure; it is persevering through paranoia of the ego. And coming out the other side shining.

Paranoia is a natural response to a culture. For if you looked at it from on top, you would see a few people manipulating the many, the boss–worker, the master –slave, the teacher –student, the parent– child. But, and still you have to look at it from above, at the overall pattern — that Buddhist distance — that is cool, yet caring and engaged.

Vibes is tuning in to an invisible nonverbal meta-language — the authenticity, the energy, the authority of how people presented themselves rather than what they say.

Square is being a slave and not knowing it. If you know it and accept it and work with it, then you are hip. Or Beat. Beat is a natural reaction, but through that you can become beatific too.

And to Dig, is to grock the fullness, that is to appreciate with a deep hip understanding of all aspects of something, with the wonder of a child, beginners mind.

Here we are: living under the 15 minute rule, that is, don't get too attached to anything, because 15 minutes is how long it takes for the intercontinental ballistic missile to fly here from Russia, and for the Cold War to get thermonuclear hot and to end life as we know it.

I think I had about two people stop.

Later I got into telling a crazy story about running with the Comanche in Texas at a time when the white settlers were taking over, and cross fencing and running the rail road. It was an alternative history, which sought to explore the idea of what would have happened if the white *hombres* had learned to be natural and indigenous like the Indians instead of raping the old West. It was a *roman a cle* about some Viet Nam vets I knew who were into drugs and guns and who were survivalists. They wanted to escape the America they had returned to, they wanted to "go sovereign" — every man a citizen of the universe, part of nature's unfolding, living back in the tribes of the frontier before it all got spoiled. In a way it was a kind of religious sci-fi about seeing through the lens of metempsychosis back to the prior lives of these men who channeled the ethos of famous gunfighters and felt like outlaws in their own country in their own time.

It was crazy because the only people to stop were French hippies. I doubt if they understood the English much. They might have been amused at the heavy southern drawl. So then I tried to transpose the story into something about Louis Real and the Metis Indians in the Northwest Territory. That didn't work either.

That was then, this is now. Now a little older, living in Montreal again, with Rayne, feeling the pressure to kick some dough into our little family life here, I thought about taking my act back to the street. Instead of writing The Great Aquarian Novel, I thought about trying to come up with something that would sell and sell quickly. I was desperate for money but not about to spare change. If I was to take it to the street, I'd have to just start saying something outrageous. And since this was pan-Catholic Quebec, I knew I could definitely get a rise out of the citizenry by launching into something about Jesu. I got the idea of a story about When Ovid met Jesus. It would be some kind of alternative gospel set in the interval of the missing years in the life of Jesus, between the incident of helping the temple elders with their astrology homework when he was 12, and the divine viticulturist incident at the wedding of Canna. This great lacunae in the life of our savior, exclued from the cannon by the Nicean council, is a favorite interval fertile to the imagination of blasphemous miscreants. Some say he got high, some say he had lots of girlfriends. Others say records revealed he tramped all over India visiting monasteries, leaving proceedings of an Occidental visitor with strange powers. May we all have such a bohemian youth. My account could be a recently brought to light Gospel According to Ovid (*l'evangile selon Ovid*).

Jesus ran away from home when he was 16, went to Rome to see the bright lights of the big city. He hitchhiked a ride out of Galilee on a tramp cargo boat driven by galley slaves that got him to Rome. Because in those days all roads lead to Rome.

And there he was hanging out being a part of the scene, and he met a cool cat named Ovid. Ovid was in his late 50s and had already written *The Metamorphoses* when he met Jesus. The famous Roman poet Ovid was the hippest cat in the whole Roman Empire during those early years of the first millennium. It was the long reign of Augustus, and all things were rising on the prosperity of conquering empire. And Augusts had himself deified as a perk. But Ovid who wasn't cool with it, had written a play critical of a god-king. So Augustus took advantage of a return to moral values hew and cry going on and acted all up in umbrage at Ovid's excesses and got the old poet banished to some Podunk villa on the Mediterranean. Which was hard on the old poet. Even though he was connected like a rock star, came from a wealthy family, was a Roman citizen and had the gifts of genius and beauty, he could not get himself legally back into the scene he missed so much. So Ovid, snuck back into Rome. He had to be completely incognito to visit some ailing relatives. And to get some canolies. And raviolies with marinari sauce. So in what we would now call the year 16, Ovid and Jesus met and they had a profound influence on each other.

It was a wild time, Romans Gone Wild, parties like you wouldn't believe — they invented the orgy. Ovid was brilliant at a young age. His illustrious legendary *Metamorphoses* insured his immortality. That compendium of ancient folklore sought to explore the possibilities of seeing through pre-literate mythologies, which are oral stories that use images for psychological states, and indeed ending up becoming the names for these feeling states. I like to think of it as a kind of primitive proto-Darwinian take, something the mathematician D'arcy Thomspson in his book *On Growth and Form*, would come to see much later: metamorphosis explained how basic functionalities were used to adapt across niches.

Young Ovid did enjoy many of the opulent delights that a vast empire offered to a young patrician. He became something of an expert on love. He had girlfriends and boy friends, as was the custom.

Ovid was quite a far seeing person, and when the soldier Octavian crowned himself emperor and took the new name Caesar Agustus that was one thing but when he further aggrandized the office with the powers of apotheosis and declared himself descendant from deity, Ovid thought that was too much. He knew absolute power corrupted, he had seen it among the debaucheries of his friends. And this guy was the ruler of the world. It is the height of megalomania and yet the plot of every sci-fi story. Ovid was trying to figure out what to do about it, when one day he met this radiant young man named Jesus with the wispy beard of youth hanging around the Tivoli Fountain.

So, what's next. We could have Ovid being shot by Cupid's arrow and fall in love with the teenage Jesus? No that's too risque. I had been raised a Catholic and though I had fallen away, I had not fallen *that* far away. What about having Jesus learn to party with the saturnalian Ovid. Being able to convert water into fine wine, and multiply a few loaves and fishes into dinner for several thousand made him a great wingman to have on the party scene.

What am I trying to say here.

I am trying to understand something about the Universe here. Lets see now, how did Jesus and Ovid influence each other. What does Jesus say to him?

Ovid is presiding over, and being the hidden dramaturge for a production of one of his plays to satirize the idea that a seat of supreme power would not be filled by people of supreme ability. And then this Jewish boy, Jesus a shows up and Roman patrician Ovid took the Palestinian Jewish peasant youth under his wing because he saw some amazing aspect to the adolescent. The young man was very advanced. Jesus wanted to overthrow the stranglehold that the Old Testament had on *his* people. His mother and father, Joseph and Mary were nice people, but it was lonely being an only child, you had to market yourself to adults all your life. Especially since his earth-father had passed away, leaving him the eldest son to support his mother. It left him looking for father figures. When Ovid and Jesus met, they felt Fate conspiring. Jesus was pretty sure it was his real father God, laying down some influence but Ovid felt it was Fate.

Ovid was looking for a supreme satirical angle. And inspired by Jesus, he hit upon the idea of giving his characters a godlike power over fate. He decides to use Jesus as some kind of force, the background of this play. He offers young Jesus a part in the play.

Of course we, in our time now, don't really believe in Fate these days. And it is mainly because of Jesus that we don't. Jesus would go on to enthuse a lot of people with the idea that kings are not gods, and gods don't really cause things to happen, (this would be the beginning of the scientific revolution). But in those days, you had all kinds of systems, cards, and astrology and the I Ching, to court and understand and try to foresee what fate's fury had in store for you. It is like the hippies now. A lot of people, priests and magicians and doctors and scholars were all making a living at that kind of activity. So Ovid used the power that people give to random chance and dubbed Fate as his literary device. Well didn't the Greeks have this, the Furies, the Archetypes — the representations and emanations of Psyche standing on the sidelines singing in unison as the chorus. How did Ovid amplify that, to use it in his satirical play? His satyr-lyrical play? He started working in the metamorphoses trying to get the big picture of the thread of influences, the higher multidimensional source that goes way back and informs form.

Ovid from his work in *The Metamorphoses*, understood how all living things on this earth are related, there are parallels, across niches. Look at how flight evolved four times on Earth. Metaphor is a reflection of that. In mathematics we would call this mapping of similarities across domains, homeomorphisms.

Of course Ovid didn't have the concept of DNA, but he did, from Lucretius, have the concept of atoms, fundamental constituent elements that are part of the whole; he had Plato's Idea and Essence as the similarity rule that allowed things to be contained in hierarchical groups. He might even have had the idea of monad. And he certainly would have had the idea of Parmenides, of the Neumonal One.

Ovid starts his *Metamorphoses* with this: "I want to speak about how bodies change form, to come to know the Form of forms — that which from whence the individual forms arise."

The Metamorphoses tries to capture the hypnagogic mind as it is remembering its many bases — the myriad functional dependencies: animal, mineral, spiritual, botanical, fluid, upon which it has evolved. The mythological mind gives these ancient parts of ourselves voice through characters, giving them representations in history and culture. Ovid is finding them in mythology, for that is what mythology is: an attempt to know across schema and in an unfiltered way how we got here and where we are going and what are the forces carrying us — to where.

Jesus saw the rich Romans and their servants coming out to see the plays in all the various amphitheaters and playhouse and community centers they had. And the slaves went home to tell the other slaves of the household, and that is how Christianity started. Jesus got the idea of how Christianity would propagate among the down trodden slave class from Ovid's theatre in Rome. Christianity was started for and among slaves, and people conquered by the Romans, peoples with little or no hope, that clung to the idea that they were not just the instruments of their conqueror's will, nor was even their own fate under the control of the state, certainly not their state's gods. But that they were recipients of a legacy, that connected back to The Great Spirit of All Things, that was behind the universe unfolding the way it does.

In an earlier time the poets invoked the gods for they were closer to these transparent forces which are metamorphosis. It was a good hypothesis at the time but moderns tend to rely on the concept of Force more. Thanks to sage Newton, we no longer have need of the God—hypothesis, but lets keep it anyway, for it is inflected with reverence and appeals to everyone.

Then, I heard Rayne come in from work.

This of course made me uneasy, cause here I was being stoned and writing instead looking for a job.

Hi

Hi.

How's it going. Rough day?

Yea, pretty rough. What did you do all day.

I always hate it when people, roommates, live-in girlfriends, ask me that question. I become defensive because I was a man home during the day. I didn't appear to have a job. But I said, "O, I've been working on this story. I'm trying to write something that will sell."

She looked kind of dubious.

Then I said, "Wanna smoke a dubie?" Cause of the way her eyes light up, and she never refuses. This got her going, and she launched into a hilarious rap about "having to whip up on these twinks around here."

But I'd be seething in my mind. It is really difficult to be interrupted at play. It is hard to turn your concentration mind away from being engaged in this fantasy of aesthetically controlled hallucinatory schizophrenia that is art. I'd be running along these lines: *I tell ya I can't write no more. Writing can't cut it, I want to really effect the world, want to work some kind of alchemy or science or something. Maybe I should run for political office. Or maybe I should buy a piece of land and move out into the country. I'm getting tired of the city.*

But I try to maintain.

Somehow I was not able to say the right things to keep it cool and we drifted into fighting.

She said, "You make me feel like I am responsible for your not writing."

Now my thoughts were more defensiveness about survival in the relationship. *I swear I wish I cold quit fighting with you woman. But there ain't no way I can have peace with honor. I'm tired of listening to your double bind mind.*

I started to think that this love affair was turning into a senseless masochism. I imagined how lovely it would be without this woman to contend with. *Rayne, she would easily forget me, be like water off a duck's back.*

Suddenly she hears someone outside her open back door yelling "Help!"

She had come home with Bruce David, a Jewish hippie, who was pulling the engine out of a rusted, busted-up '56 Chevy truck who suddenly yells HELP! from down in the alley. Rayne gets it into her head that he's trapped under the motor, so Rayne and I rush out the back door down the stairs, through her apartment and she yells in the hall: "Bruce David needs help! He's trapped under the engine! The car has fallen on him!"

We were scared now and Billy, who lives across the hall, comes running through her kitchen too, cause they leave the front doors open, and we all run out into the alleyway where Bruce David is standing on top of the cowl, holding onto the rope that leads up to the block and tackle, safe as could be and he says, "I need your help pulling this here engine out of the truck."

So we all grabbed a hold and gave it the old Heave Ho, and she's pulling hard beside me and grunting and moaning loud, and I make some crude remark that she sounds like she's having a baby and she's breathing close to my arm, cause we're all together in a clump holding the engine aloft for a long time so they can push the old truck out from under it and back the other truck bed up where we can set the engine on the back bed, and we are all yelling "Quick! Cause we can't hold it any longer." And she's breathing on my arm hard and then as though it was an accident, leans over and kisses my shoulder!

Wow. Women on the crew. How are we gonna have women working on the crew, hoisting engines out of cars when they reach over and kiss you? It could make you drop your load right on your foot.

Then we all came inside Rayne's place, whereupon Billy produced a dubie rolled up with some shit from Colombo.

There in the living room were Beausolei and his friend Wolfie. They were watching some grade-B parody about some hippie cult leader leading his children through a bone orchard. The two boys were tranced out, sitting in awe before the 25-inch color screen. A bunch of interference was coming through the speaker and a soup of electric jelly-bean snow was percolating like water sprinkled on a hot griddle. Rayne starts giving the TV some light hits upside its square head. "The Glass Teat," she sighs in dismay. "The Cyclops, with huge eye staring into all our homes, hypnotizing us."

I thought of Norman Mailer. Now there was a writer who tried to get into politics, even wrote a book about running against the Machine. Norman the Barbarian, in a lion-skin loincloth swinging down on a rope, trying to fuck CBS in the eye. Tell it Nomon has hurt me.

Rayne cusses at the TV set. "This damn TV is totally fucked. All we get is static and interference. I'd like to get a new one." I felt bad, that I — the TV-tech — had not been able to get a better signal in this apartment.

I had Eddy trying to write something that would sell and sell quickly. Something topical with a global threat. But what I really wanted was this penetration into Time. Some kind of trans-generational Montreal as a topological manifold, of boroughs and warrens, of subterranean tunnels and of elevators and stairways and rooms some of which lead up to or down from or out to or in from a soft surface that was only quasi-real, for it was not in a dimension of space but was in a dimension whose structures were not eroded by time. In this Aquarian novel exploring the underlying Proustian aesthetic of time as a river, it would all come together under some wicked awesome metaphor that was really a function on this space, one that we are starting to see through the many pathways in by living out an aesthetic apperception of some of the significant ideas of our time: chaos, fate, Jung, projective geometry, the strategy of genome.

How to Fight with Girls

Many preconceived notions about women did I have to be delivered from when I hooked up with Rayne. It was not all hearts and flowers. If I had to pinpoint a lowest moment it would be the night Rayne taught me how to fight with girls.

Rayne is upset, and when Rayne is upset, all hell breaks loose. Maybe it is just her time of month, maybe she gets exceedingly stressed to come home and find me not gainfully employed in making money. Rayne was feeling extremely stressed, even more than usual. Maybe kicking some ass or getting knocked around or humiliating someone else would make her feel less wretched.

It was after some kind of argument, over something. I was going to leave and walk around and I didn't have my own key, so I grabbed her keys — the car keys and headed for the door.

She was giving me some kind of test. "Where do you think you are going!?"

I was out the door and down the stairs and I didn't know she was following me. I was about to step off the last step into the foyer, when she jumped me, from the landing. A flying leap down a whole short flight of stairs! The harpy flew through the air and she grabbed me by the hair and I was so shocked I was stunned and couldn't do anything but be dragged down to the floor. My knees buckled and I went down to the floor backwards, struck from behind. She had me by the hair.

She was wearing this blue flannel nighty, that made her look like Wendy of the lost boys. She had hair on her legs, and tough bare feet. She was 5'2, eyes of blue, I was 6'3"' and looked way more dangerous than I was. She had a perfectly round Coppertone bum, a good stance, and the lightning like reflexes of a mother. Sometimes she could look as mean as an old Quebec grandmother at a funeral. Most of the time she had the playful look of a 13 yr. old just finding out about sex.

She was pulling me down into her. Here we are rolling around; two silent strangers in a struggle. The muscles in our necks were standing out like cords. We were two hells looking at each other. She was showing me a face, of rage and indignation. Out of all the millions of women, I had to get this one, who must have been my mad sister in hell in an earlier lifetime. She just has to bring it all out in me. She's the evil child. She hadn't bathed in week, and she smelled like cunt. It was attractive.

Scream!? When in she going to scream?

What's wrong with me? I've never in my life so much as raised my voice to a woman, and now I'm rolling around the floor with one locked in mortal combat. What if I should hurt her, what if I've lost control.

Rolling around on the floor of the foyer, at the bottom of the three-story tiered gallery, her dragging me down by the hair, I imagined people would hear us and start to come out of the their quarters, and look down on us from the gallery with contempt and alarm. Having been dragged onto my back and looking up I could almost see the faces of her neighbors and friends in the building, they would be up there looking down on me, judging me. I was a *bomme*, a *pique-assiette*, an *outremonter*, a *petite-bourgeoisie* with no ideas. Then the men would come down and pound and stomp my worthless personage for causing grief to one of their own favorites.

Some kind of demonic angst was operating in the air.

At any moment her friends and the supporters of this little single Mom, would leap out of their lairds and carrying long terrible carving knives, come down to the bottom landing at the center of the gallery to inflict many stab wounds into the person of this evil male interloper. The walls would be splotched with arches of blood splatter.

Suddenly the walls dissolved and I could see myself at the center of Montreal, all roads leading to and intersecting right here at a point in the center of this landing at the bottom of the three-tiered gallery. From here all the skyscrapers in that three-point perspective of looking up at surrounding tall, tall elongated buildings made them seem to stretch up into the clouds. Each building had thousands of windows, and at each window an angry face, many the offspring of Nosferatu, looking down at me with cruel vampire eyes, chiding me, shaking the head, going tsk tsk, what a low life. It was one of the lowest moments of my life.

With great effort I managed to turn around and I saw my "love" she was wearing her giant Wendy moo-moo pajamas blue with little tiny flowers. All flannel with different cream orange flannel collars. Around her neck she was wearing that little black velvet band with a cameo image of a porcelain doll inlaid in it that I liked so much.

Truly I am one of the damned now, I am in hell, and I can see the demons right here beside me gloating, sickly, subhuman. Monstrously cruel, looking at me as if I weren't even a person, vulnerable, fighting for my life here, well maybe not that dyer, for my freedom, my sanity, my sense of self on this plane.

But then suddenly self-preservation asserts itself, and with a sudden surge of power I grab her by the neck, and pin her against the floor; he's hanging onto my hair like some deadly leach, and I get on top of her, saying, Let go my hair, let go of my hair! Are you gonna let go of my hair? And I'm about to nail her one to the floor. She looks up at me and says, "DON'T you know how to fight with girls?"

She's looking into my fear panicked eye. "Well, no," I said, slightly taken aback.

"You should fight back exactly like they do," she explained. "Not slug them or kick them like you would a guy, but pull hair and arm wrestle and roll around on the ground."

She paused and looked like she was enjoying my incredulity and added, "Try to get her hot."

So I did, I grabbed a handful of *her* hair, and put my hand on her tits.

We rolled around some more on the floor, she on top of me, me on top of her. I was pulling her head back just as hard as I could. I expected people to come running out into the hall at the violent melee. At any moment all the guys in the building would probably come down and put the boots to me.

Then a sudden inspiration hit me, and I let go of her hair, and grabbed her ass. About all I could think of was that horny little ornery face that she threw at me, coming all the way up from childhood. She had really showed me that she was a force to be reckoned with. But then finding ourselves in the position, some kind of automatic sex-machine thing kicks in. I feel a red itching in the loins. Is that love? I'll have to get this thing straight between us. Man and woman, it's a hard one. I'd *like* to beat this bitch with a cane and yet, I hate to admit it, I can't help but admire a woman who would jump on a larger man and pull on his hair. And I had that power on my side — most of the time.

She looked up at me, shining, her eyes making fun of me, "Kinda turns you on, don't it."

She gave me the thousand year old look of a slave

looking up to her master. I think of all the velveteen cameo dog collars that she wears, she likes that fashion. Around that still graceful gazelle neck. That I could just about strangle! And I thought about how fine she is, and how sometimes she cried for me, sometimes how she would curl up like a ball in my hands.

I took out the keys and handed them back to her. She let go my hair, and took them in that hair pulling hand. We separated, set about restoring comportment. But, so that the feeling would not be lost, with a forceful look, I picked her up and tossed her over my shoulders and carried her back up stairs. To the two or three people who *had* come out of their doors and were looking down at the end of our spectacle, at this newly affiliated couple rolling around on the floor at the bottom of the stairs I said, "Newlywed. What are you gonna do." And I carried her back to the bedroom and plunked her down on the bed.

"Watcha gonna do?" she asked grinning with power. She looked down at my crotch. I jumped on top of her and pushed her back on the bed, and lifted her nighty over her ass and hips, above her belly, over her tits up all the way up around her neck, and I stretched my full wait on that hot brown nude body and pinned her to the bed. I raised one knee to press into her cunt. She pulled the nighty the rest of way off over her head, and was nude but for the cameo around her neck. I loved that. I pulled off my shirt and pressed my bare chest against hers. And like a snake, crawled up and kissed her behind the ear, and pressed her down, and kissed her down the neck and said, "I'm sorry," to my little slave. I kissed her breasts, and pulled my pants and underwear down to my knees. I started to rub my cock around her dry cunt, I reached down with my fingers and rudely separated the lips and drove it in. She winced, but then got real wet.

Now this became the Hungarian grudge fuck screwing in anger. I'd have to pump that pussy 'til it burst, just to take the sheer meanness out of her. I guess it's true, every man is a rapist. There it is raising its ugly head. I'm guilty: the penis will exchange for the power or not.

Then inspiration struck. I rolled myself over on my back, and pulled her on top of me, staying inside her. I said, "Here, you get on top for a while." I pulled her on top of me so that she was straddling me. I had got one of those really ferocious boners that won't be knocked down short of orgasm cannon to the moon.

"Watcha gonna do now," she said looking at me from on top. I just kept on lifting her off and pulling her back down on my cock. She was quite helpless all spread out like that. I started to tap her bum very lightly in time to the rhythm of the strokes, then tapped harder so that I smacked her ass to force it back down over my prick. She'd raise it up for more and I'd smack it into her. Her ass was getting slightly roughed, and she was squirming and wiggling, and cooing and squealing and grunting and trying to break free and I just kept smacking it into her, open hand on the fleshy part of the ass. And soon she was moaning, unhhh, ahh, that hurts you son of a bitch, ouch it feels good, harder, harder. And she was moving up and down on me now, and the juice was just dripping out of her, as my hand would occasionally spank between her legs, then back cupping her asshole, than back hard onto the ass again, until finally, like a beached porpoise, she flopped up flailing and heaving in orgasm. I brought her around under me like a passed out rag doll. From on top of her and moving in and out of her, still holding on tight with a hand on her ass, I came explosively and the rage left me.

A Wedding in Vermont

Rayne was a lot of fun to run the back roads of Vermont
with. And who wouldn't have enjoyed it. To get back beyond
those hills into the country, to slow down and get into those
little pastoral lanes bordered by split-rail fences winding
through fields, fields manicured by gentle tanned cows who
meandered on paths to and from wine-red barns with yellow
trimmed windows — as beyond, the genteelly rolling sylvan
vistas demarcated by hills led to other valleys of friendly folks
— was to go back into time. A time of nature and of our
primogenitors.

Next we went to a country wedding. I had not been to
many weddings. Only my younger sister's and younger
brother's. At my brother's wedding I felt like the bearded
odd-ball brother wearing secondhand corduroy sport coat
with professorial elbow patches. (Actually to put it more
correctly, I felt like a mud rat looking over a white picket
fence at decent people.) And at my sister's wedding I wore
a rented light blue tuxedo with a ruffled shirt. (There I felt
like a werewolfe looking through the bushes at humans.) I
had never been to a wedding as part of a couple before. I
guess Rayne and I were a couple now since we were living
together.

I washed and waxed the Mercedes for the occasion. I
used to do that in high school and was pretty good at it. I got
a bottle of Turtle Wax from an automotive store on Decarie
and some old soft sweat shirt rags and washed it in the back
alley being careful not to get any water in the broken back
wing window for which the money to fix was not yet forth-
coming. I felt bad about that. I got a parking spot across

Staynor street in front of the park and in warm Montreal autumn sun got to work waxing the venerable touring car. I was able to bring out that sweet emerald green sheen pretty keen.

Somehow I talked Rayne into wearing an antique garment she got from the 1800s. She did not subscribe to the pretty girl requirement that it was an obligation for a woman to always look attractive. She did not shave her leg hair for example, and did not wear any makeup. But on the other hand she was a sexual adventurer, and did understand the psychological component of tease. This genuine Quebec antique garment, probably worth hundreds of dollars, was laced up the back and it had a high neck and it was all black with lots of lace and bindings. It was hot, kinky. Looked like a cross between a straight jacket and a something a biker babe might wear to a B&D session. Though in its day, it was probably worn to a funeral.

I drove my 'old lady,' she wearing her resplendent attire, in the supremely buffed, stately appointed touring car down Greene to Dorchester to the Trans-Canada where we crossed the Victoria Bridge. We drove along the St. Lawrence river, passed the Expo Dome nestled into its permanent home on the edge of an island in a bend in the river, and headed on down through the Eastern Townships to a hippie wedding across the border in Vermont. She in her wonderful top and me with my British bus driver's coat. We were a pair.

We got to the wedding reception at a picturesque farm outside of Barton. They had set up large white pavilion tents in case of weather, but it was a gorgeous warm fall day. Banners flowing from masts made it look like a medieval encampment. The pre-Raphaelite hippie girls all dressed up in their finery, in long flowing dresses, looked like acolytes in robes at the altar of love. There were throngs of sinuous young women, in elegant fluid attire and bearded men in jeans. There were some girls in miniskirts, and long flowing hair. And hats! The ladies were taking the opportunity to exercise their right to wear big floppy glamorous hats that made them look like exotic flowers in the hot house of the wind.

Groups of women were walking arm in arm — though that was not usually done as it is in Asian and Mexican cultures. And there were mostly couples, men and women together. Some big tall skinny guys with their hands in their jeans pockets, very long hair looking perhaps already a little wasted, a little stoned. The women were astute, a lot of bustling here and there.

It was a lovely day, the sort of day that touches your heart. Everything was in harmony, the hills undulated with waves of sea green grass, the birds flying so swiftly south stroked the air in unison. The abundance of verdure rose to fill the air with a luxuriant scent of healthy sweetness, the colors of fall played brightly against the shadowy covering of the tall evergreens all along the road. The whole vibe was love, it was intoxicating, contagious. A hippie wedding — everybody on their best behavior, comporting themselves like young ladies and gentlemen — yet intoxicated with the atmosphere of love moving in the trail of flowers in the bouquets dotting the tables and the whole beds that had been set about.

Rayne was delighted; she is an extrovert and at ease in community. When she is in the country she utterly loses her head and is just plain happy. It is a joy to see. She knew quite a few more people there than I did. I, on the other hand am a shy and modest man, and not much of a socialite. My partying style (if you could call it that), developed in Texas, hadn't evolved much beyond "hanging back by the keg swapping lies with the good ole boys." I had that writer's reticence and ability to split off, to be both here and not here. To be able to observe myself as though from behind my own eyes rather than just through them, to observe myself observing. It is a kind of amplified epistemological awareness, a querying that over time becomes autonomic. Though it could be misconstrued from the outside as a dissociative stare. I was content to be a fly on the wall amongst the important unfolding events; I had been this way since childhood mentally able to generate, through the practice of silence, exile and cunning, an undetectable force field of imperceptibility. It was that sense of being a catcher in the rye on the fly, an outrider on the periphery observing through the arras, looking for the place where the veil of maya moved on its own, where it parted, was rent or thin and might not hold but fall down altogether and reveal the inner workings of the universe. I was pretty good at one-on one conversation though. I liked intimacy. So I was content to be on my own while she did her thing and went to greet and meet and be more a part of the scene. I hung back under the shade of a tree.

A band was playing across the way. They were a high-energy dance band with fiddlers and guitars and drums and a piano. They were a little bit dressed up: some of them, with long hair of course — but not outrageously long, played beautiful light-colored wood guitars, that glinted in the setting sun when they swooned and grooved. Some of the band men were wearing sport coats and turtle necks though it was sunny and warm. Throughout the evening they played all kinds of music: there was bluegrass wafting through the air; Western swing and country favorites for the old timers and parents there; straight country ballads; hippie country; and, some blues and rock and roll. Something for everyone. Soon people were dancing on the veranda and on the lawn. You had guys in tuxedoes, next to guys in lumberjack shirts, next to guys in frilly tuxedo shirts — without the tuxedoes — wearing a necklace of puka shells, next to a couple of beautiful girls, one red-head with a voluptuous figure and gorgeous legs in a little mini skirt suit. Her top had extremely wide white collars, so did the trim on the cuffs of her sleeves.

The house was a great big Vermont country white house with black roof with many gables and a big wrap around porch. People were sitting out on the porch, pretty girls leaning their behinds on the railings, playing with their long hair. Most of the crowd was in a big field boarded by the long driveway that went up to the house. Quite a lot of these Vermont women were wearing sensible footwear, boots, (with long dresses) to walk around the grounds in.

I looked around catching glimpses of couples walking, holding hands up the drive way, or further away by the fence. There were planted gardens with beds of bushes and ferns. And placed here and there were stately urns filled with bright sprays of colorful flowers. In the tents older people were sitting at tables. And off outside were long barbeque pits with meat roasting. I was back by the keg not venturing too far in, though I would have liked to meet more people.

The bride came through, and walked among us. In her heels she was being conducted, holding on to the arm of her new husband with one hand, stepping gingerly, and with her other hand lifting up her long dress. The ladies in her retinue were also gracefully circulating arm in arm with their beaus. The bride, she was stunning, with long auburn tresses, and thick eyebrows. A beautiful face, so young, maybe not quite 20. She was resplendent in an off-white all natural cotton, long maxi dress with a corset-laced-bustier. The sleeves where three quarter length, puffed and gathered and made of sheer lace, the scooped neckline drew the eyes to her robust twins; lace and ribbon embellished the bodice, a high empire waistline was swathed in long ties that wrapped around her slender torso and tied in the back at the waist in a large bow. Fortunate indeed would be the new spouse to open that gift package. The bride, our queen of the gathered tribes wore a crown made of woven daisy chain, as did her attendant maids. The groom was also young and a bit stern looking, with thick mustache and a big head of curly hair. They looked so young. He had on a white, high-collar, Nehru sport-coat, and seemed a bit uncomfortable in it. He was accompanied in the tour by his best man, a serious looking hippie with long dark hair and Zapata moustache; he had dark eyes, and looked messianic.

The band was serenading them, playing to them. The lead singer was wearing a stylish fedora; he had a mustache and goatee. They were playing *Moondance* of Van Morison. The young drummer was spanking the zildjians softly; the base was a tall guy with jeans and a sport coat, hitting the downbeat.

The banquet tables had been set with white tablecloth and silver. People were taking seats. They moved casually toward the food being served near the barbecue pits. Some took their picnic away into the tall trees at the edge of the field as the Autumn sun was setting and the light was so inviting. The light made the shiny sequins of the girls dresses spangle. It poured down like honey and made the highlights of their flowing hair into luminous rivulets. Beams angled down through the forest canopy and defined webs of demarcated spaces like convex hulls, or chi squares of field influences from the ecology. While the band jammed on a long quiet instrumental jazz standard.

Rayne appeared at my elbow; she had changed out of her antique biker ensemble — it was too risqué for this fine crowd. She had slipped into her comfortable man's flannel shirt and a car coat with fringe and was ready to party in her mountain hiking boots.

We sat on long benches in a group of her friends I didn't know, and partook of the sumptuous ceremonial dinner.

After, we headed over to where they were toasting the newly married couple, who were standing side by side with his arm around her waist and her arm around his waist, and she looked so sweet with the garland of daisies in her hair, and her stalwart blue gray eyes gazing with keen interest and power at the assembled people there in her honor and he looked pleased, with his long hair falling down his chest, and every man had his arm around his girl and every girl had her arm around her man and we were all just one of the many swaying to the music, moving slowly in the procession and the bride was a symbol for the Other who was the focus of all our hopes and wishes for marriage — truly it is a moment of great commitment and change. I felt a wee bit nostalgic for my own future, longing + hope? A homesickness for one's own real home, for his own wedding should it ever occur. Like all the lovers and married people at a wedding, you feel your own commitment. That was a nice feeling for me. I felt really proud to be with Rayne. I was trying to remember: I don't think I had ever been to a wedding while in the state of living with a girl. Though I had lived in a state of monogamy and connubial domestication with three women already, Colleen, Dianne, and Terry. How odd.

And in the glowing light of the setting sun, people's faces were softer. And everywhere I looked there seemed to be still-lifes in impressionistic lights, the young girl playing with her dog near the little lake at the bottom of the property, another maiden in a green chiffon dress and auburn hair and light wisp of green eye shadow had her eyes closed for a long time as if she were tasting something delicious, there were people clumped together, flash bulbs going off as group pictures were being taken, the girls looking so satisfied and kind of stoned, the men tanned and happy content, looking stoned too. The band was back on stage and really letting loose: some guy in a serape was genuinely enjoying the music, shaking and howling; some guy in a velvet jacket and scarves and a mullet haircut was blowing marijuana smoke rings. (But I didn't want to get too high because I was going to be driving Mz Luce.)

And the great old house was witnessing from its place in history hosting there with its white porch pillars and the wisteria vine climbing up the far side, and a willow tree in the yard; it was just so pretty: men in white shirts and vests and bolo ties seemed to be in the grooms retinue, they were dancing on the porch with the maids. A beautiful hippie girl with long flowing hair and a long green frock coat was smoking a cigarette as she was talking and laughing with two bearded men.

And the newly married couple finally emerged and people pressed around their car, which was a Volvo sedan with the long sloping back, and there was Just Married written in soap across the back window and a white cardboard sign cut in the shape of a heart and attached on the sloping trunk proclaimed Cathy + Tim. And the back side was festooned with ribbons. The saucy bride waved an unopened bottle of champagne out the car window as they lurched down the driveway. Ribbons fastened to the bumper were dragging a tail of Budweiser beer cans which did not make much of a racket on the dirt road driveway as they were heading out to the highway, and into their new life together.

And I felt my spirit as I was swaying there in the soft crepuscule of gloaming twilight as it floated up to meet the setting sun. From on high I could see that car as it got further and further afield and I could see the hills against the last of the orange sun setting in a blue sky beyond the farm roofs, and I was able to look down at the revelers from this ancient shamanistic eye in the sky perspective and I could see me and Rayne were there among them and they were dos-y-doeing in a flow pattern of the dance like eddying whirlpools in a stream, like star clusters reflected in a pond, and it felt like the wind was a river flowing through the valley reflecting the archetypal flow that simply was and was poking into all our lives and how we encounter each other where it flows. And we were all flowing on this river as it passes to and fro, breathing in it like fish.

La Tour Jetee

Rayne showed a film *La Jetee* by the French *auteur* Chris Marker in her class. She made sure I was there that day to see it. I was absolutely stunned. I had to hide my reaction, for I might burst into tears; I walked around like a man in a kind of aesthetic shock. To experience a film about sci-fi time travel with primary psychological processes touched my soul and I felt that now and forever it would be a little more complete. I would not die empty or hollow. (I felt like that about Joyce too. And the theory of vector spaces.) When I heard that Palumbo was going to show it in his class, I told Rayne that I had to see it again. Rayne was indulgent, though she did not like to stay around school any more than she had too. Palumbo took the canisters of reels home and showed it at a film party at his place a couple of days later. I made sure I was in attendance at that soiree too. I couldn't get enough of it. In fact it precipitated a phase, a phase I might refer to as my Tour Jetee phase.

The black and white film as we saw it was the 16mm — projected through one of those old jumpy projectors with the light intensity shifting and fading. It was French with English subtitles. *La Jette* starts off with a terrific sound of a jet engine blast. The roaring sound segues into a singing chorus heard reverberating in a vast cathedral. We are at an airport where we can watch jets take off. It is like listening to the chorus of deep male voices in the basilica of St. Joseph's. One is watching and hearing. In the voice over, we hear a world-weary *philosophe*, with a voice harsh from endlessly chain-smoking Gitanes say while we read: *Ceci est l'histoire d'un homme marqué par un image d'enfance.* (This is the story of a man, marked by an image from his childhood.)

It is a film in the form of a slide show, like a *photo-roman*. I was very familiar with these, they were all over Montreal: large format magazine with frames from films and printed captions from the scenes. It was my favorite way to study French because it was so *au courant*.

The scene puts us on the jette of the Orly airport looking at a clock tower with the sun behind a haze, and we hear about a *troisieme guerre mondiale* (third world war).

At this point the movie projector goes into fits and starts; it has to be restarted; our minds are struggling to understand the French with the English subtitles. The narrator voice in the film mentions how parents take their kids to the airport to watch the parting planes. I remember how my parents used to take us to the airport on Sundays too, to watch the planes depart.

The boy sees *un visage de femme* (a woman's face). And also he realizes he has seen a man die.

The philosopher narrator voice-over says something about memory and that *ce visage qui devait etre la seul image du temps de paix a traverser le temps de guerre*, (that face he had seen was to be the only peacetime image to survive the war). Then the scene cuts to an image of an El Greco sky over the Eiffel Tower, making the tower look ominous like an alien standing over a burnt out landscape. I recognized black and white images of war destroyed Europe, which someone my age would have seen as a very young child at a newsreel at the cinema. The images almost seem to flicker with the jumpiness of the projector. But there is no mistaking it, we are in a photo roman, a series of stills, a story board of a film.

The 3rd world war, (choir of voices) force the people to live underground. Above ground it was *inhabitable* (unin-habitable) due to *radioactivité* (radioactivity).

Underground the survivors (they are called victors) stood guard over an empire of rats.

There were others, the prisoners (*Les prisonniers*). And these prisoners were subjected to experiments *(étaient soumis à des expériences)*.

In the experiments one hears people talking in a whisper, and some guy laid out in a hammock with pads over his eyes. These experiments caused *les autres etait morts, ou fou* (some to die and others to go mad).

We see a series of haunting images of a man, lit from above so that his eye sockets are dark and hollow; below the moustache his face vanishes. A hollow man. This scene of the man's face dissolves back into the underground bunker, by going through a geometrization in the transition: where the nose is just a triangle, the eyes squares — it is a masque or some ancient stone head. Or the radiation symbol we had all grown up with in the cold war, the triangle with center three black splotches.

They choose one prisoner in particular: *l'homme dont nous recontons l'histoire* (the man whose story we are telling).

He was afraid that the experimenters were mad scientists. *Il pensait se trouver en face du Savant fou* (he was prepared to find himself in the presence of a mad scientist). But he meets a reasonable guy who tells him that *la race humaine* (the human race) *etait maintenant condamnee* (was now doomed). And that it was cut off from space and that the only hope for survival lay in time. They were preparing him to travel through *un trou dans le Temps* (a loop hole in time).

In addition to seeing just the stills jump-cutting across the frames of darkness, when the scenes are held, the jiggyness of the film's luminosity intensity projector makes the light in the faces of the people shift as though it was an aura shining in their visage.

That was the task of the time traveler to *appeler le passé et l'avenir au secours du present* (to summon the Past and the Future to the aid of the Present).

To do this *le choc était trop fort* (the shock would be too great).

The experience of looking at this film about time reminds me of what I feel when I look at the early cinema of Georges Méliès' first efforts when he trained a camera on a stage, or a set into which people moved in and out — one that flickers and dances in the light. It felt like we are looking at some kind of primitive artform almost like fireflies glowing and moving in the forest at the edge of an encampment.

They were sending the subject into a different Time zone (like the air port jets taking people into different time zone). The experimenters must concentrate on subjects given to very strong mental images (*se concentraiet manitenant sur des sujets doués d'images mentales tres fortes*).

To be awakened in another age meant to be born again as an adult (*se révelier dans un autre temps, c'était naitre un seconde fois, adulte*). They were going to send the experimental subject to see if he could re-inhabit lost time.

They had chosen this subject because of his obsession with an image of the past. *La police du camp épiat jusqu'aux rêves*. (The camp police spied even on dreams.)

The subject gets an injection. Big frightening needle. He puts on soft goggles, a masque with electrodes, over the eye piece, presumably to detect REM. It has other wires at the temples to detect brain waves. Maybe the experimenters can see what he is seeing, of if not that, at least sense that he was seeing.

All the while in the sound track we hear whispering; sometimes sharply, conspiratorial. Always we see in the black and white underground world, the soft shape shifting movement of lights flickering in the analog frame, almost like a gray-scale aurora borealis.

Au début, rien d'autre que l'arrachement au temps présent, and ses chevalets. (At first he is ejected from the present and its certainties). (At first he experiences nothing out of the ordinary but an arrestment, or rearrangement of the present and its certainties.)

And here as if by magic, the film makes all kinds of leaps about in its projector, like it was some kind of Bergsonian synchronicity, the machine picking up the message and acting in concert with it — the projector has picked up the time of the message! And the flicker is like the current frame of reality breaking down or drifting off it tracks into other times. What a fabulous coincidental mergence of subject matter and object allowing this form to inhabit itself for its presentation.

The sleeper is watched. The sleeper is touched by the scientist. *Le subject ne meurt pas, ne délire pas.* (The man doesn't die nor does he go mad.) *Il souffre.* He suffers. Here the sound tract is the lub-dub of a heart beating, getting faster and faster. This artist Chris Marker is relentless; the images are strong, still. The subject starts to experience the past. A real bedroom, *une vraie chamber. Des vrais enfants* (real children). *Des vrais oiseaux.* (Real birds).

When I went outside after the showing I started piping up lines from the film. The first was *des vrais oiseaux.* When I went to see it at Palumbo's party, I took notes. Even asked Palumbo to back it up and let me look at the sub titles, to get the English. I was at the party earlier to help set up since I was underemployed and Palumbo was showing it just to make sure it would work. So I watched it again. *Des vrais tombes*. (Real graves).

Quelquefois, il retrouve un jour de bonheur, mais différent. (Sometimes he recaptures a day of happiness, though different.) . . . *un visage de bonheur, mais different* (A face of happiness, though different.)

He is retrouving, capturing.

A girl who could be the one he seeks. *(Une fill qui pourait etre cell qu'ill cherche.)*

She smiles at him from an automobile. *(D'une voiture, il la voit sourire.)*

The man, and the woman he has met in the past, go into the museum of memory, with many images of the past — statues and artworks. The head of a statue dissolves into the subject of the experiment in his mask glasses, and we are returned to the experimental present.

The man and woman meet on the 30th day in the past. He is sure he recognizes her, — *dans cet monde sans date qui le bouleverse d'board par sa richesse* (in the middle of this dateless world that at first stuns him with its affluence.) We see pictures of being in a Macys or some kind of big shopping mall. Just like here, just like now.

We are hearing the whispering of the experimenters only in voice over now, we have left his present and gone into a past.

The subject gets hung-up on the materials of this world. *Lorsqu'il sort de sa fascination,* (When he recovers from his trance) *la femme a disparu* (the woman has gone).

Time rolls back again, *(le temps s'enroute a nouveau).* He goes back to her again and again. *Elle l'acueille sans étonnement* (She welcomes him without surprise).

Ils son sans souvenirs, sans projets. (They are without memories, without plans.) *Leur temps se construit simplement autour d'eux.* (Time builds itself painlessly around them.)

It is an idyllic scene of a man and a woman on these dates, on this kind of honeymoon, they walk in a garden. She asks him about the warrior's necklace he wears, from a war that was yet to come. He invents and explanation. *(Il invente une explication.)*

He feels waves of time coming over him, thinks it is the experimenter giving him another injection.

Puis un autre vague du Temps le soulève. (Then another wave of Time washes over him.)

He sees her asleep in the sun. Sits beside her. It is a beautiful Warhol moment — watching the sleeper.

He realizes that in the world he comes back to, to be with her, she is dead (*elle es mort*).

Now there begins a kind of floating, lilting love afair between the man and the woman, the slideshow of scenes are like snapshots from a photo album. The viewer is invited to sashay along with them in the park on their the sojourn with love, as they meet without plans. Just an unspoken trust *(une confiance muette)*.

Then we are back with the experimenters, after a dissolve that juxtaposed a wall, a barrier between them.

They do more experiments, in which he would meet her at different times.

And then one of the most beautiful moments in modern cinema occurs. We move for a moment out of the slide show of stills into motion, in the blink of an eye.

The film has up to this point been sequences of stills that rapidly change in succession. They show sensuality and tenderness contrasted with bleakness and control. But now we are touched with animate motion. For one poignant, brief, moment, the camera has zoomed in on the woman's face, and we see her blink and smile; it is almost a wink, a nod, certainly a meta-communication to the audience from the artist. The sound track is a cacophony of birds rising to the flapping of wings taking off; it reflects the flutter of eyelids. Then we are sharply returned to the slides of the black and white stills. At this point the film, in its meta-communication about seeing, has become self-aware. The objects we are looking at are in some sense looking back at us. Is it that they have been so imbued with the vision of the artist? It is a sense that time has taken off in this motion, we feel that it is out of our hands. We feel the larger forces outside at work that make the happiness of this couple doomed not to last.

Then a startling jump CUT from that moment to the dark face of the experimenter looking down at us. Great use of camera angle.

Next, the man and woman are in a museum *plein de bêttes éternelles* (full of timeless animals). This romantic sojourn in a natural history museum among a vast plethora of preserved animals, a mooneyed hippo, a noble tiger, suggest the long time of evolution. One senses the facility of human cognition among all that instinct. There is a sense of evolution as emergence, of evolution using matter to give opportunity to these animal forms. It is a most joyous long scene of romance. The music too is exquisite, romantic — like we are waltzing in some kind of scientist church, all this amazing creativity evidenced in the species all around them. The faces of the stuffed animals seem to be smiling, endearing; implicit blissful innocent hippo faces are looking on the human couple and are looking out of the scene at us.

Again the eyes of the objects being seen are looking at the viewer. The animals seem to be looking back at the couple through their glassy-eyed eternal taxidermy stare and at us from creation. This reflects the dawning of the awareness of ecology, in my generation; we realize that they are looking at us to save them from extinction. They are almost like equals in the world.

The man, *qui apparait et disparait, qui existe, parle, rit avec elle, se tait, l'ecoute et s'en va* (who comes and goes, who exists, talks, laughs with her, stops talking, and listens to her, then disappears.)

They go into the butterfly exhibit. Even though the film is black and white, the view of the butterfly case is a feast of entities of light.

Then suddenly we are back in the experimental present, and the subject knows something is different. *Il sentit qu quelque chose avait change* (He knew something was different.)

Now the experimenters start to send the subject into the future. He realizes the encounter with the woman in that time at the museum was his last.

The subject starts to fall or zoom over the landscape of the future. He sees Paris as a place with thousands and thousands of streets he does not recognize, like the city of the future was a three dimensional maze, or the etching of an integrated circuit. So dense are the streets of the future that they look like a close up of the cellulose in the matrix of a leaf.

The people of the future are waiting for the subject.

They have little organelle / machines / a third eye? at the center of their forehead, about the third eye.

They rejected him. The beings of the future are not very

welcoming; he is referred to as a "leftover" from another époque.

The subject uses a trans-time sophism to argue with these advanced beings of the future. One that he has been programmed to introject. He tells them that since they are proof that humanity has survived, they cannot refuse to help the humanity that gave birth to them.

They give him the power unit, *et les ports de l'avenir furent refermées* (and again the doors to the future were closed).

The subject of the time travel experiments is released from duty and sent away from the lab. He realizes he is expendable. He was their instrument. And now he has the memory of a twice-lived fragment of time *(en lui le souvenir d'un temps deux fois vecu).*

In his isolation back in the underground camp he is visited by the time travelers of the future. For them it is easy. They offered to accept him as one of their own *(parmi eux).* But the subject has a different request. Could they send him to another time? Rather than this pacified future *(pluto que cet avenir pacifié.)* He wanted to be returned to the world of his childhood, *(il damandait qu'on lui rende le monde de son enfance),* and this woman who was perhaps waiting for him *(et cette femme qui l'attendait peut-etre.)*

And now the film viewer sees that we are looped back again to the beginning of the movie, to the Sunday promenade on the grand jetee at Orly airport. It is a place where he could now stay *(ou il allait pouvoir demeurer).*

The time traveler realizes the child he once was should be there looking at the airplanes, but first he wanted to find the woman. The viewer sees her lone figure way out on the quay *(au bout de la jette).* The man starts to run to her, running through the crowds. She turns to recognize him. But as he is running toward her he sees someone from the camp, one of his handlers with the bug-eyed glasses. And the running man understands that there was no way to escape time (*il comprit qu'on ne s'evadait pas du Temps.*)

And on the screen the viewer sees a staging of one of the most famous war photographs: the one of an Italian soldier at the moment of his death. The soldier is seen with his arms out-stretched beneath a clear blue sky with a few high cirrus clouds looking down. We see him falling, as though we are very small from down below, as though from within the trench. Or that child.

And the subtitled text on the screen is "at that haunted moment". . .

And the subject understands that this moment he was allowed to see as a child, which had obsessed him was the moment of his own death *(ce etait celui de sa proper mort)*.

Requiem voices overhead.

FIN.

I was stunned. What had I just seen? I needed time to regroup. Time to not mumble incoherently about the intimacy and intelligence of French cinema.

Wow, is all I could come up with.

I walked to Rayne's office like a shell shocked zombie, making my face look like the stone masque of the time traveler who had been destroyed.

I started seeing myself in a movie, like *La Jetee*. I would stop in the middle of things and consider something then deploy my most weathered old *roué* French *comte* accent. *Mais oui.* And *On recommence.*

It started in the parking lot as we walked out of the CEGEP St. Laurent after seeing the Marker film. I started making a rectangular frame with my two hands: the index finger going across to meet the thumb on the other hand. Like a director or photographer might be trying to frame a movie or a shot. (Or just to annoy the people I was with.) I'd zoom in so that I could see their face in close-up. When I went outside I started piping up lines from the film. The first was *des vrais oiseaux*.

Scene: *Looking up the little hill at the edge of the college parking lot, into a stand of maples, dancing in the autumn breeze.*

Walker: (indicating) *Des vrais oiseaux,* (real birds). (Touching the Mercedes) *Le vrais voiture* (the real car).

Scene: *He looks at Rayne as though to question, Is this real? Uses the frame to zoom in on her. She is indulgent, smiles.*

Walker: *D'une voiture, il la voit sourire.* (She smiles at him from an automobile.)

Sometimes I'd translate for her, because she's not that into French.

CUT

Scene: *When they went to pick up Beau at the day care.*
Walker: *Des vrais enfants.*

CUT

I tried to get my voice to sound like the voice of the French *philosophe* in the film. A gravely voice from a lifetime of smoking Gitanes and drinking absinthe and listening to Edith Piaf records.

Scene: *Entering their bedroom.*

Walker: *Une vraie chamber.*

CUT

In the next few days, after I saw it a third time at Palumbo's house, I had taken notes, even got Palumbo to back it up and let me listen to the French and associate it with its English sub-titles.

Scene: *Rayne and Walker are in the supermarket. The light is bright and glowing in that stark shock. She is looking into the frozen food behind a glass. She is looking pensive.*

Walker: *Ils son sans souvenirs, sans projets.* (They are without memories, without plans.) *Leur temps se construit simplement autour d'eux.* (Time builds itself painlessly around them.)

CUT

Scene: *Rayne has left Beausolei and Walker together at the table and gone into the kitchen. She can still hear what is being said.*

Walker (to Beau): *La femme a disparu.*

CUT

Rayne had brought home a little golden hash oil, that the locals smoked by daubing a bit onto a cigarette paper, then rolling up a pinch of tobacco into the paper.

Scene: *Walker reclines back on the couch, his eyes looking up out of the top of his head, past the ceiling to a very far gone place.*

Walker: He feels waves of time coming over him, thinks it is the experimenters giving him another injection.

Puis un autre vague du Temps le soulève. (Then another wave of Time washes over him.)

CUT

Scene: *Walker and Rayne are out at stylish Montreal pub, walking down rue de la Montagne. He takes her hand, looks into her face.*

Walker: (loudly, so that the French speaking Montrealers nearby can overhear the lovers)
Un jour de bonheur, un visage de bonheur, mais different

Scene: *Takes a pensive pose. Waits for the others nearby to look at him.*
Walker: *Et alors. Encore je suise la.*

I did this — speaking French out loud on the streets of Montreal — a few times because, since it was not really my mother tongue, I was liberated to act a parody of how the French show passion in their language.

Rayne was indulgent of this phase, even got into playing in this movie.

Rayne was a very good photographer and lugged around a huge, gigantic camera with a long lens. She was quick with the camera, was on some kind of quest. It was a peripheral, sudden shoot-from-the-hip intensity she could muster. What was her desire with that? She did not speak of it to me. It was pre-articulate?

There was a kind of . . . not sadness, a starkness, a clarity, the real . . . to her photographs of subjects — places and people. I don't know how to put it, the only photographs I had ever taken were shooting other members of my family when they wanted to be in the picture. I had never owned a camera.

Photography was Rayne's passion and she was too wise to get into a light conversation about it. Perhaps she thought I was too unsophisticated to talk to about it. She was self-assured. Was she narcissist? We both were. When two people are in a passionate love relationship, one's desires take president over the other's desire. Her desire became my desire — for a while; then you have to struggle to maintain your own desire. You must. It was good that she was an artist on the quest too. She could at least empathize with my struggle if not relate to the result.

The invisible character of desire had gotten us, together and was, like Cupid — except not with bow and arrow but with still and video camera — was flying about looking for opportunity to insinuate its agenda, its program, to satisfy its urge to exist into the situation.

She took photographs of me. Sometimes when I was lying on the bed, she would get on top of me, straddling my chest and shoot close up portraits of my face. Or when we were walking around Montreal.

Scene: *Walker looking sexy, vamping for the camera, with his long hair.*
Walker: *Le subject es etudie.* (The subject is studied.)

CUT

Scene: *He makes a frame of the camera, zooming in on her photos when she shows them.*

Walker: The experimenters had a device for freeing moments of time.

Under her tutelage I learned how to look through the big camera too. I took some really nice pictures of her. All you had to do was take your eyes of love and look them through the view finder. Shoot subject through the eyes of love, capturing them in a moment of being themselves.

Another time I ducked into an alley to take a piss and she followed me in there with her camera! I tried to get away from her, ducked into a doorway, and turned and shot a stream of pee arching out into the cobblestone alleyway. She took pictures of this.

Scene: *Still photo of a parabola of pee arching out of a doorway into an alley.*

Walker (shouts) : *Il sentit qu quelque chose avait change* (he knew something was different.)

CUT

Scene: *Whispering.*

Me and Beausolei got into a kind of whispering jag where we would tease Rayne by whisper talking nonsense among ourselves. It became our in-joke, our experiment in how to tease the mom. Rayne would look exasperated.

Scene: *Walker is handing Beausolei his lunch in a paper sack, while Rayne is looking on.*

Walker: These are the inhabitants of the future.
They have traveled into our time, but it will be only a memory for them.
They are not wholly here yet. They are coming in.
We are grounded in the real.
And we are not able to push this will; but we can receive this will; and we can touch this will; and we can move with this will.

Scene: Walker is regarding a shape in the air he has molded with his hands

Walker: If we can feel the web, the membrane, the bubble

— around all things — with our hands, ever so
ambivalent and ready.
The body now is more than the eyes and the brain —
a vehicle to get into . . .

Scene: *Walker is reading stories out of a big book to
Beausolei sitting beside him.*

Walker: "And the very hungry caterpillar eats a hole through
the leaf."

Scene: *Zooms into Rayne's face and holds it for a long
time. She demurs; acquiesces to his gaze. Camera Zooms
into the child's face. Child's face looks patient, in the
game, in the moment.*

Scene: *Walker is carrying Beausolei on his shoulders,
when he gets tired, and he is so very tall. Beausolei is
enjoying looking down on his mother who is rather
petite.*

Scene: *Walker has made some kind of goggles out of
cotton and tape. He is lying there with these over his
eyes. They look like a homemade sleeper's mask.*

Walker: These experiments caused *les autres etait morts,
ou fou* (some to die and others to go mad). They had
little motion sensors in them when the subject drifted
into the REM state of dreaming.

Scene: *Walker is holding a flash light under his chin and
the light is making his face look weird, shadowy. He
looks over at Beausolei with a caring solicitous nod of
recognition, trying not to be scary for the boy.*

The Lunch Monitor

I got a little job at the Westmount Park elementary school as a lunch hour moderator. A little job indeed. A catcher in the rye but in an urban setting. I would walk down Ste-Catherine Street toward Westmount Park. It wasn't long before all that preparation and coming and going for one hour of pay began to seem absurd. But I felt needed. And I thought it might be good for the kids to see a man in the middle of the day.

They didn't do much of a background check. I just followed up on a notice I saw at the Westmount Library.

I was starting to feel quite confident in my parenting skills. My experiences with Beau returned my big brother proclivities. I occasionally kept him and Wolfie and they could be quite rambunctious; they quickly found I was a push-over, not really an official mom/dad unit. In looking at him my mind drifted into memories of my self when I was that age. You can't help it, that's what children do; that's how they humanize by activating your empathy, and your sympathy. It was new territory for me. They give you an opportunity to set things right, to right perceived wrongs. But they also just as much become the situation in which wrongs are repeated. Of course these elementary kids were older. I could say things like: "Hippos have a windshield wiper on their bum," to Beau, but certainly not to these middle aged kids.

Westmount Park Elementary must have been desperate. They were probably thinking about a retiree. And here this guy shows up, who is not otherwise engaged during the middle of the day. It paid $20 a day. Among the kids there were some unruly groups with gang aspirations who wanted to terrorize the younger kids, so that's probably why they hired this big guy.

I interviewed with the headmistress who was the main walking floor monitor; she was a righteous French Canadian woman, without any trace of accent. The elementary school facade was dark red brick with wide flat columns of white brick running all the way up to the roof. Tall industrial windows with steel frames. Inside, the halls were wide corridors of yellow industrial ceramic tile. It was fun to watch the kids. For the most part they were very well-behaved. There were some big, hefty white boys, well-fed, spoiled from the wealthier families of Westmount. There were some poor kids too.

In particular there was one little guy from Vietnam. Straight black hair. The other kids pointed at him and said he doesn't speak English. This was pretty much an all English school. It was odd that he was here with all the French in Montreal. I spoke French to him. When I first encountered the 4th grader, he was lying on his back underneath one of the swings of the swing set kicking his feet up in the air defending himself from a couple of the big white boys. You had to hand it to him, it was a pretty good strategy. They were trying to reach in past his flailing legs and grab him but he kept kicking the bouncing swing into them and lashing out with his feet. And they were not succeeding at getting their hands on the skinny boy.

"Hey!" I yelled. "What's going on here. Stop that!"

The teachers there were harassed. They had a fairly cynical attitude developed from years of seeing this bullying from the overenfranchised scions of the wealthy. There was one head hen. I liked her, she was French but spoke to me in English. The head mistress rang a bell and the kids lined up like little soldiers at arms length apart and shuffled single file back into school. The vacant yard fell silent and I returned home in that brilliant slant Autumn light. And later in the snow.

I took a special interest in the Vietnamese boy cause he needed it. Some other kids ran up to me and told on him, "He's brought matches to school!" I think he had cigarettes too. Whenever I saw him moving around the playground he always made sure his back was up against a wall or a bush, so he couldn't be attacked from behind. I think he was a refugee, his family from the former ruling class of Vietnam. I imagined he had seen more brutality and fear in his few years than I had in my entire life. In his delicate, sad yet resourceful face I saw that he was coping with some really big changes in his world. I could relate. I was undergoing metamorphosis too. I did notice that the Vietnamese boy seemed to be friends with a couple of girls. I think they were the girls to whom he was showing the fiery matches. They told on him.

I got in trouble with Rayne and Linda in a similar way. Linda and Rayne were the best of pals always coming and going freely in each other's apartment. Linda would come in the back door in the morning while I was having my coffee at the kitchen table, and wait for Rayne. I never saw Linda with a boyfriend, she was devoted to her pottery. We became like an extended family, one man, 2 women and 2 boys. Once Rayne came into the kitchen, lifted her skirts and jambs a tampex up into her. Linda and I just looked at each other in surprise.

Our apartment had a much looser discipline going on, we had the Wall and let the kids write on the wall with crayons. It looked pretty chaotic. Sue got high and tore the old sole out of my Texas tennis shoes and put it up on a ledge that runs around the top of the kitchen wall. I made a painting of a face on it after I noticed a face in the arch. Called it Old Soul. It was cool that she is a spontaneous crazy person. She just gives away energy. I got some ill fitting shoes from the free box and made it through the snow to my little job. I wrote my mother and had her send up my paratrooper boots from high school ROTC. They were Viet Nam surplus paratrooper boots and had a most amazing non-slip surface. They would be a great to wear in the snow and ice. I used the skier's trick of putting a sock, then a plastic baggy, then another sock to have warm toasty feet no matter how cold.

Rayne would come in and sit on the thrown when I was naked in my bath. She would bathe Beau in the tub, there was a little yellow rubber ducky and a blue boat and other various kid toys. There was some kind of holder device for setting athwart the tub, to hold various toys, soaps, shampoos or a book.

One day I got into my writing, and refused to go to Wolfie's 5th birthday party. I was just trying to get some time for myself. Besides it was going to be all moms, and I didn't have a present to give him. Rayne got pissed.

Rayne was the princess of the documentary film / art world, if not queen of the whole underground. I'll be her roadie, factotum, hopeful swain, boy-companion, lover, dog's body. She was working on her own films and I would go to help her in the editing suite at College Ste-Laurent, which was quite a well appointed setup. She was able to use the razor to cut and splice film, and also bump and edit on the 2 inch video tape machines they had there. I learned how to do this from her. I was a help because come what may, she could apply her artistic energies much better after she had had her mind blown out by orgasm, so that her attentions were reset away from the mundane workaday considerations of the single working mom, to those of the artist. Consequently I now have a fondness for the ergonomic height and smooth surfaces of editing tables and the industrial sturdiness of swivel office chairs.

Intimations of Archetypal Light

Two of Rayne's friends, Bob and Dave, came on the bus through Montreal all the way from Berkeley, California. They were a couple of actors on tour of college campuses and she had seen to it that they were going to perform at the CEGEP. They stayed with us at her apartment in Montreal. Rayne was great to use her influence at the CEGEP to reach out to what artists in other communities were doing. Rayne and Palumbo were politically savvy. They used a hard cop / soft cop routine to drive the school administration into an enriching creative direction. The CEGEP was lucky to have these artists who were using the media of their time to grow a powerful aesthetic. Canada, with its famous film board was generous; there was still grant money for poetry too. Though I wouldn't have had the career / marketing chops to get any of it. But for sure, I was inspired by the work and the earnest dedication of Rayne and Palumbo and Bob and others, and that was currency enough for me.

Rayne explained that Bob was a former lover and they were friends. Bob was a charming sweetheart of a guy, happy to be camped out on her living room floor. He was nice to me, seemed thankful that I was on the scene. Dave, in spite of being on crutches had numerous girlfriends to visit. These two were traveling writer / actors who seemed to lead the coolest life possible. They looked like wild Tibetan monks with their colorful Quebec knits and mufflers and Vermont macks and vests made by loving hippie girl hands. Bob had a thin moustache and long hair and an earring. They were traveling mystics on cross-country tour doing their solo theatre pieces in odd off of, off off off Broadway venues and converted warehouse spaces and universities.

Bob performed a stunning solo theatre piece of great intimacy about his relationship with his father called *Trunk 15*. He emerged from a trunk onto the stage. There were no sets or costumes, just pure storytelling, poetical energy and theatre. Bob could transform his face to look like his ancestors, like a malleable mask. It was shocking. He could do things with his voice that were astounding including a kind of throat singing, or overtone singing — a deep chant that was so otherworldly one imagined he could invoke strange metaphysical spirits in the sound entities. You felt like you were in the presence of someone who had spent years in the monasteries of Tibet, studying secret knowledges and powers. Truly this person might be possessed.

I used the new shoulder-mounted portable video camera to record it. It was a stunning opportunity to receive the transmission from this great performer. I was very moved by this solo theatre piece especially a moment where he realizes his father is really deceased, when he takes the man's pack of cigarettes off the dashboard of his truck. What a completely human and candid divulgence. The solo theatre piece — I knew to not call it a "play" — had more to do with storytelling. It had a lot of visual still moments like you were looking at a painting. I think this was the beginning of performance art. It certainly was for me. He acted on all levels, big physical movement, graceful gestures and even micro muscle level, doing contortions in his face, that suggested familial trait absorption. I was able to use the zoom in on this. I had never seen anything like this kind of intimate theatre.

At the time I met Rayne and Bob, I was still under the control of big media; actually I hadn't watched any TV in years and years, and had pretty much dismissed it. But being into her interests, and learning at the CEGEP, I was starting to come around to the real possibilities of video. Rayne just let me go at recording Bob's performance / ritual. She understood that a video made by such a beginner would be interesting because it would be full of process. She was always way ahead. It pissed me off sometimes. At first I was a hanger-on on some shoots. I carried equipment, I was good at setting it up, good at troubleshooting. I quickly got over the ideas from film that I was trying to bring to video: that it was a very expensive proposition, and that one had to be very careful not to make mistakes. For tape is cheap, and you can record over it and use it again. It takes the pressure off. It lets you swing into a looser more spontaneous generosity of your time and equipment, to apply to what is going on around you. I was being delivered of my preconceived assumption that people who worked in TV were just wannabe big-media types. I didn't really get it what a democratizing media video was, or could be with the right approach. It was surprising how much McLuhan I had read and thought I understood, but had not understood at all until Rayne invited me into her world and I started making inroads into my academically nurtured print bias.

I had not really had much of a good experience of theatre at that time either. I thought that it was just a bunch of attractive extrovert types playing together for a bunch of blue haired matrons who wanted to be seen at the *theatre*. So it was an awakening to be introduced to what Bob called Poor Theatre. He acquainted me with his teachers Grotowski and Artaud who I didn't know. He explained that physical theatre was about the ongoing process of its own development, it was about what one discovered while in this process. It was a kind of folk theatre from storytelling and joyous singing. To me this intimate theatre was like a transformation ritual — being present to witness something sacred. And the experience of video taping and reviewing the tape was empirical because with video you interacted much more directly with the experience then you ever could by writing about it. This intimate personal theatre on video was a whole new total art that collaborated with the world on its own terms. This kind of "writing" was liberated from the big performance, liberated from big publishing, liberated from big stage production, and liberated from broadcast. It wasn't just stick the video on a tripod and point it at the stage but, like his theatre, was intimate and vital. And it was an art never seen before; something from my generation. To use the Porta-Pak you need the camera/sound person and someone to hold the deck or have a long lead to the deck. When I recorded Bobby it was a pure interactive process. I could follow his gesture by moving the camera with him. It was like we two were in a kind of dance, when he came at me I could zoom. I got a good stance and could turn and pivot, crouch and lean in. I could zoom in to his changing facial gestures and expression, and thus capture the tremendous perception he had in mimicking familial and nationalist traits of types. I was a tripod, a pivot on the fly. It was like watching a consummate artist improvising a sketch of the people he had grown up with through inhabiting them with his own persona, the way their bringing him up had inhabited him. And in the way it got recorded, one felt more present, interacting with inhabiting.

I kept asking myself as I was recording the performance: What makes a good video, I was saying this as a mantra. It was spontaneous. I understood that the video camera was like a brain, it was an extension of my senses. I could zoom in on his facial expression for example — this is something you can't do with ordinary eyes. He made himself go into slow motion. And in rhythmic back and forth motion, he did instant playback. The experience was much more than just being in an audience, it was interactive. The experience of reviewing my footage was challenging to my introverted nature, for I was watching my own performance too.

Bob and Dave taught a writing class. It was my first.

Rayne and I took Bob to his performances and teaching gigs in Vermont at a small theatre in Bristol and various performance workshops for some communities. The theatre in Bristol was built and supported by a stunningly attractive couple, Kim and Debbie. They had removed all the walls of several rooms in their house to create a performance space. They were, along with Bob and Dave, the most assiduous and zealous alums of an experimental theatre at University of Iowa. Bob also did a workshop with the local community theatre in Barton. Some of Rayne's friends, John, Victoria, others in the North East Kingdom were players in the Community Theatre, and we went to their plays. Everyone enjoyed it. Barton was also the home of the Bread and Puppet theatre. Rayne was in touch with everything.

Bob had shown me the score for a strange poem. At first I thought was some kind of *poesie concrete* but it was written in a completely invented symbol system. He showed me how to enter into this poetry they called Sound Katas after the series of martial arts moves. The sound kata were (mainly unvoiced) breathing measures of open vowel sounds, the eeeehhh and the ahhhh, sometimes articulated with various stops and fricatives attacking the open vowel streams. One made sound (voice or unvoiced) on both the inhale as well as the exhale, precipitating a trancelike focus through musical content on top of breathing — the most vital of all life processes. Like the shakuhachi flute, it lent itself to the aleatory. And in the rhythm of breathing, and making the fricatives shhh, it was like waves breaking on some distant shore. In Vermont, Bob and I sung /chanted / performed this choral sound poem — entered into this sutra experience — in the forests as we sat cross-legged like monks in the warm shifting air. We were Buddhists chanting. He had a deep resonant voice that was unhesitating. To me the aesthetic from whence this poetry emerges was an intelligent secular spirituality. This level of work revealed an artistic mastery and penetration into being that I had not experienced in any school, philosophy, program. And he understood it — was sure of it. So that he could invite those around him to relax and just let go and be, in the moment of sound. What an art!

Something happened to me when I went out into the Vermont forest that evening to do the chanting of the Sound Katas with Bob. After Bob and I smoked some fine herb, (John, our host did not smoke) we three set out in Indian file, forth into the gloaming of the late afternoon Vermont forest near Barton village. And I came back different. As we were heading out I said, "See ya," to my girlfriend Rayne, and went off with John and Bob.

"Don't be gone too long," she said to the men.

It was like walking into a psychedelic light show because the forest was peaking in its great spreading leaf-change, it had phased into specular oranges, yellows and reds. It made a flood, a flow, a spread — the clusters of bright maples in the chiascuro of dark evergreens and shadows of valleys.

Perhaps we were following an ancient path that aboriginals have walked in other times. I was bringing up the rear and cast a glance back at the lovely Rayne, who was smiling at me, a slightly lascivious smile. Standing there, perhaps she felt a little melancholy at being left out of this monk-like pursuit of sound poetry.

I felt OK about Bob. In the new order of the world that the women were showing us, the former lover and current boyfriend, husband could get along. Could even be friends. After all, we were now brothers of the flesh.

There behind us, above us and before us the great maples undergoing the big change, resin flowing down like sweet sugar in their veins. It was a pleasant forest to walk through, not dense but airy. You walked past each individual immense trunk and looked up into their great articulated boughs, then beyond at the slant light shooting great shafts through the trees down to leaves mounding up in heaps on the ground. You could feel in every tree a representation of an evolution strategy: the leaves maximized their surface area and minimized the distances from their branches in order to maximize food production and minimize its transportation. And they distributed themselves in their growing in a way that was best for the life of each individual element, like the way sunflower seeds arrange themselves in Fibonacci spirals on a pod head so that the largest possible number of seeds get access to the best energy. The intelligent trees were quivering and swaying in the breeze, having set themselves afire to flail the sky with their chromatic blaze in the dance of slow oxidation to celebrate once again the end of the earth's journey around its star and the dying and rebirth they were undergoing. And like the star, just giving it all back to the generosity.

We left the dirt road and walked a narrower path 'neath the over-arching promontory of flaming leaves on huge dark boughs, to follow a path along a dried creek.

I noticed a speckled mushroom growing on a long stalk out of a small heap of barky earth. I picked the mushroom saying aloud: "I wonder if this is psilopsybin? Do y'all have any old-school farmers with organic cows around here?" The boys smiled.

From my studies I had concluded that next to language, it was this — Soma — that had been the impetus to change consciousness from ape to early man. Cro-Magnon paintings scrawled in flickering firelight on the cave wall were the signs of the first inhabitants of this expanded space.

"If I ping it and it turns blue we might be in luck." I popped it with a finger and it does not. I announce: "It has not become en-psy-essencent, didn't go into cyanosis." Then switching to a ridiculous British-Canadian accent, said officiously, "I'm not at all sure it's not a toadstool." And dropped it with feigned fastidious disdain. The mushroom falls slowly into the chaotic habitat of the ground. I remember thinking that I better not let these experienced woodsmen get out of my sight because I'd be pretty quickly lost.

The air was fresh; the forest is an ocean of oxygen, the smell of life, from the duff, the smell of leaves, wooden, wet. It was all as lovely as could be. (Lovely, now there was a quaint old word from my Maritime aunts, but they knew about Sugaring-off Time, when the life force runs back down the maples and can be tapped off into syrup, and Sugaring-off was a word made for it, for truly I felt like I was passing through a forest of love, for one could see the working of the creator in a most expressive way in the endless parallel arborescence of branching foliage scumbling for the light.)

It felt good to have a little company in this world, to be on the quest of a poem, to cut through the loneliness of the long distance traveler and the philosopher.

The poem was written in a strange sound language of numbers. It looked like some kind of Martian, out-of-this-world text. Each number represented a position of the tongue in the matrix of the mouth. There were diacritical markings for fricative, sustain, voice / unvoice and these operated on the basic vowel energy position numbers. Flows in time were indicated across the horizontal. I had not thought that so much language could be generated with such a small number of agreed upon sounds out of the world.

Bob had been teaching me the notation of this articulation system. Basically it was equivalent to the IPA, the International Phonetic Alphabet that you see in every dictionary. But this sound notation system expressed the whole human sound making capability in a unified sign system depicting position of the tongue in the mouth rather than agreed-upon typographical symbols. This matrix of tongue positions is, of course, the vowels. The system made it quite apparent that all of speech language was generated from just the few vowel energies articulated with various attacks, sustains and decays. Thus it was universal. Bob mentioned that there were several of these sound katas, each exploring variations around certain sound energies. The particular choral chanting poem that Bob had been training me on explored variations on the shhh — the linguoalveolar fricative at the 4 position.   Thus it was called (number) 4 + (squiggle fricative diacritical mark) = It also had movements into the open but unvoiced vowels aaaahhh and eehhh. (And there were several of these works!) But I was blinded by the one; it was like sutra to me.

Bob was an actor and always doing exercises and I was impressed by what a bracing physical attention the actor's discipline helps him bring to the world and the word. Though John was an actor too, in community theatre, he had not patience for all this — stoned monks soaring high on sliding sound sutras — and left us saying, "Just keep to the path to find your way back." Bobby looked totally OK with it, and since he was, I was too.

Bob and I spent a while hiking through the sun-dappled paths of the fall forest enjoying the warmth and silence, which was broken by a few lingering birds calling and the grinding creaking boughs swaying in the rhythm of pleasant breezes. We found a particular spot, a power spot, the way the brujos did, by letting it attract us to it. This intuitive sensing involves surrendering yourself to something like a spirit of place. The one that picked us was a shady place. Moist, it had an enclosed, turning in on itself with an aura of hallowed hollow. We sat down and Bobby showed how it was done. Putting the text (the score) down in front of us so both could see, we sat cross-legged, spine erect in meditation posture with good attention. We started to make sound, sending out into the air our feeling energy with this special poetry.

And it was such an experience to be breathing and chanting and making sound in that glorious Vermont autumn light, in the green forest fuse shot through with cascades of bright orange, yellow, and rivulets of reds. Our tongues were like reeds sensitive to the breath articulating the vowel colors from the resonance chamber of the voice, were like the leaves of fall foliage flapping in the moving air. And with the sound we were making being carried on top of our expiration and inspiration like a signal on a radiant carrier, it set up a glowing in my heart. I fell into a stony rapture brought on by the controlled breathing. A bracing sense of self, percolated in and out through unknown channels on the warm shifting air as it pressed and released its force on us. It was serenely uplifting and fortifying to the attention. We were falling into the omni-inter-accommodating spherical concentricity of it all (as Bucky Fuller might have phrased it). OM . . .

To me the sound notation was a kind of mathematics, the symbols of which were not abstractions but elements in an incantation that brought forth a world. One spoke these "equations" to invoke the energies imbuing the entities moving through the natural world. It was like being taught a kind of mimeological homeomorphism math. I was an alphabetarian undergoing a profound change being raised to a higher power or slipped into a parallel dimension. Could it be that everything moving, crashing, banging, sliding, tinkling, roaring, raging, clanking, fizzing, bonking, blurting . . . of the mechanical world could also be expressed in this matrix notation? Yes. We could finally know its true name. With the help of the insight of this notation, I began to "see" the sounds of the world in a kind of synesthesia. And to hear them as spoken in a voce from the "mouth" of a multidimensional being. The leaves were rustling, swooshing, shuffling, whispering in the trees.

I became entranced by the bright but hushed sound energy of the unvoiced vowels, while being touched by the physicality of the mechanism of articulation. I became high on the breath control and above all by the terrific melding of sound poetry with spiritual practice. I was filled with a rapture I had only experienced with drugs and though drugs were good to cut through the terrible sense of "I must prove my right to exist," and extended the perception of time and space out from under the horrendous clock-driven, market-driven, scarcity-driven impetuous of need (if only briefly), they took away any authority you might have had in living the experience. Doing the Sound Katas I became transported both away from and more deeply into this world. The level of poetry expressed showed a love and trust and sophistication for my generation that was beyond anything I had ever seen. My mind began to expand, and I got a sense of myself as belonging in the world; I was content to belong in the world; it was my right, I really belonged here.

I started noticing a phenomenon: light notes — dust motes undergoing random motions, turning and rolling in the thermal flux of the breeze so that they sparkled in the sun reflecting their motion and it seemed this stochastic motion on the Brownian path traced a shape of curling vortices. As Descartes thought, light was just another kind of stream. The light motes became musical notes in *la symphonie pastorale*, a green oeuvre played by the ecology orchestra. The fields here and there are the great pauses and silences, the sun and the shadow are the tenor and base, the rise and the fall, the movement as they are conducted by the air to rise and fall, blown from a horn that goes all the way back to the mouth of the sun. The sun is a golden white noise reflected by the wind, hushing and rushing though the spangled and shining trees, and the distinct notes are the individual flowers and blooms giving off their last in the time of bounty.

While we were chanting the sounds and resonating the overtones into the firmament, raising our voice in unified celebration prayer, a breeze picked up and snaked through the air. I felt it bathing my face, tossing my long hair. The wind moving through my hair whispered in my ear. And then the play of light on the leaves of the heaving trees, reminded me of a more frightening moment, I had not thought of in a long time. And would rather not have thought of again. It was something that happened when I was much younger, I was living in Quebec City, the summer we landed on the moon. I was going through a lot. I had been laid off from my job as a night auditor at the Chateau Frontenac, (maybe it was that my nights and days were reversed and I had gone quasi-somnambulistic.) And, I had once again gotten my heart broken in love, I had been supporting my girlfriend and she, tiring of the isolation of French immersion, wanted to be in a commune down in Montreal. (It was isolating, living in this strange city of another language.) And I had to shift around from rooming house to rooming house in the dead of night cause I couldn't pay rent. Come to think of it, I had been reading a lot of Pascal and picking up some of the terror of Pascal looking out at night into the lacy star fields of the stochastic universe and feeling that fear at the edge of things where your radical doubt is amplified by aloneness into a laser-pure anxiety undiluted in distraction by the Other as it becomes a constant companion haunting and shadowing every thought. Or maybe it was just a flashback from my first mescaline trip that summer. So that, because of all this, for a while there I slipped into a dissociative, perhaps psychotic experience, what I would later call The Green Fuse (after the Dylan Thomas poem). I had this sense that the plants and trees around me were alive and aware, and in touch with the life force and were "looking at me." It was frightening. It had something to do with this big patch of horrible looking weeds in a vacant lot. The weeds with their jagged edges looked like the mandibles of insects, or worse, some kind of cancerous tentacles. My brain tried to process it as just a weed. I tried to assuage my anxiety by telling myself: There is not some great green thing in front of me, some Jolly Green giant of weeds slouching across the landscape of my days. And laughed it off. However the image persisted for what seemed like a very long time, weeks. I didn't have anybody to talk to about it. Going to a psychiatrist would have been the last thing I would have done. I told myself it was like some kind of an externalized obsession. I went about my cognitive business, brushing aside what was perhaps a outward manifestation of an overdose of stress. I recall that I was reading Borges and Leon Bloy, a catholic mystic at the time. Perhaps the weed was some kind of rebirth symbol, something that they kill and eradicate but still keeps being reborn. Or perhaps it was just a symbol of me, a weed in this foreign landscape. It was a very powerful and frightening experience, unforgettable. I didn't understand it. But knew it was something I had to surrender to, a power. I tried not to think of it for it is frightening to remember, even now. It might even be what they call an out of body experience, or perhaps even a psychotic separation. Sartre describes it well in *Nausea*.

I feel like the quest to do art is such a surrender to a power. I would like to think of my art as a practice of Recollection and a practice of Surrender to this power. Now though, with what I am sensing in the Katas and what I am learning in this community I am trying to get at it more directly.

Dreams are related to the out of body experience. Except the dreams are a dialog of entities that have gotten within the mind. The separation experience is more like getting in touch with entities outside the mind, which are seen as representations of this a priori archetypal dimension. The place where Design comes from and Ideas; where destiny angels operate the machinery of the world like scenery of a play to get lovers and other agents of change together. It is the great chemical creativity being of water and fire and earth and air without you and within you. And it feels the abstracted, the hierarchically built-up, history of evolution from whence it came. That is ultimately what one is trying to Recollect. And it is recollected everywhere and in everything. Perhaps it as simple as what happens when binding energy is able to maintain for a time a local hegemony over the greater and ubiquitous thermal energy.

The sound of a the voices used by us "monks" [chanting of scriptures (in overtones that reflected the currents)]   is hard to describe. It reminded me of an experience like that depicted so beautifully in Jack Kerouac's book *Big Sur* where he went out to take dictation from the sea. The sea, the great wet mother of the gods, whispered "cher son" in its chanson to him. Yes we too were "dear sons" of the earth mother, trying to get into harmony with her ways.

How long we sat there lost in the masterpiece of choral chanting, I forget. I remember realizing: Oh, this is what rhapsody is. What the old poets knew going back to brave blind Homer. I thought, wow, this goes directly for the feelings. Whoever came up with this poetry has got to be one of the most creative and amazing writers of our time. I have got to somehow go and study with this guy. By the time we finished, got to our feet and headed back, I knew I had to follow this California Zen aesthetic into the future. I had to get to Berkeley. Would Rayne be able to come to?

Later when I got home to Montreal and got on the typewriter I wrote another Eddy story:

Something happened to Eddy when he participated in the forest doing sound kata and chanting with the monk. Whether it was from hyperventilating, causing a kind of rush of adrenaline speed to mix with the weed's serotonin cascade in the frontal lobes, or it might have been the awareness of the great circulation of breath (the dual mirroring of respiration and photosynthesis) in the currents of his mouth that projected the air molecules of his being out to meet the Brownian motion of dust motes on the slant rays of autumn sun shafting down through the spaces between the branches of the trees of the dappled forest, causing the trajectoring particulates to become intermingled with the flotsam and jetsam of rag weeds and milkweeds and bits of red and yellow flecked maple leaves and other particulate detritus, swirling and floating in the air there, that he was taken out of himself and invited to be present in a kind of eco-topology of life moving through the forest substrate.

Aboriginals might have called it being charmed by the spirit of place.

Rather the lufting particulates and bits of life circulating around were tracer elements that a discerning "head" could use to observe the eco-topology of the most excellent meshing together and convolving of the local proto-evolutionary forces rising from the thermodynamics and seeking order in a new aufbau (finding their place and occupying it) of ecological niches.

Later he would come to think of it as Intimations of the Flux Moving in Archetypal Light. Not just the normal light we see, the electromagnetic radiation, but of a more prior Source of which the light of a Sun or a Star being partitioned off into so many millions and billions of beings and ecologies layered strata upon strata as abstract surfaces through which the energy flowed, fluxed, diverged, curled about, dissipated through, was dispersed into.

There is . . . was the lumpiness, the fine structure, the hills and dales of time's leafings through the foliations by way of the convex hulls of seeds adrift on the wind. There was a Brownian (random) motion like dust motes in the sun rays, or a fox's tracks in the forest pathways, yet there was a treelike purposivity extending into any substrate it could poke its feelers into. Descartes saw it as vortices, back when physics was still part of metaphysics; Leibnitz saw it as monads, little yin yang enatiomorphs; von Neuman saw it as finite automata; Laplace saw it as field points. Every point that light strikes is a point of many kinds of fields, warping and weaving, diffracting and entraining into coherence like ripples on a pond. The world is book, the leaves of its pages a foliation, the pages were layers surrounding a convex hull containing a seed.

(foliation (hull (seed))) <—>(book (pages(images)))

(plane (line (point))) < — > (leaf (branch (seed)))

In Desargues, (trunk (branch (node)))

Though we thought we were breathing, it was breathing us: just as the earth was breathing in seeds and breathing out saplings; breathing in eggs and breathing out birds in flight; breathing in flower perfume and breathing out bee buzz and pollen flow; breathing in star fields and breathing out planets.

It struck me that the shape of the leaves of the lower branches, were like a lens. They were trying to focus in more of the precious light. Even though they were beneath the canopy, the had evolved organs to capture a little diffuse light. And they had those pointy edges which helped pull up water. The leaves engaged in transpiration with the sky through those pointy edges. In cooler climes, the leaves had more points to pull up water. Some leaves could distill it out of fog.

It was a bit frightening or awakening to see the plant as an evolved machine, its tree supporting this outer skin, an epidermis for funneling light down and water up. It is all about absorbing the light. Simple. Synchronistic sun-eaters every one, supporting diachronic time-binders on the run.

This land, this place, this time was a reflection of a more eternal place, a projection from the archetypal dimension and just as it is, so am I — a forest, a place full of music and systems, an ecology of trees branching in space and time like rivers and veins and in a mind out there thinking this all up, the dreaming void of long long ago, with is vortices and loop back inconsistencies and anti-entropic stabilities. Like the curlicue swirls in the path a leaf takes on a stream or on the air for the air is just a different kind of fluid, not so dense, of the general Watercourse Way.

Archetypal Light expresses the idea that there is a prototype of all light; by analogy you can envision it as field emanating from some source. The analogy from the behavior of light as radiation of the electromagnetic field gets extended to a preexistent and supra-ordinate coordinate system of higher dimensions. Relativity showed that light is the metric of space and time and that space and time itself align relative to a more abstract archetypal order. It is Archetypal Light that the ancient philosophers speak of as the Watercourse Way, the hydrodynamics, the thermodynamics with its entropy and information quantized and encapsulated in packets. And it is this that all beings are trying to partake of, in a kind of communion in the now. Excuse my mindset of catholic metaphors.

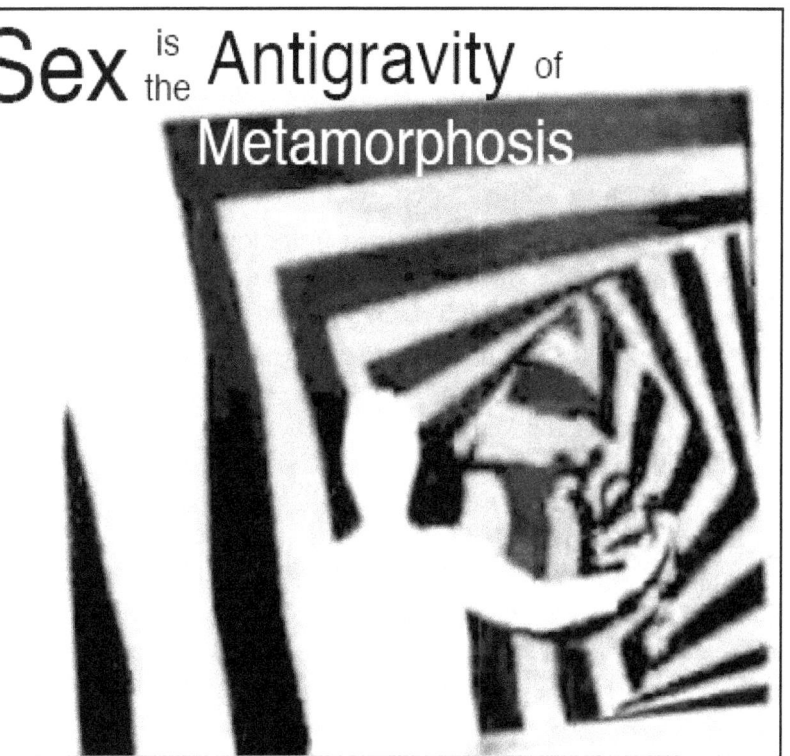

Sex ^{is} the Antigravity of Metamorphosis

Lodeo on The Main

Rayne took us to the Lodeo Café in a part of Montreal called "The Main". On the way over she was telling us, "On The Main, everyone comes out to have a good time. There's coffee houses, restaurants, bars, and night clubs. The place is teaming with cheap stores during the day and it's just as busy during the night."

The Lodeo was in Montreal's Chinatown (*Quartier Chinois*) off the Main. Walking through there you hear French, English, Yiddish, Chinese, Greek, Portuguese and India. Rayne was telling me, "It used to be called the Rodeo Café, but it became the "Lodeo" in playing off the Chinese mispronunciation of Rodeo."

I said, "Actually back in Texas the old timers say ro-day-o instead of rodeo."

Palumbo put in, "Well we better call it Lo-day-o, then." Palumbo's girlfriend Marie was there, and another teacher from school Kirkwood, and one of Rayne's former students, Roxanne. She was a dusky young beauty, Indian, Rayne said. And she didn't mean from the subcontinent.

The Lodeo was a former cowboy bar of The Main. It was the entire ground floor of a big grey-stone at the corner of St. Laurent (The Main) and La Gauchetiere just below Ste-Catherine Street. There we saw a two story tall vertical sign with the enormous letters L-O-D-E-O running down, outlined in red neon. There was a lot of neon in the neighborhood. The whole scene was wrything and pulsing with bright letters and signs. There were packs of roving young people and very shady looking characters in cheap suits, and big-assed brassy women shivering in hot-pants.

Entering the cavernous night club was like stepping back into time. It was the 40's with all these big galoote doorman standing around in double-breasted, wide-lapelled, big-shoulder suits and athletic, short, jar-head hair. There was a huge coat-check closet room, into which we check our jackets. Got a ticket.

The cavernous space had a turning ball of mirrored surfaces rotating on a rod from the ceiling, projecting moving flashes of colored lights. A spot light with rotating color filter gells in front of its lens was shinning directly on the mirror ball. This caused the many faceted mirror ball to reflect spots of color to flit spectrally around the room. It was kind of magical the way the lights moved across the dancers and up the walls. There was a catwalk for strippers to shake their booty for an indifferent clientele; behind that against the far wall was a small stage for a band with some instruments set up. There was a loud juke box. The walls of industrial green might have been quieting but had gone ghastly in the garish blacklight and the aged grit and the great din.

The blacklight made my white shirt glow bright bluish, and made people's white-toothed smiles gleam like Cheshire cats. There was a lot of sound from juke box. Blue and orange lights glow dimly through the bottles stacked in several tiers up the mirrored bar-back. Among the bottles permanent Christmas lights, the bubbling thistle kind, were hanging draped and festooned. The places where the lights didn't shine grew strange in dark shadows. With much noise dragging the chairs across the concrete floor we got seated at some formica kitchen tables with chrome legs.

Waitress comes up wearing a white peasant blouse with red thread roses, and lots of clinky bracelets that jiggle when she writes on a little pad to take our orders. Bonjour.

Kirkwood, Palumbo's good friend, is asking people

what they want to drink.

"Why don't we just get a pitcher."

Un pitcher de Labatt's cinquant, si'l vous plait.

Oui

Merci

She went to pick it up from the waitress station at the bar. The workers in the place glanced over at us from behind the bar. We were not the usual clientele though not that far off either. Just English.

I said, "This place is amazing. It is like stepping into a time warp." Black light was making white things really stand out like neon. I said, "And the bubbling Christmas thistle ornaments going around the mirror at the bar, that is a homey touch." There is a faded TV for watching sports, but it can not be heard above the music and the sounds. The place is all churning with characters from a demimonde: women in skimpy hot pants — the fashion for whores, were with men in coats and leisure suits with wide lapels — the fashion for pimps, but it may just be the style the regulars are used to. The band and strippers are on an extended break. Fun place.

Kirkwood was talking about the Parti Quebecois. "The PQ is running for election in Quebec. Going to give Pierre Eliot some trouble, to be sure." We got to talking about the Quebec situation; one lowered his tone in a place like this.

I mentioned that I had been living here during Expo 67. That was the summer when De Gaulle came from France to visit. I said, "De Gaulle came to the *nouveau monde* that summer, stopped at St. Pierre and Migalon islands in the St. Lawrence and then proceeded in a great procession down the *chemin de roi* from Quebec to Montreal. People were standing by the side of the highway as though they were waiting for the *pape* to go by."

The waitress approached looking serious, the corners of her mouth turned down. The green scheme and the blacklight inflorescence making everything look like it is coming at ya, is making the whole scene seem fairly nauseating. We pour the beer into the small glasses. And it is quickly quaffed.

Rayne and I got up and danced. It was a slow tune, and I just loved swooning and swinging with her under the mirror ball. I was enjoying the moving patches of light drifting suspended across the room. I thought to see these glimmers floating through space projected by the rotating ball and splashing against a mirror as spots of time being projected by a more *a priori* entity. It would be the noumenal sphere projecting on to the phenomenal sphere. Spots of being in which time was turned back, spots of light in which the Zoot-suited young men in fashionable Montreal in my parent's heyday were moving. They took the trolley. They danced the jitterbug like mad. They followed the Tommy Dorsey and Benny Goodman orchestra. 'It don't mean a thing if it ain't got that swing.' I had the feeling of having entered into an a scene of post WWII.

Also, besides feeling the great circulation of being — through Deadhead Sufi twirling with my love — I wanted to get Rayne away from the student that she brought. What is her name? Roxanne Luna and she was a dusky beauty. Only 19. This girl was giving Rayne entirely too much attention.

Our party was far enough away from the door not to be able to really see it but there was some kind of commotion. People shoving, and moving fast. Several stout fellows came out of a back room and rushed up front. The music was too loud, the din to dense to really pick up the turmoil at the door, but there seemed to be some kind of a scuffle. The Indian girl Roxanne came back from the bathroom and told us she saw some kind of fight going on.

"Well what happened?"

"He was throwing these bouncers around and they were pushing and shoving back. "

She told us some big Indian is fighting with the bouncers at the front, at the door. "He is huge. They are having a lot of trouble getting him outside. I saw one of the bouncers try to hit him, and he threw them all off, they knocked into some tables."

She laughed, "The people just picked up their drinks and stepped back. . ."

Palumbo and Kirkwood went up front to check it out.

I was left with the girls; Palumbo's lady friend Marie was there too.

One never thinks about the Indians. I used to see them in New Brunswick, sadly hanging out by the government liquor store. Roxanne says she was Indian. I asked her, What tribe?

" I am descendent from the Huron."

"Wow." We just looked at her. Here was somebody with roots that go way back. Somebody with depth to their personage.

I began thinking: Better check if there is a back door out of here. There's gotta be.

Roxanne Luna was talking about the Indian. "Montreal even back at the start, the ancient people called it some big long name; I can't remember, it is some big long name, that means "big waterway." My ancestors, they were Huron and this place was the fish market because it is an island at the confluence of the Ottawa and the St. Lawrence river. What did they call it before?"

"I don't know."

Rayne said, "And it has been like the cross roads of the world, the Europeans coming in here, the refugees, it is a lot easier to get in here than the States. It is like a no man's land, the boarder, the jumping off place for every refugee trying to get into America."

Kirkwood is back and is looking troubled.

Rayne leans over and whispers to me, "Lets go down to Vermont this weekend."

"Yeah!"

"We can help with Larry's log cabin."

That will be fun. You know I like those people. I like all your friends. Mostly."

"But . . ."

"Well, this is all so intensely urban. I'm used to Texas and less density and . . . siestas." I smiled, sung a line from a Carmen Miranda: "*Manana* is soon enough for me."

"I need to get out of this rat race too" she agreed. "We can have some time together down in Vermont."

As we walked out, petite Rayne takes Indian Girl's arm and hooks it around hers and they walk arm in arm. There's lots of police activity out on the street. We get to a large dark parking lot down the block and Rayne says, "I gotta pee." She goes behind a big dark car and squats down out of sight as we all walk on toward Palumbo's sedan. We are standing around waiting for her, and as she strides up to us I notice a trickle of her pee running under the big dark car, she had just come from behind. It is trickling across the asphalt.

I think: Maybe they didn't notice. I did.

Palumbo was talking to the cops, comes back with a report. "They cuffed the Indian guy who was indeed making such a ruckus, pushing and shoving at the front door. Hauled him off to jail."

He looked at me and said, "Canada has the aboriginal guilt like the US has black guilt."

We headed out into the neon signs, and the crowds back to the west side of town. Spellbound by the dazzling strings of gaudy neon lights and red lanterns swaying in the breeze in the *Quartier Chinois*, and applying writerly spy technique of using peripheral vision and involuntary side scanning sonar of certain mathematical / linguistic /semiotic theorems (theo — godlike, rems — rapid eye movement in dreams) that went oblique into time, I became — I believe — able to tell fortunes.

The Green Car

We are seeing out through the windshield of the green
car, down the hood, the green Mercedes is pointed down the
long vast St. Lawrence river as we are about to get onto the
Victoria Bridge out of Montreal. Rayne was fun to run the
roads with and we did, down to Vermont whenever we
could. This trip she said, "On the way back lets come home
the long way through Burlington. I want to show you where I
grew up."

Lovers, try to share their whole being with each other.
They naturally want to take the other into their past. It was
generous of her. I had to try and put myself into her shoes.
How would I take her to the place I grew up and show that
aspect of myself to her. I did want to take her to Texas. I had
not been able to show her too much of my own past here in
Montreal because I was trying to find it myself. We had gone
to a diner with Denis Coutour an old friend who got me a job
at Expo 67 and she had met Ian Lavoie at the Rainbow. I
imagined she might feel some fear in the intimacy of showing me how it was for her growing up. I would try and be
sufficiently sensitive to it. I didn't know what to expect.

Down river to our left we can see the islands and the
dome. We've got thermal underwear, look like space children, and we've got that "on the road again" excitement and
that "get out on the highway looking for adventure" edge.
We are not asking each other how long are we are going to
stay together, we just are.

Snow has come and the skies are looking powerful and
grey, yet there is still green in the distance. The weather is
going to get powerful and kick our ass in the shorter and

shorter days ahead. We don't care and are heading across Quebec into the Green Mountains of Vermont in the distance beyond the hood ornament peace symbol of the Mercedes. We are crossing the wide river on the steel span, its big girders swooshing past. The fabulously wealthy houses in Montreal climbing the hills are left behind as we head out for the wilds. The emerald green German touring machine was great. It seemed a little big on her. Made her look like a small child behind the wheel. It was more like a man's car. The Mercedes-Benz 280. Light green exterior, leather tan interior. It was a beauty. I washed it and waxed it for her, even though I could not afford the expensive repair job on the window. I had done a neat job of taping it up with duct tape and cardboard.

Looking up toward the mouth of the St. Lawrence it seems to go on and on forever. Summer is only a memory with all its green vines and foliage. I have such fine memories of the fleuve and its backwaters, its little bays and marshes and spits.

When we passed through the small towns of Vermont, it was cool to see our emerald green conveyance reflected in the large window glass of the shops on the main streets of these perpetually pastoral American towns. And to see ourselves as though from outside through a window.

I get excited when I travel. It is stimulating and I start blathering a heady pastiche. I had been waxing enthusiastic all the time about Richard Grossinger, about how he was investigating the topology of dream space in *Spaces Wild and Tame*, about how he was an anthropologist, like Castaneda, taking field notes on all kinds of phenomena and who understood structuralism, and Freud and semiotics He was also engaged in a kind of magical warfare using occult, astrology, Jung, oneirology, and literature of awareness. His journal IO was indeed a Whole Earth Catalog for the mind. And he taught at a school in Vermont.

I told Rayne how his books came into my world. "It blew my mind when I ran into his books at a book store in Austin. This was an amazing book store, they used to have readings outside under an oak tree. It was right beside Oat Willies – that's a kind of cowboy head shop. I had just finished at UT and was drifting, hanging around the university trying to become a writer, and there in this bookstore were these Grossinger books turning up. *Spaces Wild and Tame* was wild. Here was some guy trying to figure out the connective projectivity of things seen in dreams."

He seemed like a nice unassuming guy in his picture in the blurb of his Black Sparrow books — young, bearded, looking pensive and cool. He was my hero. It turns out he was a professor at Goddard in Plainfield. Rayne suggested meeting him. "We have to come back through Plainfield. Why don't we look him up?"

So after our stay in Glover checking out the community theatre play all her friends were in, and going to a big dance at the co-op, and generally helping with Larry's cabin, we headed toward Montreal by a different way. We started early in the morning. At the beginning we are bumping over the back roads of Vermont, the grey crushed rock roads with ruts from the rain. The sun was throwing long shadows across the road, making the trees look like columns. Ancient boulders and rocks on the hillside, moved there from the last ice age, peered at us like stellae that had seen much. The way was straight out of Glover through Crafstbury and Greensboro to Hardwick. Then a bigger highway through Marshfield. Plainfield was on route to her home town of Burlington.

To see our reflection in the store windows as we slowly drove through the eternal towns in our stately sedan, we looked like minor gods or royalty passing by. But I was nervous at the prospect of actually meeting the Great Man. We wandered on. I yacked. "Topology in *Spaces Wild and Tame*, it was just thrilling to see concepts from math and science and structuralism being used in stories about people in our time. His writing has that great hippie wonder and sincerity and truthfulness, he was not afraid of telling the truth no matter how unpleasant. The material about his brother's psychosis in *Martian Church* was a personal human divulgence about his family life. His essay on Simon and Garfunkle and the movie *The Graduate* was a sophisticated critique with great insight.

"In the Dream Issue of IO he had stuff about the Worfian hypothesis. The Worfian hypothesis had a huge influence on me when I was younger. It is about how language shapes your reality. Language formulates time sequences, for one thing. As an idealistic young philosopher, trying to explore mind I figured we'd have to get beyond the Worfian programming that language does on your mind. That was the main reason why I started to get into math, because it is a non-protoindoeuropean mindset. The mother tongue, learned from the mother, is about expressing need and desire. Math is the most psychedelic thing you can study. Everything has its own center of mass, even things in motion. Everything is projected, objects cast shadows reflecting the incident light unto subspaces. Probabilities project coincidences. Motion follows curves that are there from the world of forms."

I could see she was getting a little tired of this and interjected some humor: "But what is it that does not even cast a shadow? That's what I want to know." (I could really get going.)

She listened to me. I could tell she sensed my shy nervousness at meeting the Immortal.

We stopped at some of the little Vermont towns along

the way, because they were lovely. We stopped in Bristol to visit the theatre run by Kim and Debbie. It had snowed in the mountains but as we got to the center of the state toward the lake it was just melted and wet. I stepped ankle deep into a puddle of freezing slush and almost got my Texas discount store tennis shoe nearly sucked off my foot. I needed some boots!

Walking around in another small town, blathering me was edifying the divine Mz. Luce on topology: talking about coffee cups and sugar bowls. "The teapot has a spout which lets the inside out. It is a torus of genus 1, which means it has just one hole all the way through it."

Then Rayne started singing the little children's song: "I'm a little teapot short and stout / here is my handle, here is my . . sp." She hesitates. She's got BOTH arms going out and coming in, hands on hips — instead of one hooked up as a spout. "I'll be damned. I'm a sugar bowl!" she says in mock surprise, looking at her arms. We both laughed.

And right about then we saw the Stein painting. And thus began a strange sequence of events encountering these cool paintings across Vermont. I noticed one in a window, another in the bus depot of Bristol. They were typical, almost banal Vermont landscape paintings — little white ginger-bread farm houses, sentimental covered bridges over a lazy stream passing by an old mill with a water wheel. But when you looked at them, they had a subtle kind of cubist / surreal aspect. For example you would be looking at a covered bridge over a river into a little hamlet, but then in the hamlet you would be looking *back* at the covered bridge. It made it as if the viewer were standing in two places at once. It was wonderful, shocking. This duality filled a viewer with secret delight. I thought it was a perfect, head on view of a Mobius strip or a closed, saddle-point negatively curved universe (a

Klein bottle) that flowed out of itself and back into itself. I immediately recognized these paintings were like the visual paradox designs that Escher exploited but painted with much more subtly and with deft humor. It made you feel like you had entered a magic space.

"Who *is* that guy?!"

His name, as he signed the paintings, was Stein.

I wanted to find more of his paintings and did find some others. A large one in a bus terminal. Another much bigger one prominently displayed on the wall in a bank behind the rows of teller cages. It was a similar idea but much larger, a mural with great golden trees like scenes in Maxfield Parish. I wondered if the people who worked there knew. I ask one of the girl tellers; she had no clue. Huh!?

On the way to Goddard, Rayne and I wondered if all kinds of people just showed up to visit the great writer. I said, "He must have long lines of VW busses, with long-haired people pulling up to his house, if one could find it, or looking for him on campus."

Rayne said, "I can see us pulling up in our green Mercedes, asking the locals in the village where is this great brujo writer Richard Grossinger."

I said, "They must get a lot of outsiders pulling up, on the quest for the real and the hyper-real self in the modern world." I was being overtaken by my affliction of terminal shyness at meeting the literary light of my generation.

"Well," she said, "we'll go out to the college and check the Anthropology Department. Maybe he has office hours."

We got into Plainfield, and asked around to where Goddard College was. It was a second town square, a little jog from the center of town. We drove through the campus, past the eccentric and cone-roofed, church-like structure of the college that looked like something you would find in a Swendenbourgian utopian cult but by then I was backing out, for fear of interrupting the great writer. And Rayne was certainly not wanting to be dallying too much for we still had to get to Burlington. Since that was where she was born and grew up I was relieved to pursue this more intimate insight into her life. I was relieved when we got back onto the big highway and zoomed toward her past. And she seemed much more interested in that.

When we got to Burlington we spent some time wandering around the wharf on Lake Champlain. What a beautiful city. Rayne wanted to show me the home she grew up in. It was close to the lake. Being close to the lake must have made living there warmer, because there was just the occasional drift of snow around in Burlington, not like the mountain cities we had just come out of. We were walking in this nice neighborhood, and suddenly she took my hand and led me up a driveway. "This is the house I grew up in," she said in a whisper. There was a big hedge shielding the driveway from the neighbors. There were tall hedges and bushes and trees so we went right up to the house unseen. We stood and listened. I noticed an outside door leading into the basement was open. I casually peered in. She wandered further down the driveway to look in the back. When she came back to me, I took her hand and we entered quickly into the basement. She let herself be taken into the basement of the house she had grown up in. The house full of memories in which she had been a little girl. Little girl Rayne: I tried to picture her. Did she have long hair? I made a note so myself: Ask her to show you the pictures of her childhood.

Was it breaking and entering? Well we didn't need to break into the house but we entered it. The basement was still full of the old furniture that Rayne had grown up with.

Her parents still owned this house, and rented it out — the basement reserved for storage. It still held many of the furnishings she remembered as a child. They had rented the house to strangers who now abided in the storehouse of memories but were not of them. Perhaps the house had been lived in by many. Now *she* was an interloper, a trespasser, a home invader into her own past.

The footsteps and voices in the house above us could be heard ominously. We were below in the shadowy recesses of the basement; it was dimly lit through little windows here and there around the top of the basement wall. There was bright green color coming through a green trellis lattice covering the underside of the porch. We were among masses of furniture, desks, fine stuff with thin legs. There was an antique couch.

"Lets sit here a minute," I whispered, and edged over to that elegant sofa on slender legs. It had a white covering that was stitched, brocaded like a tapestry of needlepoint or weaving. (I don't know this stuff.)

She had brought me here and I had facilitated an encounter with her past that we could both be a part of; we had entered together a subspace of her life chronicle. Where there memories of times spent here in this room under the house? Playing on cold winter days, when it was too cold to go outside. There was the giant old furnace, that clanged and banged when it started up, did the grill over its flame look like a mask over sharp teeth when she was a little girl? She no doubt would have come down here to be cool on hot summer days. Had she ever come down here to feel herself? It was just stuff to me, but to her there would be recollections of life story attached. I felt her, felt her mind moving on narrative. Why had she brought me here? To juxtapose me into her childhood somehow? What did it mean to be sharing her past this way?

As she looked around, she seemed to be recognizing some of the objects: tack from a horse she had once owned, a Tudor table made of walnut or was it maple, a wooden rack to dry clothes, some heavy curtains. I wondered. I imagined her mind could go from room to room seeing these objects in their place in the family homestead. It would seem vague: things missing — lost. She had told me that she had a dog, a border collie; what was its name? It had died. And dolls, where were her dolls? Did little Rayne play with dolls?

Standing amid these things I had been brought into her past. Perhaps she saw herself looking through the glass out the front door, then going off to school, then being at school, and wondering about boys. Where were they now, the kids she had grown up with, the people in their synagogue, that had been so important to her mother? Where was that community with all its knowledge and rules and singing? Who from that life was still in her life now? How *do* you know who your friends are? Who will stay, who will go. Are we just here to fulfill the obligations to our past?

I wanted to stay a while and inhabit her past. I sat down on the sofa. I wanted to dwell a while in that cool shaded quiet with her where she had brought me. I motioned for her to sit beside me. But she was off in her mind. I knew she must be feeling what it was like to be back in her mother's house, even though it was her father that was the powerful one, and the one she took after — it was her mother's house. Did she remember being in her room, feeling like a captive, yearning for more feelings? With boys? And with girls? Had she always felt like that? Androgynous, as much masculine as feminine. We're all hungry for feelings, and would rather avoid knowing or understanding or experiencing how that need made us feel so vulnerable.

I took her hand and pulled her down beside me. I patted the cushion with its ornate Victorian curlicues of plants and blooms. It looked vaguely Freudian. I don't know why she brought me here. What meaning does this have for her, for us. Yet I saw something in the way she was relaxed. Safe. Within her self here. This intrusion instead of being an exciting criminal act of home invasion was a quiet sanctuary. We were silent. We could hear the people walk around upstairs.

I pushed her down, supine; she pulled me down, on top of her. We kissed, her lips parted. She felt pliant, willing. I cradled her neck like she was a little girl and she leaned back. We played, me kissing her cheeks, she turning her head, twisting and turning, feigning flight, but not hiding the smile and blush of delight. She would not have been able to do this when she was a living at home with her parents.

I reached under her skirt. She was not wearing any panties. As I was kissing her and she kissing me, I was running my hand over her bum. Sweet white bum. Then I slid off of her, sat back up, took one of her feet and lifting her leg, placed it way up on the top of the back of the couch. She looked good, spread out like that. I looked into her eyes, she said yes with her big slightly scared but excited eyes.

I went down on her. Parting the lips I kissed her clit. She thrust her hips up into my mouth. Then, mindful of being on home intruder time, I sat back up, undid the belt of my jeans, and in one swoop pulled them down along with my underpants. I got back on top of her. But she pushed me back to sitting and swung her leg over me. Her white thighs opened at the crotch and the nervy, venial, flushed, tumescent, purplescent standing coconut tree was planted at the mouth of her cave. And she ooched herself down, impaling herself on my cock and gasped as it slid in. She lowered herself down on me, and her hands reached over my shoulders and grasp the top of the couch.

There was a mirror behind us, I hadn't noticed it, at first, but she had. I couldn't see it anyway, but she had looked at herself in that mirror many times in her life. Now she could see herself in it again. She thought I hadn't noticed it. She didn't bring it up and I wouldn't have wanted to see myself in it anyway but she was intrigued by it.

She slowly rocked back and forth with me inside her. She began to thrust and rock harder. We both became flushed and a bit dizzy as she kept fucking me with her tight wet cunt like a salubrious glove.

She knew she must be quiet but little moans and chuffy aspirations escaped. I gasped. I was a wee bit distracted keeping one eye on the lookout lest the householders be coming down. Listening, we could still hear them talking and tromping around upstairs.

Her hand was tightly grasping with clenched grip the back edge of the sofa, the chesterfield, near a rusting bicycle wheel. She could see herself in the mirror, but thought I hadn't noticed it. It captivated her.

She would forget herself and be rocking and rolling riding me, and then look up to watch the faces she was making having sex (as she could see herself in the mirror.)

I reached down and got a hand on each of her hips and was forcefully moving her backwards and forwards rocking her harder and harder and she closed her eyes into little slits and let out a gasp of air seething out of her mouth as she bit her lip to not cry out, (as she could see herself in the mirror).

She quietly leaked slick liquid over me. Looked at me as if to say: Do you want me continue, do you want to come?

I lifted her off of me. There seemed to be even more noisome activity above. I said, "We better get out of here."

And I stood up and pulled up my pants and tried to tuck an atrocious boner down the left pant leg of those sturdy tight blue jeans, and I had to bend way over to keep it from breaking off. I had to hobble out in the most egregiously humorous bent-over, old-man kind of way, because it was ever so slow going down.

We slipped outside and moved as quickly as we could back down the driveway with me hobbling and her holding onto me by the elbow side by side. (I felt at that moment that we might grow old together.) Two old hobo bohos hanging close to the hedge along the property line, for fear that someone would yell, Hey! You!

But no one did.

We both breathed a sigh of relief as we hit the sidewalk and started to stroll in the neighborhood — all be it a bit roughed up. But then comportment gradually returned as we tucked and smoothed and buttoned on the move.

She laughed and beamed with pride, said, "My, we are becoming quite accomplished at the art of the quickie, aren't we."

I was proud. We had become lovers, so attuned to each other that we could do the quickie, moreover one that sunk deep into psychology.

< Perhaps lovers use the other to have it stand next to the super-Other [Mother] to use the force of the new Other to confront the old Other [Mother]>.

Or in vector space notation we see that love is an operator in a psychological space spanned by |other> and the projective space |Other>.

So that the Love operator, $\mathbf{L}$, is <other|L|Other>.

Love is the projection of the other into the space of the Other.

Chrysalis

One morning I brought up the proposal of essentially kidnapping her kid and the three of us going on an extended road trip to California. Here's how it went down. So me and Rayne are laying there in our new queen sized bed that Palumbo had built for us because I asked for it. With a head board and everything. He came over one Saturday, showed up with skill saw and wood and we built a very sturdy platform and now we had a real bed. And my, it eased my mind to get off the floor with winter here. Now here we are — safe in our cocoon snuggled up ready for the winter with all kinds of her silky draperies and inner sanctum satins, in the private sacred chamber of her secret sachet. The clock radio is tuned to the jazz station and some cool riffs playing soft and low had come on. I get very stimulated by jazz.

We had just been making love, and were drifting, listening to some cool jazz, thinking man's music, on the radio station CFOX, Montreal. I was being drawn in by the syncopation. I am following the theme, it is McCoy Tyner being in a groove, being in the pocket. It isn't really anything you can see. It is a head nodding entrainment, a cascade of serotonin in the frontal lobes, a feeling of well being, que sera sera. Plays that big stride piano like a drum, giant steps.

We are traveling in some vehicle, feeling a rocking to and fro from its motion, feel that there is some thematic unity, or at least some conversation among the players. They are talking in the moment and letting us overhear. They are like porpoises with a purpose, able to communicate with sound waves directly into the brain from bouncing off the terrain and reifying the images in their refrain.

Can you feel it?

Me an my lady were so tight that when her heart went lub my heart went dub. Lub, dub! We had a synchronization going. Sometimes it felt like entrainment. A groovy dance but sometimes just being stuck in a groove.

I thought about how the embryo's heart beat is syncopated with the mother's heart beat in the womb. How I loved jazz. Because that is where it gets its power to draw you in. From the womb. What could be finer than to be lying close to your baby, swinging with the lady you love, dancing within the heart through jazz, on a windy winter's night in Montreal. Syncopation. It is periodic, but the signal in each interval changes. It uses various harmonics of the main periodic wave. Jazz is syncopated syncopation. Is phase-shifting phase-lock. Is a celebration of push, of accelerated acceleration.

And I am feeling her, her body pressed into mine, with a force of melding. We two had become like one — entering through the doorway of her pussy into the presence of soul. You had to rock it, send out waves into a body that was a charged battery and let yourself be rocked but not shocked by the wave echoes coming back. Thrusting probe and echoing shudder. Seismic, man! I dig getting into sex with this women. But psychologically she was changeable. She could be sweet, gracious and charming and she could be angry and vituperative and crushing and cruel. And she could be just gone, no one home; not there. But now there is this lady beside me, she is all swaddled up in her flannel nighty, looking like Wendy of the lost boys.

If I'd have caught another ride, or gotten a late start or followed the woman I saw on the Metro, I wouldn't have been standing out there by the Magnetic Lake at the exact moment not two seconds before, or two seconds after but right at the time she came to snap me up.

Y'see I wished I coulda talked to the girl cool like that and make everything copasetic all the time, but I am one of these guys in search of some kind of god thing, and the sex thing is a way into the god thing, sometimes. The god thing is also kind of mathematical. What I am trying to say is that like a lot of people from a French background I get my Eros confused up with my Logos. On the other hand maybe all of that mental activity is a running away from the feelings that being with a woman bring out: they get you in touch with — they threaten you with — your own feminine side. I think a lot of men are like that actually, if by logos you mean the ego, the decision processor. To get out of this introspection my mind drifts into time series sampling and phase portrait of jazz. A phase portrait is where you observe something unfolding naturally in time, but also notice how its *rate* of unfolding, is related to its change. Sometimes these developments have odd shaped relationships, where they bounce and hover around stabilities, then break free and then flux down into some other stable point or come back to the point where they started. The picture of these stable points about which the etiology moves is an attractor. It is music — doing variations on a theme and coming back to it.

I was lying in bed drifting, in and out on a dream, some where between wakefulness and sleep, in that in-between state, the hypnagogic, where you can halfway control your dreams. And halfway be taken on the ride of your life. I was down by the river and I was really small, your proverbial fly on the wall. In the hypnagogic state, I = eye. It's privileged. It's a gift. A gift in the form of knowledge transmitted in image, not just visual images but whole body kinetic and audial, and tactile in a kind of synesthesia that is so real.

The eye pulled alongside — arrested by a dragonfly and a damselfly mating in the aerial dance. The bi-wingers have exquisitely delicate gossamer wings. Their exoskeleton insect bodies of bluish iridescence is segmented like bamboo sections — the designer is reusing the plants. Their helmeted heads are in a leaning forward, hunched forward attitude. They look like jockeys stooped forward on their wicked rides, so well capable of roll, pitch and yaw. They have their plumbing hooked up and they fly united.

Then, over a curved green leaf which was like looking up a small hill in a neighborhood, our eye flies. Our eye is tiny now. We see two butterflies back to back connected by their tummy. Same species with similar markings on their wings. I wonder how they met. Probably in an upscale fern bar somewhere down on the river nearby. Their wings are in a folded up position, I wonder if they were to be startled by a predator, would the female fly backwards being dragged by the male — like Fred Astaire having Ginger Rogers doing everything he did only backwards and in high heels.

The perspective is pulled back, we see winds coursing through a forest; beyond, it is making a field of corn wave.

In a bed of bright flowers we zoom in to a hideous and hirsute bumblebee with horns — buzzing as it is coming in for a landing. We see from below as though at an airport, into the golden highway of the sun, as he alights; then crawls, ungainly, stumbling and slipping and grasping all over a lovely flower, getting all kinds of superb pollen, golden nectar from the anther into the grocery bags of his hairy legs. Thence, off to another flower and if it has a stigma to receive, the cross pollination occurs.

Now the eye zooms into, onto the curved space manifold of the flower, sees that she can select the pollen or not, by facilitating with wetness its flow down the tube. She can be sticky to receive the golden nectar of life.

The eye is the point of perspective, and the sun is the vanishing point. The sun is one point at infinity and the center of mass of earth is the opposite. Between these two poles everything grows. All things are a projection between these two points at infinity. And just as the beings need two eyes, in order to appreciate and navigate the symmetry of space, so the beings need two sexes to navigate the symmetry of time. And if we zoom down into the egg, it is so huge, as big as a planet, a moon! compared to the spermatozoa swimming, boring in. And the female sex accepts only one, only one is admitted. And the tiny little gametes meet and divide to become one again.

There is more life in a handful of dirt that we walk on under our feet, than anywhere else that we know of in this vast universe. We take it for granted like children, the gift, and we waltz on through like puppets on the shoulders of giants who are on the shoulders of giants. Taking giant steps.

And then the real McCoy band outside the dream is doing a little elegant cymbal work, soft brush strokes rubbing the high hat. I see the word Sex with the serpentine S, being pulled upward and downward, and the outward exploding ex. The slithering S-ex extends exogamenous.

I was a s-existentialist looking for s-experience. Wanting to become a s-expert in the art of love. Listen while the world s-explains it all to you. The Genome has a strategy a design. It is s-explosion, by s-exegesis.

In the dream the eye sees in the sea beds great forests of coral waving in the currents, the polyps on the sea floor spew their gametes (eggs and sperm) out into the water in great clouds. They drift out in great clouds on the ocean currents, away, mixing, like flower pollen spreading in the wind. Sex: the rising and falling are one and the same. The great designer has the carriers coevolve in the movement of their precious cargo; a gamete flying on a gander to a goose or floating in the water out of coral or whirlygiging down from a tree on a bean pod or hugging on to a furry body or floating down a river. It is the eye of seed, peering into the unknown vicissitudes of the ecosphere. The genome cares only about dispersing teams of genes that better fit the challenges it faces as widely about the population as it can. The unknown ecological disasters, too much heat, over population of parasites and other bad wigglies. OOOhhh. Ahhh.

Then the tune on the radio outside the dream changes. It is Alice Coltrane. Great, big, rapturous, ranging, phase-shifting harp filling the space with its strong presence. I think surely hers is the harp we will hear when we go across and enter through the pearly gates into heaven. And that reminds me of death. And that death is rapped up in the strategy of sexual reproduction. The idea that great trees have to fall to make room for the little saplings to grow. Genome casting seed as far away as possible from the parent is not enough; it requires death in a way that asexual reproduction does not.

Sexual reproduction requires signaling in the presence of dangerous predators, requires being able to read the signal, peacocks signaling of love, moo cows calling out of love, wolves howling out of love, orchids getting interesting bumps on their skin to attract flies to carry their pollen out of love, out of levity – divine. Signaling signs for thems that can read.

Sex is expensive. Look at the lazy lion, that the pride felines have to feed and yet it is dear how it makes the sexes preen and shine for each other and anticipate and have strategy and forethought in their anticipation. Even the lowly nematode is leaving a trail in the dirt beneath our daily parade.

Sight is like orgasm: they both continuously seek to go out of the body across space and return. And in that move-ment of the gamete across space it is snapped up and "seen" by the appropriate receptacle – or not, in the blink of an eye, in the flutter of eyelids, in the flutter of a bird's wings, in the flutter of butterfly wings. The genome is permitted to see through the movement of the sex that the beings enjoy in order to rend a veil and see through physical reality what we see by analogy.

The eyes fall upon the things in the space as genome creates a path into the flesh. And we cruise down that path into the hollows and spaces it creates for itself as it creates us, with all our perforations to take the world in. And just as the eyes close, so sexual reproduction must drop us in darkness forever, because it is variability and opportunity that must be maintained.

The genome is burrowing into time, it is raising itself up off the planet, in the great aggrandizement of apotheosis $f(x)$: Sex = Antigravity (Metamorphosis): $>|< = .../...([...] \times [...])$

I see my mother's face. She has green eyes. My father has dark navy blue eyes. My sisters have brown eyes. My eyes are the color of the sky.

I was lying in bed in a spoon close with my woman and felt a swoon of empathy so strong, that I had to hold onto her and bury my face in her shoulder. For she seemed like she was somehow me in a prior lifetime or that I had know her before. This feeling was not just the *post coitum tristess* all lovers feel; it was more like you had taken part in Lovemaking, that you were part of the fabric of Lovers making love going back to the dawn of time, raising waves in some great tantric sea. This ran deeper than that. It was like reincarnation or metempsychosis. I started getting an image of what I might call the Light Cone Butterfly.

It had to do with the transformation of the Light Cone. Did you know that at the edge of reality you come to a boundary surface and it is the surface of a cone of light? Like a street light or a lamp in the living room. Everything within the cone is possible— it can be reached by light which is to say is within reach of causality (which may not exceed the speed of light). For every second of time, the light travels a distance of ct. It is linear d=ct, which is a line in time, from the point, and in space this line sweeps out a cone. And the inside of the cone is the possible; outside is not. Cool, and actually it is a double cone, one going out from the present to all points it can reach and one cone coming from the past to the point at the exact now moment of the present. To me the present moment has these light cones attached to it that look like wings. >|< And the transformation is from the spacetime of one observer to another. (It's OK if you can't visualize this. It's just an objective correlative of a feeling in the central metaphor of my time.)

I felt this connectivity with the woman. And I felt like I was undergoing some kind of apprenticeship. I had learned it in my body, but it had always been there. I could see images of myself running along my life line, from the time I was 4 years old until now, when I was 26. 0, love . . . o love I felt like I could sail along in an airstream above the clouds, I could sail into time, like I was looking into a time warp, like looking in a tunnel and the me of past times could see himself at the other end. It's beyond my power to describe.

When I drift into the universal reverie of maths, I become a different person. It is like participating in the thoughts of Mind, in the sense that we here on the planet are living beings in a universe that is giving off energy, but on this planet there are forms and organizations that take up the energy and life is solving the problems of keeping the energy from evaporating away by investing it into forms. It is doing math. It is doing poeisis.

The after sex glow so relaxes my spine that another me emerged from there, like some kind of *hombre mariposa* with wings, floating hovering fluttering being. >|< I loved the feeling so much, I wanted to never come down. It was an out of body experience. I want to create a world in which these things are always present.

Like I said before, I get Logos and Eros confused. I can feel passion in the movement of ideas — find them sexy and see forms. And sex percolates over into my intelligence. (Or maybe it is my mind getting all hyper so as not to feel the empathy and the vulnerability?) So I couch it in esoterica erotica.

I was lying in bed thinking all these things and out of the corner of my eye I see her wild mane splayed on the pillow. And I feel a rustle and WHAM she elbows me in the ribs. And she raises herself up in the bed and is looking down at me and says, "We've been living together for 60 days now. And I'd like to know, how do you like living together so far?"

Wow. Eyow!

I'd like to tell her of my love, but conversation is such a shallow and untrustworthy communication medium. While I am thinking of an appropriate answer I am probing my brain for a flexible way of broaching the subject of us kidnapping her kid and absconding across international boundaries to the other country of California. So I could study with Bob and the others who developed the sound poem. Cause that's where my heart is really at.

Quickly I try to draw up a quick sketch, a portrait of our relationship. This is some kind of a test. We have something, a *thing* going on, call it a romance, or being shacked-up or, god forbid, that once in your life you allowed your youthful self to indulge in a satyromaniacal saturnalia.

What is she asking me? She's asking me if I am finding any critical infrastructure vulnerabilities. She's asking me to assess system vulnerability in terms of probabilities that the system undergoes significant changes, or even disintegrates under progressive stress of my continued underemployment. It's some kind of a test. And above all at that moment I knew a QUICK answer is required.

"I'm really digging it." I said. "How about you?"

"Yea, it's really fine," she agreed.

"I feel like we have been married for a long time," I said.

And my mind is turning and I think if I pose the trip to California question, what is that going to do? The stress could result in three kinds of distortions, of the portrait of this perfect scene we see there be. It could be an innocuous distortion: that preserves the phase portrait topology and thereby system stability; it could be a crippling distortion: that changes phase portrait topology and thereby our saga's stability and this could severely alter the relational stability but not enough to destroy completely our remaining in a together state; or it could be a catastrophic distortion: taking the system out of the realm of love and quickly flipping it into its complementary state, hate, and thereby having it disintegrate. Ooooh don't want that.

I went for the received idea, astrology: "You and I are very much the same. Are you sure you aren't a Cancer, a Moon Child."

"Nope, Aries," she said, "The sign of the Ram."

How could I tell her that I loved her. Tell her about how I am thinking that we are destiny, that she is the shining light of my destiny.

My mind works quick, recovers, trying to come up with something, "We are like two peas in a pod. Or as my mother used to say, like two fleas in a fit?"

I decided to blurt it out. "I was thinking about the three of us traveling in the green car across America. Heading out to visit California. We could stop in Texas and you could meet my folks. And we could visit your parents in Coop-er-teen-o, and Bob and the friends in Berkeley. That would be cool wouldn't it?"

And before she could protest, I continued. "We would be like Swift Family Robinson traveling across bicentennial America and it would be interesting to write a hip travelogue from the point of view of a family stopping in various places and seeing how it felt. Make *documentary*!"

She was not totally surprised: "What! That would be crazy!?" Pause. Considers. "And kind of fun."

I talked it up: "We'd be traveling it the great green touring machine, driving the back roads, the blue highways, dipping into America's small towns, stopping to walk in fields, to be part of the ongoing Bicentennial Celebration. It is goin' to be cool, the whole country is in an open-house, partying mood. It was going to be one yearlong Fourth of July picnic, and we could just drift on into it. You've got your summers off, cause you're on school time."

She looked like she was listening.

I continued: "We'd take the back roads that meander off the freeway, so that there's not so much traffic. We'd camp out. You love to camp, and you are really good at it. Go from camp ground to camp ground like gypsies. We have the whole winter to put enough money in our jeans to travel the road; no doubt other opportunities would open up in middle of America. It would be fun? Can you feel it?"

"Well, yes. It would be fun," she said. "It is something to think about."

I noted a slightly dubious downturn in her tone. "Beau's father would never go for it."

And as Rayne feigned feasibility I broached the idea of kidnapping her son. "Well, we'd have to kidnap him then."

"Oooohhh, they don't like it when you take — abscond

with children across international boundaries."

"Well we'd bring him back."

"I could tell his father that I was taking him to visit my parents in Cupertino; it's near San Francisco."

And there we were. Trying to make a home. With all the connotations of home that we bring to it, whatever they were.

And I am thinking about all the trips that we have taken, running the roads and how cool she was to travel with. Yeah.

"We could go many many many other places. Along that long and winding road."

"Riiiiight."

I got going on a letter, to gather information about a travel book. If I have only one life to live, let me live it as a travel writer.

> Dear Sir, Madam, or Ms. as the case may be,
> I am preparing a package tour guide for the Canadian Trucking Company containing information about your locale. Hopefully to be displayed in truck stops from coast to coast, the book will be a compedium of information for the Canadian or really any adult tourist vacationing in America.
> I would like to have information on the following:
> Local Points of Interest, churches, forts, night clubs, Natural wonders, boutiques, restaurants, galleries, fish hatcheries and haberdasheries. . .
> Local History, stories and Lore. Canadians are, by and large an unsophisticated race of travelers, they have an eye for what is really down home. Like one of the most interesting pieces of mail I've receives was the local newsletter for a logging mill in Maine, or the minutes from the Gulf Coast Shrimp Fisheries convention. Also Maps and Brochures from Historical Societies would be greatly appreciated.
> I find that the prices of things rise so rapidly and so often these days that I need to include more of an economic picture

of your locale than most tourists information Books carry. In fact I would need to know the prices of xxxxx restaurants and garages in your area. Do you think you could find it within your official budget to send along a newspaper from your town? Perhaps some of the free ones, or an old one if readily available. Something like the "Goings on about Town" papers that they give away at the major hotels I would find really useful. I would be most greatful for the price index this would give me.

But most interesting of all, will be coming to your 200 year old birthday party. I would like to know what Bicentenial projects have been undertaken in your area. This for me is really the most important and interesting part of the book.

Thank you very much and I'm looking forward to hearing from you. And Happy Birthday.

I was surprised that this hideous and error strewn letter, it even had crossed out words — it was so tedious to write on a typewriter, started bringing in an inundation of promotional brochures and newspapers to the apartment on Staynor Street.

Belles Lettres

In the few letters I saw written by Rayne you could see they were written with great force and speed in an integrated emotional intellectual burst. Having gone to McGill it was second nature for her to use sophisticated language, moreover to develop the closely reasoned argument.

Still I was the more prolific writer of letters. I was always into correspondence by letters. There is nothing like the spontaneity of writing to a person, especially if it happens to be someone you trust, someone you want to touch with your humor, someone you trust to let know you.

I was staying in touch with my brother Roux, and an artist friend Ben White. I even wrote a few letters to my friends from the Brother Heuman Hour, and the Church of the Coincidental Metaphor in Austin. But they were not the *belle lettres* type, be they typed or handwritten longhand, several pages long, stamped and delivered by the post office. I was delighted by a letter in a story of J.D. Salinger in which we see Seymour Glass waxing manically intelligent to a librarian (who somehow represented the refuge of the cannon of all that was great about literary expression and self-understanding). Under his influence I wrote some ungodly embarrassing fan letter to Grossinger. Hopefully he didn't save it to be unearthed in his archives in a library somewhere by a future scholar.

I occasionally wrote to my parents, since I was in their home town, taking the opportunity to ask them questions, something I had not done before. But now since I was "en famile" I felt somehow on a more equal level.

My mother wrote back to say that I might be crazy. I

found this disturbing. I was trying to understand Freud and Oedipal and all that and might have asked some inappropriate questions. I had never been in psychoanalysis, nor had anyone in my family. We weren't those kind of people, and yet it is incumbent upon the philosopher to know thyself, no matter what the cost. I don't know that I would say some of the things I said in letters if I were talking to the person in person. Words on paper are kind of blazé unless you amp them up to make them intense.

When I showed the letter from my mother to Rayne, she was somewhat taken aback. She got busy and banged out a letter of her own, addressed to my mother.

Dear Walker's Mommy

Enclosed find shopping list for household of 3 (2 adults and 1 kid) for 2 weeks.   Now triple the milk and bread amounts and you have 2 weeks worth of food for $40. Ergo 1 wk. for $20 ÷ 3 (this in unequal cuz child's lunches cost more) and you got per capita $7 and per diem $1. That is what it costs to feed your son Walker, the big guy. If all he did was eat his total in the debit column would be $365.25 per annum. Slightly more than the cost of a pack of cigarettes a day, money I've saved when Walker helped me stop smoking. A man of simple tastes say, but scarcely a bum, a lech, a leach or a loss.

Now I introduce this balance sheet to develop the following idea: that the easiest way to get out of touch with our sons, friends and loved ones is to confuse our expectations for their reality. To whit: so anxious was I to believe that my camera stolen that as soon as it was not where I expected it to be I assumed that it was stolen and didn't proceed on a thorough search into the bowels of the car where it actually disappeared. For a long time it remained 'stolen' fulfilling my expectations until someone, Walker in fact, found it. My point: I was so ready to believe that I knew its whereabouts and never questioned these assumptions.

Now before extending this to maternity and lost and found

sons permit another digression. When Beausolei was 3°
he started playing outside with other children without my
being present for the first time. He was reluctant but I was
insistent. A sensitive and socially 'at ease' child who
makes friends instantly with all manner of adults, he was
apprehensive about the bigger children in the park. Sure
enough a terrible 4 year old SEAN a rough and tough
terror of a bully of a brat, made threatening gestures and
through the literal sand in Beausolei's eye and Beau went
somewhat limp with apprehension. There followed many
weeks of argument between Beau and myself. I was of the
fight back school or the ostracize the bully or the you can
work it out and find allies etc. etc. cautioning him that at
least his mother would not interfere between his tormentor
and him and that he would have to find his own solution.
Then one day it occurred to me that I was only offering
him the most aggressive ways of resolving his problem,
that I had proffered the solutions that I would choose,
completely failing to take into account Beausolei's own
and radically different personality.

   Beau despises all conflict; I relatively thrive on it. I had
forgotten monetarily that he was not a miniature of myself.
I had solved the problem for myself in my way but not
given him possibilities for himself. With that realization
came the corollary: : I had encouraged the most masculine
and aggressive of solutions. Had Beausolei been a girl he
would have had other options. So I extend my postula-
tions to include ones fitting to me of the more convention-
ally 'feminine' responses (ones that I rejected for myself
and never thought a boy child should have in his reper-
toire) and almost immediately Sean began to consider
himself Jesse's friend and cease to terrorize him. The point,
I reiterate: I had seen only my reflection of myself and my
own choices. I failed to consider my son's personality and
his own viabilities.

      Now closer to your home, a place I have no business
but a growing interest. Casting off your son in the sense
that you sent a brief letter relaying your disappointment
and concluding essentially that he was lost to bad ways

seems to accomplish the losing of the camera (gone forever and irretrievable) by the device of projection: 'be tough or smart or rich or chic or any quality I admire.

There is that classic quandary of parents of when to stop parenting. My 60 year old father complains his 87 year old mother still tries to educate him. But beyond this is the projection of our own expectations on our children and the resultant DISAPPOINTMENTS when the child doesn't achieve what we want them to, or get what we want them to get. Usually we want material comfort and security. Now is it fair to castigate and repudiate a child let alone a grown adult for making his/her own choices? By rejecting what I choose him to be he/she is not rejecting me, but rather finding his/her own way. Isn't this a true sign that the child has been successfully raised and an autonomous individual to make decisions etc. etc. If we are disappointed in what lifestyles our kids choose isn't it a fact that we are usually only disappointed that they didn't confirm our choice of our own lifestyle by choosing to duplicate us. Really, why are we so threatened when the young forge a new way. We haven't lost them as people we loose them as disciples. Except if we get confused and reject them as unwanted people. So before you 'give up your son, before indulging full vent to the disappointment and bitterness your letter contains, try to consider the following catalog of virtues of your selfsame son.

1) Your son is not a parasite. He balances on the true scales of give and take. He is taking advantage of no one. Therefore he is not a thief.

2) Nor is he a murderer, a rapist. A common money dodger. No-one starves as a result of his greed, in fact he seems to have no victims.

3) He is a fair man even-tempered and sensitive to other peoples beauty, joy and grief. Deserving of scorn? Merely because he is not butcher baker indian chief. A dead loss as a human being? No certainly not and if not, the apple of his mother's eye than it is because his mother wanted to behold her own beauty in the mirror instead of allowing herself to see her son.

Wow. Well. What does one make of that? True it was a put-on, somewhat dripping in vehemence though on the surface it was supportive. A double entendre? No doubt she was pissed that I had quit my little lunch monitor job. I just called them up one day and said I wasn't coming in, was too busy writing. I of course didn't send that letter to my mother though kidded I might. Rayne said it would be OK. It was insulting in a humorous way. You can see her confrontational style and the elegance and well reasoned presentation, point by point. It just gushed out of her.

There was something about her, she was just wild. We'd swirl up to a club, she waring a long elegant, dare I say starched, cotton scarf and freebox tweed coat and pleated dress and peopled wanted her at their affair. The doormen and ticket sales people at clubs often just waived us through. *I'm with the band, man.*

She had amazing abilities with slight of hand to match her steady nerves. Once when I had parked the car in a wrong place, and it snowed, the green Mercedes got towed. It was the first snow of the season, and the policy in Montreal is to have the snowplow crews, and their fleets of tow truck, make a bunch of noise with horns so that people would get up and move their cars. You had just a little time to get dressed and go out in the freezing blizzard and move your car so the snowplow could come through. I didn't know and the Mercedes got towed before we could get out and move it. There we were standing outside in the freezing dark. We went down to pay the fine which with three twenty dollar bills, which was a lot of money to us.

And somehow . . . she handed the cash to the official government agent who set it down beside the cash box to make out a receipt, and while he was making out the receipt, she, the sly she-bear, not going to allow the alpha male take food away from her baby, deftly reached over and with the lightest two finger move: slipping a nail under the bills and gently clipping them between her fingers, extracted the money back! I was so scared I was about to faint, but she pinched it and palmed it like a pro. The guy was slightly suspicious, but had been enchanted by the sexual force of her mind-field aura. Or he just couldn't make himself believe that this diminutive attractive single-mom citizen standing in front of him, looking fine, would take his money like that.

I fell for Rayne pretty hard. At first it was that she was beautiful and I really wanted to stay a while in Montreal. But as I got to see more and more how beautiful she was, and it was just good company, even though she could go into a dark mood. Perhaps it was her monthlies. I had not lived with a woman in a while, and never in a situation with a kid. Nothing in my previous dating and shacking up experience had really prepared me for the forceful animated energy of the full blown mom! My sister, somewhat, to be sure, but I was way peripheral, avuncular to that. Motherhood is indeed the most potent spell on earth.

Women deliver a man to stand before the other, which is his feminine side. The feminine side connected to his mother, and on the one hand he wants to serve and protect and on the other, wants to be liberated from.

Boys and girls make such fun for each other don't they?

She seemed better than me. She was multi-talented, a cinematographer, a writer. Writing gushed out of her in an angry burst of cogent chaos that went off in all direction of feeling and worldly wisdom. Her writing was fast and furious, and full of emotion. Mine seemed plodding and abstract by comparison, totally utilitarian, enslaved to the big idea while deprecating the smallness of gossip and detail. And she was an artist, a great photographer, and she had all the chops required to make good political real films.

Here is a note she wrote to me, after we had had some disagreement or hassle over something, maybe housework. It shows a vulnerable side of herself that she didn't show very often. She had said to me, "If you fuck any one else, I'll kill you." I felt possessed.

Sky I'm trying to reach   it but it's high and altitude wasn't something I was born understanding. Now I can tell you all sorts of things you never noticed about ground level. But while you were standing at one end of the line in gym class I was at the other, and that's why it's important and more than important its critical that you stay here and I keep you here....you fight your impulse to flee and I fight mine to drive you away.

I said we were therapeutic the other day and I was more right than I knew ie the sense of therabeautific ie between where my feet are and where your head is, and my hands and your heart, whaddya say pard what I'm trying to say Walker buddy of Beau-son is that I love you to the point beyond the distraction of last week because on the other side of that I have found the greatest goodest gaga tonite you have never been as beautiful as tonite with it all taken for granite I mean I don't want to tell you your a good cook I want you to know I think that I mean I wouldn't really kill you but would momen-tarily feel like dying I mean instead of soap 1 would have it be anything ever you wanted, Le three lbs. of renown, minus 67OOO qts. of distress, one iota of understanding in mother (and yes of course you can use the letter to her if after reeeeeel careful consideration you think it will work) mostly now I mean that my gruff and barbed edges disguise mostly for myself the Lost incredible fears, the most the most....Walker do the dishes, the coffee, the kid. so i see you really care. i know its fucked and know as symbol it shits but fuck and shit Walker skyfuck I LOVE YOU and in addition to not knowing the protocols for these sensations I have this enormous fear I keep trying to get myself to tell you about but always find several digressions to follow instead   see? anyway this fear goes something like we're back at the Busy Bee and we both smile knowingly into 'each others eye and with a nod to the 'affair that might have been' you go out and stand by the road and I let you male you go and I know that 1 will NEVER again have this chance, but that I was too afraid to take it and will live forever safe and sterile, everyone's favourite eccentric and nobodies Person. You see it is no longer and it never really was sufficient for me to be someone's mommy. I want to spend time

and time and norm and shine getting to know You and showing you me.

did you know for instance that I cringed tonight with the image of people tiptoeing around me? Now after some thot I see that maybe even I've cultivated that...certainly at the college so the pedestrians would leave me alone, prob. among menfrens so that the SUBJECT would never arise...in both instances it was an ungainly but expedient device so as not to get   involved etc etc all of which I   could see for the first time not merely because you told me 'tiptoe' but because I cringed at the knowledge that you tiptoe' too. that doesn't work. that terrifies me. fuck I feel so fleshy so soft I'm a pink 'n blinded mouse baby, I'm Beausolei's squirrly rabbit, I even see the colour pink when I think, my equivalent of creampuff I suppose I AM ALL BELLY and you are afraid of my SPINES

it is so awfully ironic so oppositely obvious when the bitch is in heat she wants more of YOOOOO crusts are there only to keep the juice in, wanna have some pie sky? Wanna lie? wanna lay? will you stay? will you try?

what do you want to be when you grow up? An infanant, and love's the way, baby. when you come in will you fuck me while I sleep?

A Stockhausen Moment

I am driving and Rayne is sitting close beside me like the way girls used to in the 50s and 60s — slid over in the bench seat. It feels good to be on the road again with her, free, cruising in the stalwart green touring machine. We are the only ones on the road. High in the mountains of Vermont, it was clear and dry. The night sky was a panoply of stars. It was cold and cloudless. You could see the lacy structure of stellar clusters spreading out their filaments into the depth of black space across time. In the crystalline night, the universe had put on its most supreme regalia, had brought out the finest gems for our drive. The road could lead off the edge of the world, and continue on an upward path, into galactic *Voi Lactic*.

We could be floating over fields. There wasn't another soul on the road, and I leaned back in my seat and enjoyed the pristine view. In her dress sweet Rayne was nestled into me with her slender girlish gams tucked to the side like she is riding side saddle on the hump.

She is enjoying being chauffeured. We had just come across the boarder into America from the north country and we were on top of the world. It was a windless crisp clear winter night with a full moon illuminating the white snow mantled mountain valleys below. Down below in the little patchwork of farms, the rivers and creeks could be seen to crinkle and glisten in the moonlight cloisonné .

"Wow," I says. "It looks like something in a holy card." I half expected the moonlight filling the snowy silent landscape to turn into the star guiding the wise men to their savior. I looked at her and teased: "Oh, that's right. You're Jewish. Did y'all have holy cards?"

She shakes her head. She has that happy look on her face

whenever she is going into the country. She was like a big playful doll, hair flouncing.

I said, "I have never seen it so clear. I wonder if we are getting into a skip situation."

"What's skip?" she says, her face going all pretty like a school girl.

I think: She has thrived in my care, the lover's *en loco parentis* care.

"That's where radio signals from all over the world are bounced off the sky into our locale," I explain. "It is kind of like skipping stones on the surface of water but here the surface is the underside of the top of the atmosphere."

"It's like a kind of echo. When it is clear like this they can get up higher before they bounce. They can bounce farther, even change carriers. We might even be able to pick up some hams on our little car radio here."

She gave me a mischievous sidelong glance; she flaps her wrists like a concert pianist sitting down to address the keyboard; she lays her hands on the radio like she is going to heal or about to play and she says, "Lets see what we can pick up." And she started turning the tuning knob, sweeping through the channels.

Music: symphony from Boston

Music: radio burbling between channels

Music: French ye-ye rock'n'roll from Montreal.

Then she uses both hands on the radio dials: one on volume, the other changing channels. And with her pinky she started flipping a little slider around the volume knob to send the sound to the back speakers only, then bring it forward.

She is starting to play the radio as a musical instrument. She seemed to be trying to change the channel on a beat. There would be some blues rhythm then the rim shot would take us through static into a high opera female voice.

She is flipping through the channels, and moving the sound

around the space, randomly picking up her cues from the soundscape itself, and we are getting a crazy cacophony symphony.

Music: radio burbling. Between channel.

She begins wiggling around in the seat in a sort of dance, rolling her shoulders as if standing in front of a band stand.

"I'm having a Stockhausen moment," she says.

I was surprised and sat bolt upright. "Stockhausen!? Yes!! I am surprised you've heard of him."

"Oh, he was big at Expo 67."

"Yeah, I was there too. It was amazing, the Musique Concrete soundscape in the French pavilion."

Music: bass drum made to sound like a human heartbeat.

Music: Screech of channels changing.

"Stockhausen was amazing," I said. "It was like a lesson in weird math, and group theory and syntax. I remember studying the liner notes on his albums. I have to admit I enjoyed the liner notes more than the actual music. Especially *Moment* — trying to figure out what he was up to. He had Functor diagrams!"

"Functors!?" she echoed, mocking my enthusiasm.

"Yes it was like some weird transformational grammar on groups of sounds in permutation."

She does some more moves on the radio.

"And I remember just being amazed at his idea of the Moment," I exclaimed. "Because the moment is a big concept in math and statistics and physics. Yes! The Plane Rotation of a Slab." I laughed. " The Moment of Inertia."

"Oh, I've heard of that," she said. The moment of inertia, is that like the moment after Thanksgiving dinner when you realized you've eaten too much and you can't get out of your chair." She smiled, admiring her own cleverness.

I picked up her jest. "Yes, the engineers have a symbol for it. It is big I. In a body, it is the axis about which everything folds and rotates. Your center — martial arts is hip to this — that, depending on the force coming at you, you will either be sent spinning or knocked down, but you can make it go around or go past if you have centered your big I in the right place.

"But I was thinking about the Moment in statistics. It is about the various measures reaching out from the mean — the standard deviation and normal distribution are moments about the mean. It's like dwelling in a deeper and deeper moment, ringing, tuning, harmonizing."

I can get rocking on a concept, zinging, going universal, riding out on humor intelligence feeling.

Rayne said: "Stockhausen had a big influence of the Beatles. And Pink Floyd. Remember that cash register ring going ka-ching in *Money*."

As I was looking out the window at the valleys below I thought: Somewhere in the high atmosphere over the US, the cold fronts have resolved their differences and dissolved into a stalled quiescence in which we are the only ones moving. Fate has precipitated out this moment where I am with this girl, the first girl in America for this long ride over the mountains, watching over the fields partitioning themselves into a patch-work of sectors on a curved orb through which and around which vectors fluxed and curled. We find ourselves alone — together — suddenly, placed like a satellite gliding through space hovering in the crystalline night. From out stationary eye in the sky, the earth is rotating beneath us. If we stayed up there long enough we might end up hovering over Chicago. Out there beyond the headlights, radio music was traveling at the speed of light penetrating the veil where the convolution at the surface of its wavefront condenses like water out of the vapor of the love cloud on its carrier. Its spacetime light cone flower, going way beyond the cone of our headlights |< where the future can be seen by light and beyond the edge of which there is not even a possibility.

Where the hippocampus runs wild in the fields of the cerebrum, going round and round like a horse on an elliptical oval trying to avoid crashing into inevitability, starting to tarry with the intuitary gland. We are just us too, the last man and the last woman, Adam and Eve, Eddy and Flo. Flo takes hold of the knobs on the Mercedez-Benz radio. Channel and volume, and a little switch to send it to the back speakers only. And punching the buttons to preset stations.

We were working with 4 channel mixing in our media work at the college.

Music: Heard from far away — conversation, whispers.

She was oscillating back and forth among some big band sound and a violin solo.

She says, "All this music they send out into the world. . .

I say, "Yes, it's traveling at the speed of light past our aerials and out into the night. . . . Where it travels forever across the galaxy getting weaker and weaker perhaps to get picked up by aliens. It carries feelings and love and blues and grooves and flings it out. Changes the mindset of countries. Maybe it will change the mindset of aliens, for that is the first thing they will pick up from us. Old radio broadcasts. Then they will know that we were advanced enough to at least achieve radio."

She scoffs, "Yes I heard one of the first TV shows the extraterrestrials will pick up is *I Love Lucy*. That ought to help them make up their mind whether or not they should invade."

One night at a dance put on by the North East Kingdom Co-op in the town hall of Barton, we had another kind of musical experience. A young friend of Rayne's, named Michael Cooper played his base cello when he sat in with a rocking R&B band. It was one of the most amazing musical performances I have ever seen. Up there with Thomas Ramirez playing sax with Jazzmanian Devil in Austin back in the day.

Apparently Cooper got set up quietly; it seemed like the other players were surprised by his coming, because they were shocked and stunned like the rest of us. He launched into playing this most reckless chain-saw cello, solo — it was savage — bowing the low open C-note as loud and as hard as possible. This seemed to enraged the other band members and they cranked it up to chase him. The drums and guitars began to shadow and resist the cello solo in a threatening, antagonistic way, like their integrity had somehow been attacked. The musicians began to engage each other in a struggle for supremacy and we were privledged to witness their free for all brawl. Cooper might have had extra amplification, because when he started sawing on the cello it completely walked over all the other amplified guitars and drums in the rhythm band. It was like somebody was using a chain saw to cut across all our focus (foci?). He just starts and takes off at terrifying speed. He must have been driving at resonance frequency because this sweet profound cello sound of deep resonant wood, soared like a solid physical floating vibe of undeniable presence. It was like: This is classical music raised to the power of rock. Now I don't know an arpeggio from a cadenza, but I am sure it takes some serious fortissimo to let yourself go wild in a controlled way like that. It was wild, untamed, uncouth. But as we came to see, cool. He carried us all away on his raging, tidal wave riff. We were in shock and awe.

And just as quickly it was over.

Michael played in another song, a waltz and it was much more in keeping with the others. Rayne and I danced. Amid the stately wood paneled community town hall, I waltzed that graceful girl in her swirling skirts around the floor.

East End Dayshift Concierge

The one job that I did manage to keep the longest was one that I called Janitor in a Slum. Slum is not the right word, especially in respect for the slums of Calcutta, Rio de Janero, South Africa; public housing, would be more precise. I was a janitor in a public housing facility east of the Main. It was a bunch of poor people's apartments, lots of immigrants and French people, who were very poor yet very fastidious for the most part. It did not escape my notice that here I was — after some 20 years of schooling — put on the day shift, a short distance from where I was born. I still wouldn't have been able to afford to rent one of these on my own.

I liked the job because it came with "The Janitor's Closet". This was a good sized room, about the size of an American living room. It had some junk in it, but it had a couch and a table and lights in there and I could hang out (but no heat). My manager at the agency, was extremely harassed, and this is how he explained to me the discharge of my duties: "You need to make yourself seen in the morning, sweeping up outside, putting the trash back in containers, and you need to make yourself seen in the afternoon going around mopping the landings of the stairs, or just picking up." It went without saying that the rest of the time you just needed to be available, kind of around.

With my first paycheck I got an old typewriter at a local haberdashery / junk shop, and lugged it into my closet / office. Maybe I could get some writing done.

In addition to settling in to "married" life and a job, I wanted to have some of my own friends, possibly some writers? Who weren't academic? I met an old Jewish writer named Saul Zimack, in the old El Dorado cafe, on rue Ste-Catherine, just a few doors down from the Vehicule Art Gallery. The El Dorado was like Wellensky's but even funkier. I was having a cup of coffee in there and I noticed this old guy with a big beard and dark intelligent eyes writing in a Big Chief tablet with a pencil stub. I got to talking to him. Yes he was a novelist. He was working on one.

"What's it about?" I asked.

He looked a little cagey, indirect. "It's political, about the wasps and the PQists tearing apart the country."

He said, "Pretty soon it will be that you can't get a job around here unless you can *parlez-vous*. Now people are VOTING in the Fascists."

He liked to rail against the hippies as well. "They are fascist too. But thank goodness they are so passive!" He raised his eyes with relief as though it was disaster averted.

I might defend them with, "Well they are apperceptive. They are trying to be aware of the self, in the sense of awareness of the gift of being in the cosmos."

"Cosmic!" At the hippie cant of "cosmic" he quickly took umbrage. "Please don't say cosmic. They are always changing selves! No commitment. And they let media define them!"

Sarcastically he taunts: "Come and look at us, we are for free love. It's like how the beatniks went around quoting Oswald Spengler about the decline of the west, and now they are the ascendancy, the chosen ones. Beatniks are fascist. Hippies are fascist beatniks."

During the day's lacunae in my janitorial duties, I could explore the environs, going further and further afield. I was back to what I suspected was the neighborhood where I was born, Avenue de Lormier.

In my wandering I was undergoing metamorphosis from a random walker to a butterfly walker. The random walker sees all the other walkers joining and leaving some thing — a point of focus — that radiates its call. I was looking for something, something I might recognize. When I look at my birth certificate from Quebec, it is a baptismal certificate from St. Dominic's Church, Montreal. In Quebec, in those days, your baptism certificate IS your birth certificate.

I went to St. Dominic's Church on Parthenais between Rachel and Sherbrooke. I see it is right by Avenue de Lormier, and I remember my mother saying we lived on de Lormier. She also said Rosemont and rue Beaubien too. This is in what would have been the French section of Montreal.

And lo and behold, at St. Dominic's Church I recognized the side entrance to the church! I realize this is the church my parents were married in. I can remember the picture, the famous picture that they always keep on their bedroom wall, of the happy young couple coming out of the church together. It had been black and white but my mother got it artificially colored. Her in her sweet 40's suit with the floppy collar, and hair styled like a movie star; and my father athletic and young and they were just the handsomest couple. Just married, heading out into life together. And there they are, beneath layers of time, boldly striding forth with all the hope of being committed to life. This would have been in 1945 — the Battle of the St. Lawrence was still going on. German subs from across the Atlantic had earlier come through the Gaspé and come down the river and sunk ships. My father had joined the Royal Canadian Navy against his father's orders, under threat of disavowal, and was stationed on one of the river frigates out of Donnacona, patrolling the St. Lawrence Seaway. These *canaliers* they were called were big ships but not too big to fit through the locks that connected the river to the Great Lakes.

Avenue De Lormier is a straight shot down to the Jacques Cartier bridge. I wonder if my parents stayed there because it was a fairly quick to get down to the docks, and the Navy work. I wonder if my father was still in the service when I was born. No I think not. Because they paid the bill at the hospital for me. It was like 12 dollars total for a birth. State Run medicine. I cost 12 dollars to bring into the world.

I began to undergo metamorphosis from a random walker to a butterfly walker, that is one hovering over and visiting only memory sites that might present persuasive possibility. A time butterfly looking to sup in the enchanting nectar of vanished time from the curved, droopy, memory flowers of spellbound time, holding succulent secrets of joy in their delicately infolded spacetime surfaces.

I have a memory of some pictures taken in a little park. Then I went a few blocks to Baldwin Park to see if I could get lucky and recognize that this was the park in which I had my picture taken when I was about 3, or 4. Because my sister was with us then too. But not yet my second sister (or at least she wasn't yet in the picture).

I had found there were fuzzy suggestion surfaces attached to things, scenes, in the streets, in the neighborhood in which you could go back to an early part of the time loop, where somehow the game was saved. Lets call them Proustian operators on a phenomenological vector space, like a remote with a rewind button. A pause button. But no fast forward. And there was something wrong with the playback heads, things weren't aligned correctly — making the tape jumps its tracks.

What was I doing with all this? Trying to go back to the source? What was I going to do then? Crawling up into my mother's womb?! Crawling back into the gleam in my father's eye when he slipped into the bed with her? I suppose I was into some great, impossible to know quest, not sure what. The events surrounding my birth. The matrix, the milieu, the engendering initial conditions — to come to know my place in the great world wheel. Perhaps knowing some kind of initial state I could understand my primary processes. A theory might develop with algorithms of how to be and a great hypergeometric multidimensional differential equation that predicted who I was, how I was going to unfold, and for how long. Lines from that great old tea-head of time, T.S. Eliot would be running through my head.

> To come back to the place we started from
> and to know it for the first time.

And more of *Burnt Norton*. How did it start?

> Time present and time past / Are both perhaps present in time future, / And time future contained in time past. / If all time is eternally present / All time is unredeemable. / What might have been is an abstraction / Remaining a perpetual possibility / Only in a world of speculation.

Now THERE is the mature artist contemplating the mysteries of Time. Time was musical — it was *my* theme song, the music being played in the background of my movie.

In my janitor's closet I got to work writing a modern *Metamorphoses*. I wanted to write an alternative Metamorphoses, based on Darcy Thompson, on *Growth and Form*. The deities would be equations, like the partial equations for the flux of material in, getting dispersed onto the edge of the diffusion spread. Or instead of the god Titan impelling and compelling it would be gravity, Big G, $F = Gm_i m_j/(r_{ij})^2$

One of the great pantheon of inverse square forces governing all phenomena.

It would have Freud and Piaget in it too, about how space and time start when the Mother goes away. Also multidimensional vector spaces. I got going on some kind of poem about cosmology. It was an alternate beginning for the metamorphoses to man.

In the mind as in the beginning, in the beginning of the Mind, there is no time until a separation is felt and with the space of waiting —complementarity — time begins.

The Other is in motion. It comes and goes in space. And in the waiting for the Other, time and space produce motion for motion is the ratio of space to time. And it was a long time before we understood that the motion of the other, was not necessarily with respect to us.

The change of the rate of motion in time produces acceleration. And it is this motion and acceleration of motion — the Force — the Change, that produces creation.

And it was the spinning of the motion that changed light into dark and bound the elements together. All is change and inertia — resistance to change.

And force convolved with space produces energy.

And force convolved with time produces impulse.

The turning of the energy from potential to actual gave opportunity to the forms, the designs, waiting in a higher dimension to be enacted.

And the spinning, turning took change to the nth power, Moments became richer ranging around the mean.

And starting from the central sun the spinning energy produced the moon and the earth and the heavens and all living things partaking in the synchronistic sampling of means — local in their time dimension.

And when we entered that dimensionality the world was born anew and grew and grew into the metamorphosis of forms across niches, the isomorphism of forms across niches, the homeomorphism of forms across niches of the nth dimension.

I became the random Walker adrift in Montreal. I would be the old tea head of time who tells all. I'd be working on the question, what is our purpose here. How does the brain interact with the mind.

In the poem there would be several old tea heads of time, to consider. Weiner for the cybernetics (I was a cyborg); Fuller, ergodic geodesic isoclines; Prigogene, for he was literary and knew Bergson; Jung for his synchronicity; Dirac for his valiant attempt to pursue beauty from the subatomic quantum to the universal scale relativity, and for his willingly radical acceptance of phenomenology.

I wanted it to be like the perfect communication in mathematics. Where you are lead carefully, lovingly along a difficult path, a path you must construct in your mind, by a skillful and nurturing and enthusiastic guide.

A fluttering of theorems, like the beating of wings.

There is nothing as dreamy and poetic, nothing as psychedelic as mathematics.

Time's Arrow flows in the direction of entropy.

The apprehension of energy by living structure circulates and reverses the direction of Time's Arrow, because it temporarily and locally reverses the course of entropy.

Uh, huh. Uh, huh. That's what I'm talking about.

The life force scaling a diffusion limited aggregation skein to the perimeter occupancy probabilities of the cluster tips.

These are probabilities for a random Walker to end up being able to throw a perimeter around memory sites, sites that are clustered around and contained within a convex hull of past time, centered on the seed of him.

> The old tea-head of time sees the moment —not as the point where the light cone to the past meets the light cone to the future — but as the center of a web whose four main strands cut the wheel into quarters, like a cross through the hub, in a system of four domains of time: time wasted, time lost, time rediscovered and time regained.
> And going around the hub in concentric, ever-widening circles, one sees that the efforts and energies, the occupations

and occasions are like isoclines of equisynchronous time and these are meandering in and out of the lines of subjective time.

And at the crossover from one time domain to another, one can travel in time freely: from wasting time to being behind the times to rediscovering time and regaining the lost time. There will be time to waste, playing games, though it is not wasted, it is practice. There will be time lost; sitting at a red light in the rain. There will be time rediscovered as you sense the parallels with life in your family again. There will be time regained, when chains of long memory are floating through your brain again.

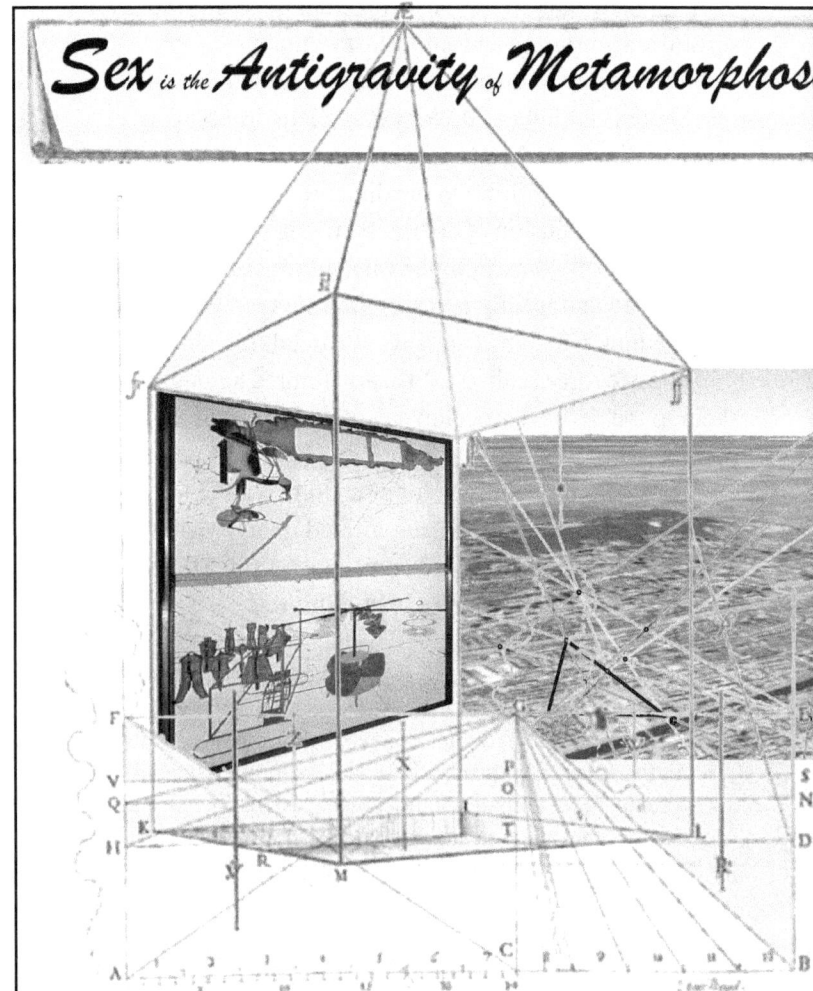

Sex is the *Antigravity* of *Metamorphos*

Snow Angels

Rayne (the Norm) manoeuvered the stalwart green touring machine through the swirling snowy night down the long winding road through some complicated twists and turns, pointing the head lights through a shadowy forest to get to the home of Dick Higgins. Her friend Michael Cooper was our guide. Snow was swirling about us as we made our way around to the back of the house.

We were going to have a steam bath, a sauna. It would be a first for me.

Dick Higgins met the three night visitors and led them in through his kitchen. It was a sumptuous room, with a big wrought iron pan-rack hanging from the ceiling over the stove. He had every known pot and utensil there ever was. I thought, he must be some kind of great cook.

I was familiar with his publishing house, Something Else Press. Higgins had invented the idea, or at least coined the term, "intermedia," which was about a synesthesia from stimulation of several sense modalities in an art work. Music, text, film. All at once, and more.

I was a bit nervous because I had smoked a little weed and it always makes me enthusiastic if not downright paranoid as it elicited behaviors not natural to my introverted ways, anyway, and since Norm was driving I had slipped into Eddy mode though was somewhat enervated by the tricky art of navigating a dark and dangerous country road in a swirling snowstorm, and further I was nervous to meet a publisher because I was afraid I might blurt out my desire to be published. Or, worse, feel like I needed to defend my own inadequate writing efforts. Or something. I was uncomfortable in these august literary circles. Plus I had been informed

223

that Higgins was homosexual, which, having been brought up in Texas I was not that experienced with at all; plus I had been told that Higgins' press had declared bankruptcy; plus he himself had just gotten out of a stay in the hospital for bad head, a mental recuperation facility. So I felt like I had to watch-it around the great man. Michael Cooper was protective of and solicitous toward his great friend.

Rayne was told this by Michael, and she took me aside to put me wise. It's not that I was afraid of homosexuals, some of my best friends back in Texas were what we called "crazy", but there they tended to be circumspect about it and the subject never came up.

Michael Cooper was amazing. He and Dick Higgins were into everything. They worked in painting, performance, and poetry; happenings, intermedia, and film; typography, book art, and publishing. Truly Renaissance men. And here Higgins lived in a castle.

So I approached with a literary complement: "I was knocked out by one book from Something Else Press, *The Annotated Topography of Chance*, where the writer talks about every object on the field of his kitchen table and how and when it came to be there."

Higgins looked at me with big eyes. "You mean *The Anecdoted Topography of Chance*," he corrected.

"Oh," I felt duly chastised. "*Anecdoted*, yes that makes sense."

I tried again: "Mr. Higgins, I know you published a lot of John Cage, and that he was friends with Marcel Duchamp. And of course a founding member of the Fluxus Group. They were a kind of art tribe all over the world. They grew out of happenings, Andy Warhol and Situationist aesthetics."

This was way too much but I knew a bit about Duchamp from the Literature of Multimedia class that Kruppa taught at

University of Texas. I was his TA. I was being my usual ingratiating self among strangers, and did want to indicate my respect to a senior artist.

I told him about Kruppa's class. Said Kruppa was the son of drummer Joe Kruppa. Made the joke about TAs being the second oldest profession and that cracked everybody up. Things became easier. Later I asked Higgins if he had ever met Duchamp. "Yes," he said, "John Cage introduced us, at a theatre in New York."

The assembled body were momentarily silenced by the invocation of greatness.

We went out of the house, on a breezeway, then back in to a building that housed a large indoor swimming pool. The pool must have been at least 60 feet, maybe even longer, Olympic sized.

There were lockers and dressing rooms, and we left our clothes in dressing rooms. Wrapped in towels, we entered the steaming sauna. I thought: The culture of sauna requires that one adopt the easygoing attitude toward nudity of the hippies, the native Americans and the Finish, and apparently Vermonters here in sauna land. I would just go with the flow. The sauna room was made of some kind of beautiful wood, cedar perhaps or eucalyptus. Aromatic. They were doing things with moving rocks, and also switching themselves with some kind of tree branch.

I was shocked when everybody removed their towel; it was only to sit on.

But I relaxed and let myself be content to just be. After a while it seemed Michael and Dick were in some kind of discussion. And Rayne and I went outside and threw ourselves into the pool. I was a good swimmer. Then we went back into the sauna and steamed some more.

After a while Rayne said, "I want to run outside and

make a snow angel." She wanted to run outside and throw herself into the snow! And make a snow angel.

I had never heard of doing that naked. "Are you crazy? It's freezing and dark out there."

"I don't care. It's part of the ancient ritual; to mortify the flesh as you Catholics say."

"Well you are seriously going to mortify the flesh if you do that."

I followed her out the heavy door. It is serious cold. Dick, the gracious host is keeping a watch for us by the door. There we were, two tenderfoot nudists tiptoeing our way across the parking lot to a snow bank on a little hillock on the other side. We must have looked furtively terpsichorean in our stark naked bodies, doing the tenderfoot tiptoe through swirling snow, steam rising off our bodies that we've just been gently cooking at around 180 degrees Fahrenheit in a steamy sauna. But any shivering is more about what's coming next, as I reached the top of the edge of the parking lot, she has gone ahead of me. She shrieks and quickly plops herself down in the snow, sits right down on her bum and leans back flat. I am amazed to see her starting to make a "snow angel".

"Get in," she shouts. "We have to get back quick."

Not to wimp out, I get down on one knee beside her and grab a couple handfuls of snow and pick it up and splash it on my chest, like you might try to acclimatize yourself to very cold water when going swimming.

"You'll pull me out if my heart stops?" I call down to the lovely Rayne — supine, on her back looking up, waving her arms up and down and her legs in and out frantically carving out the snow angel. There is a large drift of snow building up above her shoulder.

An instant later, I am down on one knee howling and

about to try it too, when she leaps up and turns for a moment to admire her handy work in creating the shape of her Snow Angel. There in the snow was the projection of an angel. The arcs swung out by flapping the hands made big wings coming out of the shoulders, other wings from the hips made by the feet looked like bas relief chaps, all fluffy, feathery wings. There was a round relief where the head had been, and rather large indentations from the bums. The beaut-tocks. Our angel has got booty. There was almost a face in the field of the head, with the arch from the neck looking like a chin and hair on the sides making indentations for eyes. No expression. Mum's the word. I quick made an imprint of a shrouded mummy, no wings and shivering uncontrollably stood up. Rayne is all red, her bum flushed. Me too, as blood surges to the surface of my skin in an exhilarating rush of pins and needles that's so unexpectedly marvelous. I'm almost hopping with excitement as we run back to the building, and Dick throws the door open for us, laughing.

We head back into the sauna, but stop and throw ourselves into the pool, for it is heated too. Rayne got out and I lingered a while in the pool, floating in the chlorine clean water. I could see the lines on the bottom of the pool. Floating like, . . . well, an angel in the air. I thought: Intermedia is a kind of floating through dimensional modalities of sense-knowing. I used to believe in angels when I was a child, thought I had sensed mine more than once. Later I would read that they had something to do with grace, and later that they were a Jungian archetype depicted in many cultures with wings and flowing loose robes and glowing with warmth and light.

I thought about the act of grace that had brought me and Rayne together, thought about it many times. It made me feel that our union was blessed.

All these things did I think about flying in the water,

thinking about an angel emerging from the intrapsychic realm of archetypes into the real physical world.

In the sauna Dick Higgins and Michael talked about music and poetry and mutual friends. They seemed aware that they were part of a great humanist endeavor to give voice to an intellectual and spiritual upheaval bridging medieval times and the early modern era together. They were into the movement. I was just glad to be there with Rayne, and not be totally ignored.

I wasn't that familiar with Dick Higgins' work, but the intuition about Marcel Duchamp and John Cage was right on. Duchamp for the visual and the epiphanic shock attack and Cage for the linguistical, and musical. And both of them for their strange and marvelous writing.

The aesthetic of these modern artist seemed to be operating from thought, they had abstracted about the nature of time and dimension and chance, then had returned and concretized, reified their abstract intuitions in their art.

Higgins, I would later find out, had been quite a political and intellectually supportive force in the 60s. He had a huge musical side, and that was another thing that brought he and Cooper closer. They were idea-based artists, and though I had come by my commitment to idea-based art through Sartre and Borges, it was interesting to see they were coming at it from what to me was a fresh perspective from a much physical musicality, a more concrete poetry so that it emerged naturally as an eye/ear aesthetic.

Marshal McLuhan too.

Frames and Feedback

Rayne was kind enough to hire me to lecture her class on something. It meant a lot to me; it meant that she was hip to what I was doing. There was a lot of respect in that. Bless her heart. Now I had to think of something to say.

Well say something she said.

Say anything.

In addition to making myself useful in the editing room and helping out with tech, setting up shoots, I was reading manuals about the equipment. The school had these new expensive portable tape recorders, 1/2 inch tape, cassettes. We also had books put out by various alternative video groups: *Independent Video*, which had great hand drawn illustrations; and *Spaghetti Video* from the Videofreaks. But the one that really impressed me was *Guerilla Television*. It was a compendium of the Radical Software issues, a cool book. I thought I might crib together my lecture from some of that. It was an activists manual about using the new media technology, cable, cassette — to provide documentation and feedback for political decision making, to show where things were wrong and needed to be fixed. It was independent, outside the Hollywood studio business and the university atmosphere. It had good, down to earth insights into the aesthetic and feelings involved with discovering and using the processes inherent to videography. It even had a good insight into the epistemology of weed seeing it was both a physical bounty somewhere between software and sacrament and a model of that eternally-returning, branching of maximum variability of possibility that was nature's way of embracing what is available now.

Rayne probably thought that though I was not political, I

was really damn handy with electronics. I didn't tell her all the details of my teaching background. I had taught trade school and junior college students before but only classes like circuit theory, oscillators, rectifier, load line, op-amps.

As a teacher I knew my failing was in having had too much sympathy for the plight of students. For example, I took my pulse digital electronics class to see training videos on pulsars, in particular the one inside the Crab Nebula. We were learning how to trap and track pulses in circuits. We learned how astronomers might use this to find other planets, because the tiny planets would cause a tiny blip of pulse in the light intensity from their central star when they passed in front of it in their yearly circuit. The discovery of other worlds required the capture of that pulse. I also took them to see William Burroughs, who they had not heard of because he had written a trilogy about denizens of the Crab Nebula, *The Nova Express*. His ideas — of language is a virus and animals are soft machines — were cybernetic. His writing is a hip and astute reflection by an artist on the science of his time. Now back then in Austin we had a very hip mayor, and he managed to get the city council to give the Keys to the City to William Burroughs! They didn't know who he was. But I got my crew of students to the reading at the civic auditorium, and after it was over one of them said he was "a class-A pervert". I realized I had made a mistake by letting them see the liberal artist side of my personality. They were students at a trade school and they were there to learn a skill to get a better job. It was not my job to expand their mind with literature. After that I could sense their respect for me eroding as they saw me as more like them. I told myself: Must not let student get too close, they will disrespect you.

So I started to ask myself what could I possibly lecture about to Rayne's class that would be of use to this group of students studying filmmaking and videography — and not have her regret giving me the gig. I did notice that the students tended to separate into two groups: those who wanted to be in front of the camera and those who wanted to be behind it. Rayne was always trying to deliver them from this Big Media / Star System mindset. But the producer types just really wanted to "get the talent in front of the camera" and get the thing going. So I thought it might be good to reinforce what Rayne expressed from a different voice.

Hubristical it would be of me to try in one lecture to lead the budding artists of the future into a realization that they are in pursuit of the most precious jewel in the universe: the artwork as a field in which to bring the objects of desire into tension with each other so that they may discourse in their own language of images, affording the universe opportunity at becoming self-aware through us. Huh?!

Also, for myself, a question I wanted to answer was: Did working in a visual media enhanced the mind's ability to think in terms of images? Perhaps I could come up with some kind of home made Frame Theory in regards to what they are studying — Graphic Novel, Comic Book, Film, Video. I'd like to relate it to what you project on your own internal screen. Really, that's what we are after. Descartes' a "sovereign transparency" — what a wonderful phrase. . .

To keep it relevant I could get into a bit of three movies: *La Jetee*, for the obsession with time; *Citizen Kane* for the use of perspective and space; *Forbidden Planet* for the monsters of the Id. What I really wanted to say was this: The fundamental activity of the artist is like the mystical practice of Recollection. Recollection involves stopping time. We got introduced to stopping time and transcendence through drugs and meditation and also very dangerous life-threatening encounters with your fate. Art seeks to have the same experience but in a more controlled, methodical program.

The difference between popular art and "real" art [I need to define this, concisely: popular art presents signs, real art presents signifiers. The hallmark of real art is that it is self-aware.] Yikes! How are we gonna tell young people about that. Real art takes the creator and the viewer into a journey into the real, the symbolic and the imaginary. I saw it as the difference between exploitation by slick marketing fantasy in genre literature and experiencing the loop of language working in feedback with your life in real literature. To me it was the difference between a treadmill and a Mobius strip. I saw myself standing in front of the class lecturing.

Scene: *Walker addresses the audience directly, looks nervously at Rayne.*

Walker: I am trying to come up with a useful "Frame Theory."

I think that the metaphor of the cinema: frames in time, speaks to an understanding of time as possibly other than the mechanistic clock seconds.

A thriller has the clock ticking, a movie of the sun rise seems slower than real time.

Even more compelling is the metaphor of video tape: writing code on memory tape and decoding it. This speaks to an understanding of time as a series of samples or signals retrieved, to project a world to explore. This art of frames — film, video, graphic novel, comic book — must exercise a person's internal screen, upon which they organize their personality. It would seem that people who have grown up after cinema and photography have different internal visualization capabilities.

I wanted to mention dimension, I think that is a big influence on my generation. And of course the two biggest discoveries of the modern epoch, relativity and the unconscious. They both have to do with dimension.

So basically this lecture will be a kind of hippie head,

talking to young artists coming up. But I have to be careful to avoid the "far out!" factor because it leads to dismissal. Hopefully with enough relevant insight into their practical problems, it will appear grounded and to point. On the other hand maybe they already know this stuff and will think I am still a hopelessly passé, print-dominated, literary bohemian full of misguided utopian idealism. Hopefully not.

The Lecture.
Twenty-four to thirty students were in the bleachers of the television studio at CGEP John Abbot in November to listen to a lecture / demonstration from a writer / tech about modern aesthetics of space time in literature and film. The speaker, Walker Underwood was someone their teacher Rayne Luce had promised would be a "whirlwind tour looking at some models of Frame Art, some current writers and a couple of favorite films."

Rayne introduces the speaker to her class: "This is our TA, Walker Underwood. He is going to talk to you about what he has been learning with us, and give a demonstration of video feedback." She looks down at a 3x5 card in her hand: "It is something he calls *The Mobius Surface as Model of Feedback Enclosure for Informing Aesthetic Sensibility*."

She looked over at me and yielded the floor.

Scene: *Walker stands and steps to the front of the class.*

Walker: I'd like to start this talk by thinking about some of the things that have impressed me about the art and literature of my generation. One thing the art and litera-ture has in common is a sense of being self-aware. I think this sense of being self-aware is perhaps an aspect of an art form that seeks to further the art form itself, rather than one that tells us story from within the art form.

Artform as new process seeks to discover itself in its own processes, its own capabilities. In the sense that it does not have a large aesthetic history, and if it does not try to emulate previous art forms, it is open and cool — in the McLuhan sense of inviting / requiring participation. But since my main influence is the ancient art of writing I am slightly *verklempt* at being up here talking to you. It has been quite a learning experience to have my linear print-oriented self dragged kicking and screaming into electronic media. And I think this is something some of you are going through and trying to understand. So hang in with it a minute and we'll see where it goes.

Scene: *Pause. Scan audience for any relating confirmation. Gets some from Rayne.*

Walker: The self-aware art communicates on at least two levels. In terms of linguistics it is an art more of signifiers than it is an art of signs. That's what gives it a certain obsessional, restless, free-running quality; it is searching for grounding. What I mean is, if you compare a genre art, like say a western: you could take that western say, into a space station. That's what they did when they took the Gary Cooper film *High Noon* into the Sean Connery film *Outland*. But a self aware art is not confined to the limits of genre.

   La Jette was amazing wasn't it. It was all done with stills. Every scene was a still except that one scene in the middle where the camera is zooming in on the woman's face, more and more until we are right up to the eye, and then we have movement — for the eye blinks. That was shocking wasn't it? I was thrilled. After that moment in the film we have been winked at by the author, we are brought in on the meaning, shifting at more levels. Did anyone else get the sense that we were being looked at by a knowing author?

My point is that in your student films, you don't have to be thinking of big budget or genre. And you don't have to be parodying preexisting genres. In a lot of ways those are entertaining but they are lacking in the one thing people want and need most in life and art: Intimacy. It is best to — in your own films — to open up your own life and let people in. Let yourself be vulnerable, let people know you. Art is intimacy.

Scene: *Walker looks at the student faces and at Rayne.*

Walker: Well, just to get started, since you are a group studying film making, I must mention one of my favorite films. *Forbidden Planet*. Have you seen it? You probably have. It's that one about a group of astronauts who land on a planet where they have to encounter the Monster of the Id. And they have Robbie the Robot at the helm of this long sedan, racing across the landscape. It is a most fun movie.

Scene: *Looks out at the sea of student faces to see if there is any recognition*

Walker: Who remembers the name of the character played by Walter Pigeon? He is the father of the daughter who all the astronauts are interested in. He is the only survivor of the original explorers who landed on the planet. Anyone?

His name was Dr. Morbius.

I think the name is a condensation of three names representing three concepts. Morpheus — the deity of sleep and dreams; Morbidity — Death; and he is named after a real Dr. Mobius in the history of mathematics. And this real Mobius was a geometer who invented the Mobius Strip which is the first one-sided surface and named after him.

Scene: *Walker picks up a strip of paper and like a magician holds it up to show the front and back side for the audience to inspect.*

Walker: The Mobius strip is a three-dimensional figure that can be formed by taking a long rectangular strip of paper which is two dimensional, *(there is a pregnant pause as he looks at the audience)* — like a strip of film, and taking the paper and twisting it once, before joining its ends together.

Scene: *Walker has a role of scotch tape, and is applying it to the ends butted together after the twist.*

Walker: This is the Mobius strip. It seems to have two sides but really has only one. Watch as I traverse the Mobius strip with this marks-a-lot.

Scene: *Balancing it on his knees he carefully goes around the strip with a pen, careful not to lift the pen off the paper.*

Walker: Notice I am not lifting the pen from the paper, I am unrolling the strip beneath the pen.

Scene: *Walker shows the paper strip with the black mark all the way around, down the center of every bit of surface.*

Walker: And lo and behold I have got all the way around the strip to my starting point. The strip has only one side! Even though it looks like it has an inside and an outside. As you saw, I did not have to lift the pen and go outside the edge of the strip to get to the other side. Like I would the flat piece of paper.

Scene: *He looks around the class, they look a little puzzled.*

Walker: The Mobius strip confounds our ideas of inside and outside. So I propose that we consider this idea of a space whose inside and outside are seamlessly pouring in to each other as a model or an image of the modern. Of ecology or cybernetics. As opposed to the idea of the cross, or the axis of the Cartesian X and Y axis dividing up space nicely into homogeneous us and them, mind and body, inside and outside.

Scene: *Walker gets excited and starts to rap.*

Walker: The Mobius Strip is like the feedback diagram, or the symbol for ecology, the oroborous, the snake eating its tale. What comes around goes around — Karma. We have something here like a two dimensional thing trying to become a three dimensional thing, it leaps up into a higher space. It is the unpredictable Synergy of something being way more than the sum of its parts, because it is held stable and organized by feedback.

    And now I would like to investigate the feedback of a camera and its monitor.

Scene: *Walker points to a video monitor on a table then to a video camera on a tripod. The video camera is pointed directly into the screen of the monitor. He touches a video cable coming out of the camera and follows it with his hand to the input of the monitor. He switches both on.*

Walker: To show how this relates to what we are studying here, I have set up a camera, mounted on a tripod. We have the camera pointing at the monitor. So that the output of the camera is fed to the monitor, but the output of the monitor is being seen by, fed into, the camera. This sets up a feedback loop.

Scene: *An image of the monitor screen appears inside the monitor screen; inside that screen is an image of the screen, and so on. . . .*

Walker: This setup demonstrates principles of optics, video recirculation, dynamics of light. At first it is rectangular — like parallel mirrors within mirrors.

Scene: *At the tripod he turns a knurled knob to turn the camera at an angle to the screen. The scene in the monitor switches.*

Walker: Then when I turn the camera at an angle on the tripod, the screen forms an equiangular spiral of the screens twisting into the center. It is the scanning sweep of the monitor, and the scanning sweep of the camera, and they are crossed.

You want to get a good angle, 120 degrees is a good angle to offset the camera. It is a lot easier to turn the camera than the monitor.

Scene: *The image of monitor within the monitor has rotated around into a square spiral.*

Walker: This sets up a nice spiral, as the two scans try to accommodate the change in their relationship by getting into phase. Pretty cool huh?

Its the timing of the scan lines and the changing of the camera lens angle that create a sort of moiré pattern that animates.

It is tricky to get the feedback, you've got to find a sweet spot, between the exposure, and the alignment of the camera to the screen, and other things.

Scene: *He fiddles with the camera, zooming in and out.*

Walker: Here is the zoom. As you can see you get a nice effect, when you zoom — it is like a splash into water, but the feedback decays really fast. When I do the zoom, the spiral zooms in and out turning around itself. It's like some kind of crazy yin yang machine.

Keep trying the zoom until you get a sweet spot and that means there is a resonance among the transforms. So that you get it to carry on for a while; you get a little duration before it breaks down into a steady state, not changing. The system response is the very quick-time of light and moving electrons.

Scene: *He fiddles with the monitor. Adjusts the contrast.*

Walker: Set the contrast higher.

Scene: *With the change in contrast the image becomes more broken up and pixelated. With the absence of color, there are areas of local interaction.*

Walker: That is hard to stabilize. Even as I walk around, it picks up my vibration and they fall into the feedback loop. It's like a synchronistic vortex.

Or like an interactive space.

Scene: *Walker puts his hand into the space between the camera and the monitor. It is picked up and duplicated three times around so that there are three hands, and it is swirling around making the hand patterns shift.*

Walker: This is the sound of one hand clapping. You've got to find a sweet spot.

Scene: *Images settle down, it also seems to be circulating around the center.*

Walker: There we go. Now we have got something going. I have "seeded" it by putting something in the way between the camera and the monitor, just my hand here.

When you get tired of the pattern repeating itself, you can reseed it by putting something in the way and a new series of patterns will start.

Scene: *The image triples the hand, ghosts it again, phase-locks into a stable pattern swirling around a central black dot.*

•

Walker: A running shape is going on the monitor, moving around a central black spot because here the chaotic inputs have canceled each other out. This is the still point.

At this point you should be able to create lots of swirling, spinning stuff around the central fixed point. It is a kind of chaos attractor.

Scene: *With his hands in front of the camera, between it and the screen, he is shaping a ball surrounding the black dot with his hands. We see this on the screen.*

Walker: Once you set up the interactive space, you can put a moving "whatever" between the camera and TV set. Or if we had a big video projection screen serving as monitor, or a bank of monitors driven by some external sync, we could put moving actors and dancers between the camera and TV set. You've probably seen this? We are allowing the moving whatevers acting between the camera and TV set to CONTROL the video feedback via how fast, what angle, and what distance the movement is between lens and screen. We can put lights between too.

With the idea of the Mobius surface breaking down the difference between inside and outside, you have a paradigm of something contained within itself.

If I put my hand or something, into the interactive space, the space forms a kind of hole where the "outside" is in complete contact with the arm and where the energy from my hand goes back through the space and alters what happens " inside" again as it passes from the prior image of hand. I start to have a loop which is partly uncontained — that is, the medium really senses that which is outside itself, and partly contained — that is the medium senses itself within itself. It is a form that begins to have the capacity to know about its own behavior as it behaves "outside."

Now THAT is a nice description of any creative art process.

Scene: *He takes his hands out and goes back to the camera.*

Walker: Try messing with the color — black and white is easier to start with, — phase, focus, zoom, iris, etc.

Scene: *The video on the screen changes as he adjusts various controls on the camera.*

Walker: If the camera and or monitor has automatic features, turn them all off, you get better control that way.

Scene: *Walker pulls a flashlight from his back pack.*

Walker: Or, look what happens when I shine a flashlight on the screen.

Scene: *The students are staring entranced at the undulating, convolving patterns on the video screen.*

Walker: The patterns that you see can exhibit spatiotemporal oscillation and chaos, and can be quite hypnotic. But there is usually a single fixed point on screen (that is either stable or unstable, depending on the zoom).

Scene: *The image shows structure like shingles, contrasting slabs, overlaid, kaleidoscopic around the central point.*

Walker (*getting more animated, humorous*): This looks like some kind of weird metabolic ooze coming out of the center of the screen.

It looks like we have our own little electronic Petri dish going on here.

It makes me wonder if there are proto-evolutionary forces essentially hard-coded into the laws of physics? Something about the dynamics of the field looping out and conducting feedback on itself sorts things into a kind of niche-filling order given apt initial conditions — in our case the contrast, orientation or the transformation of light. We have gotten some kind of electro-metabolic ooze here.

Scene: *Walker scans the audience looking for a laugh. They seem politely attentive, entranced by the light show but not REALLY digging it. He strikes the table and the whole imaged dips then falls apart and another pattern occurs.*

Walker: We have seen that within a few cycles of feedback, each cycle is very fast, the time it takes an image to come into the camera and get projected onto the screen — essentially the speed of light — just some latency in the picture tube. But the image quickly settles down to a cyclic, or phase-shifting but steady running pattern. We change the contingent inputs, focus, color balance, contrast, brightness, and the effects show up, but they are susceptible to vibrations of the table, and fluctuations of air currents. It is very sensitive.

Scene: *Changing the focus or the zoom, slightly makes the material on the monitor change the areas of color get more numerous and smaller.*

Walker: In feedback we have local thermo-mechanic-optical-cyclic stability versus stochastic background perturbations! It is a miniature of the competition model of animals in a forest, ants in a colony, students in a class, bacteria on a petri dish, fire in a forest, fever in the cells. There are relations of competition and symbiosis — entity and substrate supporting it — that are trending from simple bonds and links and connections among the parts that are almost like valence bonds in molecules. Thus we have here a fully Darwinian chemo/biological process! Isn't it cool!

Scene: *Walker adjust the camera a bit, causing the screen to shift into an unfocused black and white blotchy image of a face! The audience gasps with amazement, for it looked almost human, then it faded into a more predictable center focused movement.*

Walker: Jesus! Did you see that!? That almost LOOKED like Jesus on the Shroud of Turin!

Scene: *The scene quickly dissolves.*

Walker: Wow, I wonder what happened there? Where is Mary Magdalen when you need her. Evolution might have selected for that organization if it knew how to reproduce it. What if we try to zoom in and focus on this strange new found land we have discovered in the field.

Scene: *He addresses the audience directly, looks nervously at Rayne.*

Walker: Like many people in my generation I tried LSD some years ago. I experienced vivid recursive patterns of luminous color very similar to those seen here, in video feedback. I used to think it was ringing — you know like when you pluck a guitar string at its exact harmonic? That's the resonance frequency. This visual ringing is at the resonance frequency of the eye-brain system. This got me to thinking about the self-referential operation of the visual system. And by extension the mind.

Scene: *Walker turns the video camera off, then turns the monitor off.*

Walker: So I present this example here to lead into talking about an art that is in some sense self-aware. An art that doesn't necessarily seek to manipulate or persuade, but one that is more democratic, it just is, what it is talking about.

    I am trying to understand the difference between dreaming and fantasy, and imagination. Between disso-ciative fugue, and mental problem solving. One needs a creative space in order to create. That is a place to get away from the anxiety. Which is very real.

    Anyway, I'll wind it up. By going back to *Citizen Cane* and the meaning of Rosebud. Think back to your own favorite toy. A sled is not a great example, but something earlier, a teddy bear toy, a stuffed toy when you were really little. Psychologists call these transitional objects. They have a lot of magic. Art is like that transi-tional object, a place upon which you project principals with which you organize the world. The transition that the psychologist speak of is between the infant's concep-tion of the world, and the real world. The art object, a painting, a poem, a film weaves together experiences that are significant, not only for the maker but for the other who can recognize what they are looking at.

It is really a privilege to try to understand this. Like, Mobius makes a model of a space turning in on itself and then one day you see it is the clue to understanding the relationship between metonymy and metaphor. Metonymy is about parts of a whole, how like stands for the thing that contains it, for example how the crown stands for the king. Whereas, metaphor is about how something in one container is similar, parallel to something in an entirely other container. Love is like Rain. How rain which creates life is like love which creates life.

Scene: *He sneaks a look at her, a raised eyebrow of recognition.*

Walker: The transitional object is something outside which is also inside.
     So in your collage-based art, (parataxis) there are lots of like things up on the frame. Similarities, leading to patterns, leading to connective narratives. Metonymies leading to metaphors.

Scene: *He addresses the audience directly, looks nervously at Rayne. She is looking slightly askance. He notices their attention is beginning to wander.*

Walker: I just wanted to point out a couple of ideas to you. The idea that the mind is a signifying machine, that it communicates in levels of language: in dreams as pure images and experience, and in writing and art through the conventions of words and signs and media. But the process is the same. Creative work goes on in an inner level and an outer level. And the Mobius surface is a model or symbol to reflect that sameness. The ultimate art work is the dream, it is going on all the time, but we only see it in REM sleep. THAT is the art we aspire to.

The outer is concerned with *measure*; what if we were to pull back, abstract, to *connectivity* — stop measuring and comparing for a moment. To really get a picture of the world underneath all these well thought out forms — to enter the underside of reality, the chaos — we can do what Rachel Carson, suggested in order to understand the sea. Leave our perceptions of space and time and enter a world where these are connected. The other day I was swimming in the pool at Dick Higgins' house. He is a the inventor of intermedia, which is an art that seeks to situate itself in between sound and sense and the visual. In the voluminous water world, sound and light move differently and one part of this space knows about the other parts. I mean if we could look at our world and see our world the way fish see theirs — they have achieved a kind of neutral buoyancy drifting on the currents, and the waves, as these forces sift down, or are moving through us. What must it be like for them?

Scene: *Walker looks at Rayne and smiles; she looks like she is about to get the hook.*

Walker: Let me leave you with the image of those Tigers from *Forbidden Planet*. And the Tigers in Blake's poem.

Tiger Tiger burning bright / In the forests of the night / What immortal hand or eye / Could frame thy fearful symmetry?

The poem Tiger is from Blake's *Songs of Experience* after his *Songs of Innocence*. The Experienced is about how children grow from innocence and delight into experience of the real, the world of materialism, poverty, oppression, disease, war and death but also our birthright of experiencing and understanding the works of creation. The Tiger represents all of these, and yet these too are created by god to test, to train, to hone adaptation. The stress of survival matures and informs and adapts beings to reality.

The Tiger is an attempt to understand the challenges of the world through trying to emulate the creative imagination that created the tiger. The question is asked: did the maker of the tiger know what he was doing, or did he leave us here with his mistakes. And the answer is: The creator left the tiger here with its purpose being to stimulate the evolution of the prey.

In a way the movie *Forbidden Planet* answers the poet's question:

In what distant deeps or skys / Burnt the fire of thine eyes.

Our attempt to know the creator of the tiger is like the advanced alien civilization in *Forbidden Planet*, the Krell. The film postulates a highly evolved race called the Krell somewhere out in the universe that becomes able to do god-like creativity: make what they thought about or imagined, materialize. They had harnessed the fields between mind and matter. As such they had transcended their own mortality and no longer needed a body. The tragic mistake of the Krell was in hubris, in their attempt to link their subconscious minds and imaginations to their super-powerful matter generator in order to give themselves god-like powers. In their attempt to transcend the limitations of mortality the Krell like us sought to reach beyond the finite human knowing to somehow experience the infinite, through true god-like creation. It is an irresistible impetus, part of our make up too, as is the savage nature that protects us.

We come from a time where we are just starting to understand the dark energies of the Freudian id, which was certainly a big theme in *Forbidden Planet,* and a big force in Blake though he did not use these terms.

The film *Forbidden Planet* was a marvel of special effects. The Tiger in the movie is visible briefly, we see only the stripes of the tiger floating in the air, shifting and undulating and oozing like marbled patterns, like the thin film interference of oil on water. We only see the evidence of this invisible hostile enemy as it stocks and attacks; in the coils of the electric fence or the spray of particle beam weapons shooting at it, as it draws closer and closer or rages in the sky.

So Blake was coming to the perspective of experience, and that is realizing there is a role for adversity, even evil. The gift of evil or adversity is that it makes you stronger — if it doesn't overwhelm. You want to set your own challenges, or have good teachers assign them to you. Maybe not even living teachers but practitioners of your art from the past.

To draw a parallel to our video experiment, the Tiger is the monitor in our system. It provides feedback. The top predator is the cornerstone at the top of a food chain and it speaks to the health of the whole ecology that supports it. It is an expression of that ecology. We are an expression of our ecology, our planet.

The question asked by Blake is answered. The answer is a primordial field of form energy. The pattern is already potentially in the field before the pattern was formed, kind of like what we were seeing in the patterns of light that we were creating in the feedback experiment.

Scene: *Walker quickly returns to his seat, hoping to avoid questions.*

I Am Not Either, Lesbophobic!

Raging Rayne was once again flying off the handle on a tirade, being reckless, endangering our relationship. And I was being feckless about it. It was shocking because she was usually a tough customer, but when she got on a tirade, all manner of vehemence did flow. "What are you writing?" she snarled. "All the time writing. Are you writing a lot of weird lesbian shit about me?"

I was learning how to sit quietly when she's being irrational. Learning to be the rational one. When she's freaking out over something small, sit there calmly until she's done. Don't tell her she's being irrational. That's not being rational; it's being superior. Wait for her to let it all out. Little moms like it when you keep your head in the face of their meltdown. If you're lucky, anger turns to tears and tears turn into posttraumatic crazy sex.

My proposal to wander like gypsies in bicentennial America had been a destabilizing perturbation to the status quo of continued connubial bliss. I could have been more supportive. No doubt she was feeling confined by her commitment to be near her kid and the idea of kidnapping him was out of the question. So lashing out at the nearest white male oppressor at hand who was responsible for that feeling of confinement was a way to test the relationship.

"I cannot be myself here under your regime Walker, you cannot have my strength to prop up your own insecurities and weak ego. You cannot live in my head and use my energy and my strength and my ideas. Go find your own."

That did it. Women are dark ninja fighters of the psyche. I had told her the last time we fought and she was being insulting that, "Lovers are allowed to do one unforgivable thing a year."

And by implication breaking that rule meant we were not going to be lovers any more. And now this, insinuating that I was taking her ideas. This was too much! It was unacceptable. I had to keep my word and leave. Sometimes that's all a man has, is his word.

I got up, walked into the bedroom and pulled my back pack from its temporary place of repose behind the chair. I opened the bottom drawer, pulled my few clothes out and threw them into the back pack. I shoved the scattered pages of my manuscript into the backpack.

Rayne sat in the living room. I knew she was fuming.

She taunted me as though I weren't there. "I cannot express sexual problems as it makes him feel inadequate. I can't be in a grouchy mood without his feelings criticized. I cannot not pay attention to him, or he accuses me of not loving. I can not ask for loving, I must wait for it."

She got louder. "The only way you will consent to stay with me is if I am totally submissive and apologetic. Well go ahead and leave then. I am no longer afraid of your going because the only thing you have given me in a long time is your resentment of me, your constant criticism and attempts to change me. And a lasagna."

I knew I had not brought much, but it was all I had to bring. And I felt like defending it. "What do you mean!? I make divine cakes and pies and all that and you make such an issue of it, of my doing it, that I feel like its necessary to fight you on it. You make fun of my ability in the kitchen so that a man can't even take pride in that."

"I never have this trouble with Linda. She's considerate."

"Well, she's a mamma like yourself. Y'all speak mommy. Have immediate rapport and empathy, both strong single moms working in the city, living in the same building. Built in sitter, trusting each other with you own kids. I *guess* you are close. That's like comparing my living with you to me comparing living with my friend Roux back in Texas."

I continued. "We wrote and did painting all the time. How come it isn't more like that here. Everything comes so hard-edge here. Nothing rests easy."

I tried to interject some humor because I know how intelligent she is. "And another thing. I'm not lesbophobic. *Au contraire*. In fact I can appreciate their love of women — completely."

I was coming to understand the mommy meltdown. Had seen that it was required of the man to shift into some strong stoic attitude and withstand whatever they throw at you. And I could have defused the situation, but I was so afraid of hanging in through a winter with eight feet! of snow, and I just wasn't getting anywhere on the job front. I had to get back to my own community where there were some people that knew me. Where I had some of my own friends. So I chose to use this insulting fight as an opportunity to get up and go. You have to really hurl yourself to leave — to compel your masochistic inertia to achieve escape velocity. I had to go.

In less than 10 minutes I was packed, with my pathetic little Oliver Twist rucksack over my shoulder and my hand on the door.

"You call up Beausolei and tell him you're leaving!"

"No, I don't want to."

"Yess! You must. You owe him that at least. Cause he'll think it was something *he* did."

"OK."

I called the boy up out at his father's farm. Beau was glad to get a call from an adult.

I told him that I had to go back home to Texas.

I heard the little guy get thoughtful and real and he said "I'm sorry you have to go Walker, I like you. I wish you would stay so that we can FIGHT."

Maybe she thought I wouldn't.
Maybe it was just a gamble on both our parts.
I walked out the door.
There I was out on the streets of Montreal.
It was too late to start hitchhiking any where. I had to find a place to stay. I went to a phone booth and called up Palumbo, and asked him if I could crash at his place for the night.

"Yes," he said. "You can have the living room floor."

I walked over to Palumbo's place through Westmount park. Park benches abandoned, rows of Cyprus denuded — standing, waiting. Winter is here. There would be ice flows on the river. All the color has been taken out, and we are left in this diffuse gray atmosphere of freezing to death. Snow is flying big and small. The magnificent trees are bare, denuded — stark still regal, but struggling like us down here below, bent down reaching for the river. The paths are cleared and straight. No one is out. The picnic tables of summer are almost buried in drifts of snow. The lamp posts, ornate, ancient, black or a dark green are kind of symbolic some-how. Like a philosopher holding out a light to lead the way for us in the dark. A melancholy spirit fills the air, and snow slowly flies all around random particles on drifting motion.

I got over to Palumbo's place on rue Vendome and was one sad, contrite, defiant individual. He was kind and consoling and though he did nod at my irate lover's disillu-sionment and complaints, he did not enter into any complici-ties. After he left me on my own in the living room, I started to write all kinds of sad drivel on his typewriter.

One was about Kwell, the lotion / soap one uses to rid oneself of the crabs. I think it is something about my sense that she was getting into stuff on the side.

> When it's time to take a stance / against the evil wiggles in your itchy pants / that comes on like St. Vitus dance / or Indian tortures with ants / because you took a chance / with where everyone looks askance / on romance / and got an advance / upon all the raving and rants of life / try kwell.
> It's true love when you delouse together / through all kinds of stormy weather / crap crabs and clap / Lovers like two sailors in the bathtub boat / keeping it afloat against the strain / Good bye Little crabs / floating down the drain /Good bye (they say in their tiny munchkin voices) you've been a wonderful lusty host / but now it's time to give up the ghost / i.e. with our arms flailing about / as we go floating down the drain / in a sea of tears shed by the protestant catholic jewish brain /
> 2 pairs of claws 4 tiny legs and a nasty maw.

Rayne called over to Palumbo's place. And they all talked. Not me. It was like having your mom and your father plan your life without you having a say so. Somehow it was decided that I would go back down to Vermont with Rayne, and perhaps start hitchhiking back to Texas from there. It was a plan.

We headed out in the green car the next day. A melancholy spirit fills the air, and snow slowly furtively flits through the gloom. Heartbreak in the ice flows on the river, so grey so long. I was a snowbird now and it was way passed time to head south. I was starting to feel like Descartes in the castle of the Swedish ice queen — only he didn't have the sense to leave. What soul these Canadian people have to get through it.

On the drive down to Vermont, Rayne and I were cordial and decent and overly polite with each other. There was no crazy joy. It was sad. Keeping a civil tongue in her head was hard for her. Against her nature.

The farms are all covered with snow. Birds have left, the beavers and bears are hunkered down. Smoke drifting up from the cozy fireplaces of the people that have them. We ended up at Michael Cooper's house. It was a big white house, and there were some other people staying there. There was a lot of traffic back and forth to New York City, in this community. Cooper was a romantic, and a spiritual man. I think he was some kind of ordained priest. Come to think of it, her other friend, Bob the actor was too.

Us guys hung out upstairs and Rayne and the women hung out downstairs. It was awkward and difficult. Cooper read me his own incredible piece of writing titled *Reap Violet Hiss*. It was tight and sophisticated. It made leaps in mise en scene observations, like they were signs for a very astute, *New Yorker Magazine* educated observer to pick up. I was impressed, though I was also highly distracted by my situation. I was only seeing my failings through the eyes of sadness.

Cooper and I talked of love. He is a very wise young man. He said things like Love means learning to read the signs of another person.

And, Love is allowing an obsessional infatuation to take hold so that you will imbue yourself in the life of signs of another.

I thought, The sex is just to keep you interested in participating in the growth experience.

We all sat at dinner, comporting ourselves through the awkwardity like sophisticated young ladies and gentlemen beguiled by our charming host, Michael. Rayne and I smoked some dope and started to giggle in the parlor. We all got high, drank some more wine. And somehow started getting amorous toward each other. Rayne and I were going to sleep together one last time. Somehow it was decided that she would bring this other woman, Eileen, staying at the house, a girlfriend of hers, to bed with us. Eileen was young — just out of high school — a friend staying in the family home, someone Rayne had known for a while. And so, drunk and stoned after Michael retired we were going to have a three way.

I was excited. At LAST, every man's dream was about to come true.

The problem, as I began to imagine it is, what if they both want it at the same time and you have to keep stopping with one and shifting your attention, then starting over with the other one, who might have gone south in the mean time. I began to worry: What's the best way to handle that without hurting either one's feelings.

We got undressed.

When Eileen stripped I saw she has a gorgeous body. Eileen was very sophisticated in a New York way with wire-rimmed eyeglasses and had the most titful body, a hard body, lean and taunt, perfect pointed perky breasts, so sharp they could poke you in your eye, lovely round smooth taunt ass; but above the neck, that was the problem. Her face reminded me of that skinny witch on a bicycle in *The Wizard of Oz*. I half expected to see her throw her head back and hear her cackling horselaugh at any minute. I tried to just stay focused on the body, the perfect body.

We were hugging and sticking our tongues in each other's mouths, but my second-guessing interfered with my lust. I watched them trying to be hot but it was becoming uncomfortable. Rayne kept looking at me in some kind of expectant way. I think she advertised herself as being more experienced at this then she actually was. She looked a bit stricken. Maybe she was wondering if I would become more interested in her friend. The teenaged girl seemed very interested in Rayne, but not all that interested in me.

I was beginning to feel a bit dismayed to find that I was not hardly interested in her either. Much as I wanted to do this teenage body who was so taunt as only youth can be, I found my desire for her wain. I had to have some kind of feeling for the woman. It was just that this was my big chance to have sex with two women, and I wasn't about to say no.

They handled and touched each other hoping that would get me more interested. But I was just not that way. Damn-it. I was having trouble getting it up. After a while Rayne went down on me. She looked over to see if Eileen was watching. Rayne was sucking on my cock, but after a while, my Catholic upbringing would not let me enjoy it. No, way.

I was not man enough to just tell them no! And who cares if I hurt their feelings.

After a while it got awkward; they didn't seem all that interested in doing each other either.

I was into only Rayne, and she was ambivalent about this experience with the girl, though the two of them did have a lot of "lesbian" rapport. It was more political. These thoughts were, unfortunately, running through my head. Laid-ees.

Though I had been programmed since birth to think having sex with another of the same sex was unnatural, I was willing to question my assumptions around "natural". Girls are beautiful sexual creatures. Even an ugly girl has sex if she wants to. But I suddenly realized Eileen was not into men. You could just feel it. She was trying to seduce Rayne, and tolerating me. Rayne was trying to show me a side of herself that she had not shared before. I was just trying to take advantage of my big chance in life.

But it was weird, and my mind got to working overtime. Though I was hot for Rayne, I could not transfer it to this man-hating dyke type. Even though it was nice to rub up against her taunt youthful personage, I had to just say, "Sorry ladies, this is not working."

So we stopped.

Rayne and I retired to our room, and there we got it on with a vengeance.

We had intense sex, felt the risk and the loss coming into our life, which made us all the more desperate, passionate. We coupled like demons for hours — a long time to be carrying on in someone else's house late into the night, a snowy night, way out in the dark country.

A masterful passion possessed me. I was completely erect, nothing could diminish the bonification of my wood, and a kind of perverse meanness and a great intimate horniness and yet a caring energy and focus and even affection and delight for this little wren who had tried to give me the experience of two women. She sucked the cock and stroked it languidly with her fingertips. Even though it was a cold snowy Vermont full moon night outside, the moon light was bright and lit up the room, I could see very well in the dark her face, she had taken the cock all the way down inside her mouth. I was feeling mean at my inability to maintain a romance and wanting to shift the blame away from my stupidity onto someone else, I grabbed her head and forced her down on it more until she gagged. I was stoned to the eyeballs and had made up my mind to be leaving, and was at the same time feeling pushed around by my ego to be heading into this veil of sorrow. I didn't care if she thought I was being disrespectful.

In the dark it was again like the first time, with no past, no longer an "us" present, no future, just Hungarian grudge fuck moments arising.

The main piece of furniture in the room was a stiff uncomfortable couch, of some kind of rough tweed texture. It made you not want to recline nor sit upon it but only allow your hands or feet to gain purchase there. I just draped her across parts of it. She was willing to be draped

We kissed, holding each other close. We pressed our bodies together strongly, trying to push inside each other, so there would be one body, one heart, connected through one dick, one cunt: we were doing it with a dunt!

We were like two soldiers on the front of the sexual revolution, (this was before I had seen *Deep Throat*). We were in a kind of corporeal combat for the ownership and control of each other's soul. We were possessed of fiendish energies, like the energies were trying to work their way through us toward each other, burn away the bodies, like melting the snow and ice, like monks drying towels in a freezing mountain stream with their body heat, we were dripping wet, her smooth pussy juices were running down her leg, and her back was wet with sweat. I squeezed her hard with my bread-maker hands, molded her mercilessly like cookie dough.

The inner being was coming out, burning its way out, seeping in sweat.

I would be thinking *She knows I am planning to leave her. And yet she is still participating, not holding back.* Maybe she is trying to store up a really hot one. I know I was, because it would probably be along time before I find another chick to tumble into bed with.

I had been up inside her, for a long time, she had been on top, then I had been on top, at one point she was standing on one leg, with her other resting on the arm of the chair. Finally we were supine on the couch and I had a good place to push off from with my feet and I had been pushing hard up into her, so that I moved her whole body.

She was almost hyperventilating while trying not to make a whole lot of noise, but really shooting off, I could feel the juices getting squashy and squishy down there, we would have to buy them a new chair, and she had her legs clasped tightly around my middle, scissoring me in a wrestler's hold, and together we, s/he, just hung there on me, pressed into me as far as she could so that we did indeed become one entity, and I started coming, ejecting great solar spumes across the dark emptiness of primordial interpersonal stellar space. She held me tight, into her, would not let me go, "Whewey! Wow!" she said breathlessly, shaking her head in demure disbelief at the level of abandon the dance had taken us into.

I had not used a condom. It had not even been an issue. We had not thought of it.

I got off her when she let me go. Come and juices oozed from her full vulva, as she cupped her hands down there to keep from dripping on the glossy maple wood floor and made her way off naked out the door to the bathroom down the hall to get a tissue.

We both knew in our hearts that we were trying to lay down some kind of statement about our inner sexual beings, trying to let them shine and burn through us for a brief moment, before the struggles of the ego took hold again and pushed us apart. The last tryst was motivated by genuine respect if not love, and deep attraction trying to fulfill itself.

Pierrot on Edgecliff

In my brokenhearted sadness I felt like Pierrot, with his liquid bonelessness (the art the stuntman), his white flour skin, his too big buttons (to reflect the predicaments of children) and his silent smile of enigmatic goodness. That's the stoic stance of the hapless innocent possessed. Pierrot is the patron saint of cool. It would have been a cop-out for him to speak, I would be his voice.

My ride from Vermont brought me into Paterson New Jersey across the river from Manhattan. Here I was. In New York, the biggest city in the US, the capital of American culture, defended by thousands of ferocious thugs. I wanted to go into it. I felt so bad after splitting up with Rayne. My sense of guilt was coming down on me like a ton of bricks. Yet I could not yield to this punishing god within, which might lead to mistakes that would be dealt with severely. I was Pierrot the innocent in New York but I was ready to quit. Come and get me, mother fucker, Death. I QUIT. My life is a classical joke with a diabolical punch line. This and my general wretchedness — my rags, my starvation, my misplaced love, my hunger for success as an artist, the hopelessness of my material situation, the lack of response of my feeble efforts to impress the casual bystander with my art. I was a stupid, heavy-moving fellow, used to provide a target for the raillery of the tres chic and elegant. It was a dream turning into nightmare repeated, turning into madness.

I called up my contact, the NYC cab driver K. S. from West Glover and he told me in a sentence: "From Paterson take the bus to Port Authority, then the BMT train to Brooklyn. Get off at Church Ave. and walk to 19th St."

That was an adventure that took half a day. Lost in the underground maze I felt like an ingénue male *Zazie dans le Metro*.

Au clair de la lune / Mon ami Pierrot /
Prete a moi ta plume / pour ecrire un mot /
Ma chandel est mort / Je n'ai pas de feu /
Ouvre la ta porte / pour l'amour de dieu.

I crashed at his place and headed out the next day.

It's the hardest thing in the world for a stranger to hitch out of New York City. Finally after bouncing around in all that confusion on the New Jersey Turnpike, I got picked up by a black dude from Paterson.

He called himself Shine, and was 19, in the army, and returning to base in Denver. He had a "cute little butterball" wife with a kid, and he was very much in love with them.

He was driving a hot rod that obviously somebody must have built for him because he didn't know shit about boss shorts. It was a little Gremlin, orange, with a whopping 352 Ford Galaxy motor with a 4 barrel carburetor. He had cheater slicks on the back! Can you imagine it, trying to drive with cheater slicks on the Pennsylvania Pike in winter snow?! They don't plow their roads in Pennsylvania, and me and Shine were sliding all over it. Plus which, he had trouble with his throttle, which would get stuck in the down position, so that you had to romp on the gas hard to bring it back up off the floor, and this would cause the rear end to break free and the car to spin out or slide sideways in this tiny light car.

In addition to this, the spray on his windshield wiper didn't work, so that there was no way you could clean off the dirt and salt that the big trucks spewed up on the windshield. We were blind, and freewheeling, rooster-tailing, all over the highway. The breaks didn't work, and you never knew when you would just push that pedal down to the floor like a clutch. It was bracing the way you had to be almost prescient to plan ahead far enough to leave yourself enough time to quick pump the breaks to get stopped. That coupled with the fact that you had to do the counter intuitive STOMP on the foot feed in order to make the gas pedal come back so you could slow down because the linkage was so fucked up. Also we had to keep on pouring fluid down the transmission tube.

Finally I made him stop, after we'd slid off the road into a ditch and been pulled out by some very capable white farm boys. I took out the windshield wiper switch from the dash and hot wired past it to the windshield spray pump motor, so we could clean off the windshield occasionally. Then I did some other field modifications — bending the accelerator linkage to receive a stiff spring on the accelerator, so that you had mash it hard to give it the gas. It was stiff but at least now it would not stay stuck at full throttle. Then we found these two chains for the tire — they were one strand each, and we put one on each of the back wheels so that every revolution of the tire had its own bump, bump BUMP BUMP down the highway. But at least that gave us some traction, though it slowed us down.

With this regular click track being laid down, me and Shine started singing songs. We started getting into Motown sounds. Shine's daddy had been a singer, and he himself had a beautiful falsetto Little Richard voice. It was so easy to remember those sweet innocent teenangel sounds. I was surprised. I had grown on soul music, listening to station KMAC in San Antonio and almost all the lines from the songs came easily, available for singing.

Soldier Boy . . . Chains of love. . .Stagger Lee . . . Yakety Yak . . .Let the Four Winds Blow . . . Hit the Road Jack . . . Walkin' to New Orleans . . . Wonderful World . . .

Under the Boardwalk . . . Another Saturday Night . . .
Twisting the Night Away . . . Chapel of Love . . . My prayer
. . . My Cheri Amour . . . Blueberry Hill . . . the Locomotion
. . . Sitting on the Dock by the Bay. . .Splish Splash (I was
taking a Bath). . .I'm on the outside looking in . . . I only
have eyes for you . . . Stagger Lee . . . My Guy . . . South
Street . . . Hurt So Bad . . . When A man loves a woman . . .
It's all in the Game. . . You will loose a good thing . . .
Talking 'Bout My Baby . . . Be My Baby . . . There goes my
Baby . . . Baby I need your loving . . . Walk on Bye . . .
Reach out for me . . . Only you . . . Save the last dance for
me . . . All I have to do is Dream. . .Maybelene . . . Sweet
Little 16 . . . Little Suzie. . . How Sweet it is. (To be loved by
you) . . .A lovers Question. . . Will you Still Love me
Tomorrow . . . This Magic Moment . . . Smoke gets in your
eyes . . . Lonely Tear Drops . . . You Better Shop Around . . .
Rambling Rose . . . The GREAT Pretender . . . Aint No
Mountain High Enough . . . Our day will come . . . Mashed
Potato Time. . .Hi Heel Sneakers . . . I can't Help Myself . . .
Cathy's Clown . . . Venus (Goddess of Love that you are) . . .
Along come Jones . . . Heat Wave . . . Dream Lover. . .Peggy
Sue . . . Hot Fun in the Summertime. . ., That'll Be the day. .
.Hold onto what you got. . . Frankie and Johnnie . . . A
Change is gonna come . . . My Girl . . . Traveling Man . . .
Since I don't have you. . . Bye Bye Love . . . Up on the Roof
. . . No Particular Place to go . . . My Ding a ling . . . Talk to
me . . . Wake UP Little Suzie . . . Out of My Head . . .
Chantilly Lace. . . Beachwood 4-5789 . . . Hurt SO bad . . .
Tears on My pillow . . . Please Mr. Postman . . . Up on the
roof . . . On Broadway. . .They way You do the things you
do. . . Since I don't have you . . . I got you (I feel good) . .
.You keep me hanging on . . . He's a rebel . . . Then He
kissed me . . .That'll be the day . . . You send me . . . You are
the sunshine of my life . . . A place in the sun . . .

We rocked on across America all night long. We were so exhausted we pulled over and slept in some blankets that Shine had. I was so ill equipped that I didn't even have a sleeping bag. In Kansas City we were totally out of money. So we started going around to these pawn shops and bars trying to down a few things, a radio, a heater, anything to get a little bread to continue the trip. In Wichita Kansas, we met up with this hustler named Nevada 'Red' Smith. His walk was so pimp that he looked almost spastic. He kept up a continual stream of road talk, and jive, like some consummate musician always weaving stories and cons. He took us around the corner, into some dark, ice-slick street in the Wichita Projects, and said "I'm gonna give you the $20 you need to make it to Denver, and next time you through town you can run a load of whores up there to the army boys." He even talked about us taking a load of horse up to Denver. He said, "You can sit out here and your partner come in with me and I'll get what's coming to you." After a while, Shine decided that there was a gang in there and they were going to come out and whip our ass and take us for everything, so we eased on down the ice slick street, found ourselves trapped in a cul de sac. We cautiously turned around and with the utmost caution drove carefully back past the den of thieves and killers. We got outa there!

From there we split up, and I headed south on 35, which went all the way back to Austin. I caught a ride with some hippies in a van. The countryside went from white snow drifts to cold dark brown dirt as the snow disappeared. In Texas the sun came out and it got warmer and warmer.

The first thing I did when I got back to Austin was go knock on the door of my friend Roux. He's from Louisiana or Oklahoma, one of them places. Somebody tole me he was working down at the hotel, the Driskill Hotel, down on the corner of 6th and Congress. So I went down there lookin' for him. Now this is the nicest hotel in town, and I — just off the road — felt about out of place, but I eased on back through this stately elegant though rococo lobby to find master Roux, all done up in the monkey suit that they made you wear in Room Service. He was looking fine, we hugged each other. Then we stepped back and dug one another. "He had his hair cut, and a crisp grown-up mustache. He had a fine January suntan and had them round shiny black shoes, black pants, a vest with brass buttons, and a bow-tie. He was knockin' down good bucks as a valet in room service. He gave me the key to his place, and said he'd see me back there after he got off from work.

Roux had a fine place right on the shore of the Colorado River, near where it flowed under the Interregional Bridge. It was a small cinder block duplex bunker on Edgecliff Terrace off Riverside behind the Ramada Inn. It was hunkered down behind a hill, in a Zen bamboo grove, alongside the river. It had two big rooms separated by a wall. On one side was a big bedroom and bathroom, and on the other side was a kitchenette and a living room combination.

When he showed up at sunset we walked down the hill to a little ramshackled dock on the river, all grown-over and hidden among overarching tree branches. We smoked some reefer and felt like Sadus or Wetbacks hunkered down along the river watching the eternal play of light on water in the setting sun. Edgecliff Terrace is a dirt road about two blocks long; the community is an enclave of hippies and bikers and Viet Nam Vets and dogs scratching around.

"I'm coming down from love, man." I tell him, "And it hurts so much I can hardly handle it."

Roux was also in the sad state of having broken up from a love affair. He had been living with a dark crazy hottie named Lynne, when I was last here. She was the brains and talent behind a boutique we had before I left. It had been down on 6th Street, a couple of doors away from Antones. We were making the Manchurian Cowboy shirt — Lynne sewing on a white industrial Juki machine that she dearly loved. I was a pattern pin-up boy. It was hilarious to work in this sweat shop during the Austin summer heat without air-conditioning. We took a lot of baths and worked in our pajamas or skivvies. The music scene on 6th St. was wild.

Roux told me how some wild girlfriends of hers, junkies from San Antone, got her all strung out again on smack, and got her turning tricks and all fucked up down in Mexico.

We were both broken hearted and it was good to rap about our broken hearts and about women in general and about various plans to get them back. We egged each other on in our blue-moon, sad-eyed Pierrot stage. We were a sad and funny pair of sensitive intelligent young guys trying to get over the traumatic hurt of lost love.

"She was like a sister," I said, "from many past lifetimes ago, we were so much alike." & etc. etc.

He said "Say, man why don't you stay a while. Mellow down before you go out to California. They gonna murder you out their, kid. They're gonna eat you alive. And for god sakes, quit wagging yer tail."

Inside his place the cinder block walls of stark white primer glowed bright when the blinds opened to the low winter sun. He accumulated goods; I could get all my possessions into a light traveling back pack. Books and periodicals attracted themselves to various piles evidencing a confluence of creative activity here. On cinder block shelves in front of the mirror sits a small white art-deco tube-type FM radio played jazz. On a vanity desk is a crook neck lamp and an old typewriter with the name LOIS neatly stenciled on the platen above the keyboard. We had a lot of fun writing, collaborating, typing and giggling with Lois. We rolled sheets of the finest cream EGG paper into the typer and got to work. We felt that on this paper everything you wrote was destined for greatness. We hung our newly minted sheets upon the long kitchen / dining room / living room wall. It became a built up texture of poems and stories in progress, stories of UFOs, pictures of Einstein, and flyers from famous rock groups. On the wall Roux has hung some of his beautiful sexy surrealistic drawings, he was a gifted artist.

In the living room there is a sliced-up Lazy Boy recliner, where I slept. In the cupboard, there is only a large cylindrical box of Quaker oats. Near the door between the 2 rooms is a "nest" a collection of found objects juxtaposed together in some kind of living growing culture. Roux's bedroom has one bed on the floor, an antique sofa with claw feet and other baroque flourishes. There a steamer trunk and a couple of closets. A door opens into a small tiled bathroom. On top of the steamer trunk: Roux's concertina; nearby, a briefcase full of harps. He was a musician and writer of songs and poetry.

We became collage wall artist, building up vast dense collages on the Wall. We put up found artifacts and pictures and poems and clippings from the world around us. Roux was a sensitive artist, romantic and sentimental and the samples (projections from the synchronistic vortex outside) were beautifully and subtly arranged. I learned layout from him. We built stories, out of the collage of our life on the wall. It was parataxis, a formal principle of composition, like layout in a daily newspaper. You could read how we were feeling just by looking at the changed arrangement of the day's wall. This Wailing Wall got me started communicating to other people. You could do anti-zazen in front of this wall, taken on a phenomenological trip into the farfetched absurd, cross sorting the rows and columns of its matrix, weaving together the warp and woof of its diachronic and synchronic signifiers as they channeled the forces entering your world through its semantic clustering.

We'd take turns typing on Lois. I made this poem:

Metamorphosis

   She brought me into her life,
Dressed me in a fashionable winter coat;
Taught me photography,
Taught me how to fight with girls
And built me a bed.
Taught me how to make snow angels
And challah bread;
And how to be a parent.
Introduced me to some true artists,
Introduced me to actual videography,
Got me a job as a college lecturer —
Showed me there could be creative *work*
In a life that engendered genuine friends.
We had days and nights in wildlife
On road trips through sweet countryside in a fine car.
With memories of Mount Royal laughter,
Squeals, rolling like mummies down a grassy hill
And mommy's laugh soaring up the sides of space,
Ascending into blue sky high and beyond —
To another river, one that flows to the end of the earth.
In a chrysalis of creative catharsis,
She brought me out of myself
But it was too much.
I entered into boy / girl strife,
Retreating to what I knew in the old ways of my life.
I had flown too close to her light and got my wings singed.
Then plunged through the air, through despair,
Falling back across America to this slacker's lair.
Now again in Austin,
I live in a bunker like the Cong.
I have the moon and the river —
Walking into town on the Interregional Bridge.
I had lost my misdirection;
I had lost my loneliness;
But that familiar me outsiderness was coming back.

We are learning to live like the Cong here, slipping away through the bamboo grove behind the house, down by the river and to stand watch, witnessing in that peaceful place, sitting on a dock smoking reefer in a long spliff — for it is incumbent upon the artist to consider god and visions first.

Across the river lived Zack Replica and the Church of the Coincidental Metaphor. And beyond that Jennifer the co-ed. We were so far below being entrepreneurial, productive members of society that it was impossible to jump up high enough to be on anyone's radar. We learn to scan their eyes like a raster of lines to pick up the most powerful signal. We made our own world to look up to.

We met our next door neighbor one day, when he was whacked out on acid and came outside to shoot his gun at some imaginary Cong. He was a Viet Nam Vet left to the devices of his own psychological reintegration. Yeah, that's how we met him — in the middle of recording a poem; the gun shots are on tape. We went outside to answer an obvious plea for attention and found this guy standing there, reeling around, with no shirt or shoes, looking one moment wild-eyed and the next sheepish, feverishly running his hands through his hair. He had tucked his revolver back into his waist. And there we were standing around, encountering each other. We invite him in to our side of the duplex, where we are perforce explain our thing — guys recording poetry.

The drug-crazed, armed, Viet Nam vet starts off with, "Are you guys gay?" That's the way to start a conversation with two strange guys. This dude was a total red neck bad trip saying the most confrontational thing to come into his head while flying on acid. Next he pulls out his piece. It's show and tell time on the macho channel. And Roux 'examined' the piece by clicking it off into the ceiling. The flashbacking Vet had shot the whole clip except for the one dud round still in

269

the chamber. Which still could go live. There followed a
tense argument over who gets possession of the gun — Roux
says, "What did you give it to me for." Finally it is emptied.

I stood up and went outside to check if anybody had
called the police. And it is determined, that the police
probably are not going to come. I was fearful, though,
imagining this gun toting vet was one of those guys that if
you did call the police on him, he'd probably get out quickly
on low bail, go buy another gun and come around and snuff
you good. And then probably get off with a light sentence.

After a while we all went outside and he began telling us
about having been an organizer for SDS when he was in
college. And then getting drafted and going into war. And
then he got a terribly horrified and sad look on his face and
told us "I just can't get the image out of my head of seeing
my friend hanging upside down up in a tree from a rope
around his feet." The poor soldier went into more graphic
detail about how he found his friend dead from torture and
mutilation. We were shocked. I started getting paranoid that
our neighbor is going to make the paranoid connection with
us and the Cong. I am thinking he is a totally savage red
neck, out of his mind and he would kill us if he knew who
we really were. Great to be back in Texas, almost every
instant is an instant replay of a parody of normal culture.
And I, being from that culture, am not any better. I made the
crude error of telling him we'd lost the war.

He gave the standard retort: "It was my patriotic duty to
protect this country so guys like you could disagree."

But Roux, ahhh the cool and elegant Roux — to give me
a lesson in diplomacy, considered the Vet and went into this
compassionate rap. He said, "Well, how should we feel when
we talk of the dead? They are truly the real prisoners.
Envious? Indifferent? Respecting? The dead are no longer
concerned with the Mad, the Living, the Holy, the Sane.

They make such meager demands — asking for so little in the days they're dead. Only to be remembered is all they need now. How shall we remember them? Wholly."

That really touched the Vet and cooled him out. "Well that's about it fer now," he said. And he went back into his bunker.

Across the river, a girl, Jennifer, a co-ed friend of the Church of the Coincidental Metaphor. We had been sort of sizing each other up, she's a cute little heifer. Why don't I go over and sniff out Jennifer, will she leave the second floor light on for me? Will she inform me? Is she my angel? I think I'll take my new understanding about coincidence and colinearity to the next meeting of the Church.

Was it really possible to have more choice in your life? After seeing the earth from space we truly realized we were citizens of the universe, given the most supreme gift of all: self-awareness amendable to being known but requiring that one disengage from self-interest. This occurring for us now in a democratic society that could empower and enslave; en-lighten and distract. I had to leave Rayne to pursue a different dream and make something of myself. How can one remain in a long term relationship, bound to being in one place for the duration of the commitment, and yet still exercise the freedom to somehow explore other selves. It didn't seem possible.

I'm done asking questions for a while. I'm giving out answers. It ought to be possible to be in networks seeded by real, passionate work that you can trust will contract and expand through natural cultural exchange rather than forced advertising images.

What was it like the day you received your first kiss.

Dear Abby. Kiss and run away dates had started for me by age 13. I remember dancing with Mary Nell at the 8th grade graduation dance and I was embarrassed at the bulge in my pants. It was all so hot and horny. To be 13 hanging around the girls, those cute little Mexican girls in pleated catholic school uniforms, with crisp blouses and knee socks and all that soft sweaty baby fat bodies bulging out of the spongy foam-rubber breast-publishers everywhere. The nuns made them kneel down in the hall like captive slaves to check the heights of their hem. How degrading. Walking home every day, in the San Antonio heat, I would start to stand to attention under my ROTC uniform thinking about Candy Ramirez, my neighbor across the street. She was the first girl I ever kissed. For months I used to go over to her house and she would invariably say Kiss Me. Thank God for forward women or I'd never get anywhere. I was one of the boys in her B-list. There were others of greater interest. Some I knew. Like the Statue of Liberty, she was carrying a torch for a friend.

An orange butterfly with dark markings on its wing span, (they seemed to be in the shape of question marks) was startled by our presence and flitted slowly up and away from some purple pink brush hanging down on the dock at the edge of the river. The light weight creature flew toward a clump of bushes higher up the hill, but was lifted by a gust and drifted out toward the open river; then changed course and fighting the breeze, flew back toward the river's edge, knowing there was nothing for him out there. He seemed to be the last of the season, looking for a place to come to ground. He continued his way along the shore toward the bridge, and I soon lost sight of him.

We hunkered down at the rivers edge, sat and gazed across the long water shimmering in the setting sun. From this angle the river was wide, and the city beyond with its golden buildings shining in the sky, seemed to be floating on the surface of something too.

Michael Lyons, moon child, born on the last day of June, in Montreal, of French / Irish / Scotch ancestry. Immigrated to America, grew up in San Antonio, to experience a second linguistical minority. He now lives in San Francisco with wife and son. Lyons has authored a dozen literary books: seven novels, a memoir, several scattered poetry chapbooks; and several dozen technical books. The novels form the trilogy called "Little House on the Prairie" and the ongoing sextet called "My Years of Apprenticeship at Love." Rich in content, these works eschew mindless suspense and the juvenility of hero-worship plot for a more lyrical joyous expression. Love is an apprenticeship to the sign system of the beloved. What else is a poet going to write about?

The "Little House on the Prairie" trilogy

The "My Years of Apprenticeship at Love" sextet

In progress

In progress

Poetry at HiT MoteL Press

I learn to walk again
Slow baby steps after a
serious skateboard accident.
Sequel to How I spent my
Christmas Break

Happy Trails to the Infinite
Fourteen Sonnets
The influence of form in
everyday life.

Diamond Head
Return to the
place of the
Honeymoon on a
family vacation.
Learn surfing,
and the secretes
of the sea.
Do to things
what light does
to them.

Chap books and collection available **FREE**
in .pdf at www.hitmotel.com

Selected Poems

This is a selection of some 80 poems going back to the 70s up to the present. The poems are selected from all the books of Michael Lyons, including some rare chapbooks.

The poetry is usually the personal observations of the self in the world with others. There are some sonnets.

The poems are loose and spontaneous and usually humorous.

The Punctual Actual Weekly

was a literary magazine in Berkeley of 1976. This memoir of the artists and writers in the community it served presents reprints and reviews. In addition to the solo theatre presentations, the magazine format supports a graphical novel treatment of a poet's notebook, and an art show catalog of works. Besides the Abstract Expressionism, Physical Theatre, and (humorously) applying the insights of several isms: structuralism, imagism, surrealism, actualism, personalism, set in the city of Berkeley (a philosopher known for idealism) it attempts what WCW did in Paterson.

HiT MoteL Press
www.hitmotel.com
These books can be ordered from any book seller or on-line.
They are deeply discounted on Amazon, and Barnes& Nobles.
Check www.hitmotel.com for selections, recordings, to order.

Boho Novels, Memoirs
The "Little House on the Prairie" Trilogy:
Cultivating the Texas Twister Hybrid, a portrait of the artist as
a weed gardener (1998) ISBN 0-9655842-0-8 $20.00
The Secret of the Cicadas' Song, a peyote trip in poetry and
prose (1998) ISBN 0-9655842-1-6 $20.00
Knight of a 1000 eyes, about Tai Chi, movement, Laban, and
the I Ching (2002) ISBN 0-9655842-2-4 $25.00
others:
The Punctual Actual Weekly, about the life and times of a
small mimeograph literary rag centered around artists living in
a Berkeley warehouse and the Amphictionic Theatre (2007)
ISBN 0-9655842-8-3
The Church of the Coincidental Metaphor, youthful adven-
tures in Mexican radio

Novels: The "My Years of Apprenticeship at Love" Sextet:
Sex is the Antigravity of Metamorphosis, tales of romance and
hitchhiking in North America. (2008) ISBN 0-9655842-9-1 $25.00
The Indigenous Tribesmen of Neverland Bohemian life in
Austin slacker enclaves. ISBN 0-9655842-7-5 $25.00
Dolores Park, Texan joins a California Tantric Buddhist
commune (2001) ISBN 0-9655842-3-2 480 pages. $25.00
Seeing throught the Spell of Transference A cab driver's
journal of psychotherapy. ISBN 0-9655842-4-0
A Blue Moon in August, about marriage and children late in
life. (2005) ISBN 0-9655842-5-9
Thoughts on Vacation, a father is raised by his child and is
enlightened by mortality. (2005) ISBN 0-9655842-6-7

Check into HiT MoteL @www.hitmotel.com for cover art,
interactive Table of Contents, e-book sample chapters,
recordings and other mindware.

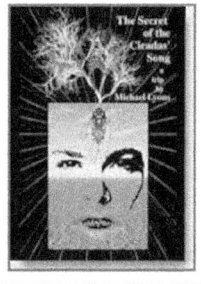

Sex is the Antigravity of Metamorphosis
a novel by Michael Lyons

Sex is the Antigravity of Metamorphosis is a comedy of manners about love told from the point of view of a hopeful but inexperienced Walker Underwood. The couple meets when she picks him up hitchhiking. She is a single mom and they immediately start living together. Though this is the 4th book to be published of the "My Years of Apprenticeship at Love" sextet, it is the 1st book of that series. The story is told from the perspective of the man but reflects what the woman has taught him as their chaotic lives seek stability in each other.

Sex is the Antigravity of Metamorphosis uses the erotic focus of male and female heat to dissolve the veil of reality allowing us a glimpse of the generative forces of fate and destiny that bring lovers together.

He is a slacker from Austin starting out on the road to making his way in the world and in American letters. It is a novel in the form of their emotional memories and creative experiences — of being in a family in his home town Montreal, after being away in Texas for a good part of his life. This sets the stage for involuntary memory to find him at nodal points in the city. These points hold together a field of time that is not a space-like time of the 4th dimension as in relativity or Verne's *Time Machine*, or in Marker's *La Jetee*, but more of a Proust-like time of coincidental crossings penetrating the vast reservoir of the unconscious through the encounter with the Other. This leads to a realization of the impermanence of personality and the perspective of the self as transcending the different époques of the individual.

Literature / Parenting Romance/ Metaphysical Esthetics

288 pages   ISBN: 0965584291 $25